CAROL MASON was born in the North East of England and now lives with her husband in British Columbia. As a teenager, she was crowned Britain's National Smile Princess and since has worked as a model, diplomat, hotel receptionist, and advertising copywriter. She is the author of *Send Me a Lover* and *The Secrets of Married Women*, both bestsellers.

## Praise for *Send Me a Lover*

"This cross between *Mamma Mia!* and *P.S. I Love You* is fast and furious chick lit." — *Red Magazine*, Top 3 Must Reads

"Her debut, *The Secrets of Married Women*, marked Carol Mason's coming out as a writer of compelling insight, with a gritty yet humorous edge. This follow-up is equally assured." — *Daily Mirror* (Book of the Week)

"*Send Me A Lover* is a sweet, sad tale about love, loss and the crazy way the world works to reclaim love again." — *Cosmopolitan* (Australia)

"This intriguing second novel from Carol Mason is a beautiful story about coming to terms with loss." — *The Yorkshire Evening Post*

# Praise for *The Secrets of Married Women*

"Mason's writing is absorbing. While reading a spicy bit about Leigh's affair while taking the bus to work I rode past my stop."
— Rebecca Wigod, *The Vancouver Sun*

"There is a fresh and vital edge to this superior debut novel. Mason has much to say about relationships. Her women have resonant characters and recognisable jobs, which give depth to their messy lives. A bittersweet narrative and ambiguous outcomes make this much grittier and more substantial than standard chick-lit fare." — *The Financial Times* (UK)

"There is a big buzz around this tale of three Newcastle wives tempted to cheat on their husbands, and I can see why.... Lots of bitchy, cackling sex talk — you've been warned!"
— *Eve Magazine* (UK)

"Full of realistic emotional twists. The characters' reactions to the challenges they face are frank and unmelodramatic; there is a refreshing honesty about the numbness that comes from discovering an infidelity, and the shame that comes with perpetrating one. Equally affecting are the counterpoised sources of sadness in Jill's life. Her marriage has faltered because she and her husband can't have children and yet she must be a mother to her own parents in their old age; it's a poignant combination." — *The Telegraph* (UK)

"What really goes on behind closed doors? Carol Mason unlocks life behind a marriage in this strong debut."
— *Heat Magazine* (UK)

"Nice comforting chick lit to be read while drinking a warm glass of Zinfandel before a cosy fire while the kids sleep soundly upstairs. It's got the raw realism of someone writing about a world she knows. A grand little book for the festive fireside."
— *The Irish Evening Herald* (UK)

"At last, a modern story of life in the North East, not a clog or a flat cap in sight. Just three thirty-somethings trying to sort out their lives. Realistic and entertaining."
— *New Books Magazine* (UK)

"This poignant novel deals with honesty, forgiveness, love, and the realities of modern-day marriage."
— *Notebook Magazine* (Australia)

# THE LOVE MARKET

# THE LOVE MARKET

## CAROL MASON

McArthur & Company
Toronto

First published in 2010 by
McArthur & Company
322 King Street West, Suite 402
Toronto, Ontario
M5V 1J2
www.mcarthur-co.com

Library and Archives Canada Cataloguing in Publication

Mason, Carol
The love market / Carol Mason.

ISBN 978-1-55278-845-5

I. Title.

PS8626.A7986I3 2010     C813'.6     C2009-907355-2

The publisher would like to acknowledge the financial support
of the Government of Canada through the Canada Book Fund and
the Canada Council for our publishing activities. The publisher
further wishes to acknowledge the financial support of the Ontario
Arts Council and the OMDC for our publishing program.

Cover and text design by Tania Craan
Printed in Canada by Webcom

10 9 8 7 6 5 4 3 2 1

**Preserving our environment**
McArthur & Company chose Legacy TB Natural
100% post-consumer recycled paper for
the pages of this book printed by Webcom Inc.

© **Mixed Sources**
Product group from well-managed
forests, controlled sources and
recycled wood or fiber
FSC  www.fsc.org  Cert no. SW-COC-002358
© 1996 Forest Stewardship Council

*For Neil*

# Prologue

Someone once told me that there's no such thing as a coincidence, only a synchronicity. That like-minded people often travel down similar paths that can converge unexpectedly. That's why you'll bump into the mother of your daughter's school friend in the wine shop at six o'clock on a Friday, or your old art history professor while touring the Louvre. But sometimes chance encounters don't seem to result from any kindred purpose. And you'll see someone from your past in a place that is so unlikely for either of you to ever be in that you can't quite explain it. You can't even read into it, because very often life, just like who we end up loving, is a random thing.

In my case, I happened to get off the bus at the wrong stop.

I wasn't really paying attention to where we were, given that we seemed to spend ninety per cent of the journey in the snail's pace of London traffic on a Saturday afternoon. What was far more fascinating at that time than anything outside the window was my left earlobe reflected in the glass — the fiery little diamond twinkling away with each slight movement of my head. I happened to glance at Mike sitting in the seat facing me. He was grinning at me and slowly shaking his head, in affectionate despair.

'It's too lavish!' I said to him in the jewellery store the day before, as I reluctantly handed the little diamond studs back to the salesman.

'No it's not. I want you to have them.' Mike cocked me a glance that said he was quite enjoying being the big man footing the bill for an expensive anniversary present, just this once. 'Try them in again,' he said.

'We can't, Mike! They're two grand.'

'We're taking them.' Mike pulled out his credit card.

He knew I'd wanted little diamond studs for a while. I'd managed to drop them into the conversation just enough times to have the hint tiptoe across his consciousness so that buying them would seem like his idea — a romantic gesture — rather than just him caving in to shut me up.

'But, Mike, we could finish our bathroom with that money. Or put it toward a new car. Or Aimee's education fund...' I thought, *Please God don't let me talk him out of his own idea.*

'You're right,' he said. 'Let's put them back.' He pretended to pocket his credit card again, and to try not to see how my face must have fallen. Then he smiled. 'One thousand pounds, Celine. What's that work out to over ten years of marriage? You don't think you're worth that to me?'

I rubbed my chin, deviously. 'Maybe I should try a bigger pair.'

Mike snapped his card down on the counter. 'Done deal.' I tripped out of there like I was Ginger Rogers. Mike said small things please small-minded people, and he was pleased he wasn't born a girl. I slept in them, and, this morning, grinned all the time I was brushing my teeth. Mirrors, windows, backs of spoons had all become irresistible.

'Come on,' he says. 'We're getting off.' He pulls me up out of the seat, spoiling my love-in with my own earlobes.

'But I thought we were staying on until Knightsbridge?' We're going to Harrods, because I can't go home to the North East of England without buying my sister something for Christmas that comes in a green and gold carrier bag. Even if it's just a box of tea. Which is probably all we can afford now.

'You can stay on if you want, but I'll hurl if we don't get off this bus,' he says, dragging me through the throng of people.

Mike and his legendary travel sickness. Some people suffer from piles, eye twitches, or gluten allergies; with Mike it's an overdeveloped gag reflex whenever he's on anything that gathers speed and turns corners. He jumps off before the doors close, pulling me with him, and for a moment I feel like I'm flying. But not in a good way.

We're only down here in the first place because Mike was given tickets to see Van Morrison through his job as a radio producer for a late-night chat show on Newcastle's Blaze FM. The palm-greasing from the station's advertisers usually just runs to tickets for a football match, which always makes my upper lip curl because I happen to be the only person in northern England who doesn't give a damn about football. So this was quite exciting. Plus Aimee is staying with my sister; Mike and I rarely get away just by ourselves anymore.

The bus belches diesel into the air, and Mike does a wet burp. I stroke the back of his head. His hair is rapidly going grey for someone not quite forty. The style has been the same since the day I met him: collar-length and side-burned — a 1950s male rockabilly pompadour. I remember when I first laid eyes on him in the coffee shop on Newcastle's Grey Street thinking he looked remotely like Henry Winkler from *Happy Days*. While this wasn't a selling feature in itself, there was something appealing about the way he didn't conform to the 'David Beckham blond highlights' standard that every other bloke did in 1996.

'Are you all right?' I ask him.

Another wet burp. 'Ergh!' he says. 'Come on, let's walk.' He takes hold of my hand, his hot and clammy fingers lacing between my cold ones. Given he's not feeling well, I will lift my ban on handholding this one time. The problem is that at five feet nine inches tall, I'm an inch and a half bigger than him in my bare feet. Now, there are some men who love the idea of doing a Dudley Moore, and I have a feeling Mike is one of them, but it's not reciprocated. I will often joke with him that by the time you put me in shoes, I sometimes feel like I'm taking my child for a walk.

'Hang on, I think we're going the wrong way,' he says now, when we suddenly arrive at Sloane Square, with its skeletal trees strung with blue and white Christmas lights. 'Harrods is back there.'

We're just turning to go back the way we came, and I'm just registering an uncommonly carefree feeling: no work, no Aimee to get off to school or pick up, the endless round of gym classes, meals to make, shopping, cleaning, work…when something shocking happens.

There is a man coming out of a building about fifty feet ahead of us. This wouldn't be odd at all if it weren't for the fact that I know this man. I know him so well that it makes my world become a surreal sort of still.

It's the stature that's unmistakably him. The height: a not-so-common six feet four. And the physique: muscular enough to save him from looking lanky, yet not so bulky that you'd think he must have to work at it. But it was the way he held himself that made him stand out in a crowd: that difficult-to-strike balance of confidence and graceful masculinity. Patrick would never think to stoop to anyone's level. Not literally or any other way. And just looking at him you knew that, and you'd be torn between admiring him and assuming he'd be an arrogant bastard.

My mouth has gone dry. My heart is a strange clash of surprise and sadness.

I am dragged back to twelve years ago. Me, just twenty-one, on an around-the-world adventure, not knowing that I was about to find out what falling in love is. We met in Sa Pa, the misty mountain village in Vietnam, in the famous Love Market — the place where young lovers find one another, and old ones come to remember. We were the only two Westerners there. Patrick was twenty-eight, a Canadian foreign correspondent working in Asia. He was in the Love Market looking for a story. And I had heard all about it, and the concept of it had taken hold of me. I remember how he stood across the square and held my eyes, and never once looked away. And in that moment, I knew I was going to have a grand, ground-breaking, heart-crushing romance. He was it. Nobody had to make the first move. It was somehow already made.

But it can't be him. Patrick lives in Canada. How could I possibly find myself in London for the weekend and see Patrick, who doesn't even live in this country?

But the butterflies in my stomach tell me it's clearly not impossible, it really is him, even though I can't see his eyes because he's wearing sunglasses, along with light jeans and a smart-casual olive-coloured jacket. I would know him anywhere.

My hand slips away from Mike's. The blare of horns, a squeal of brakes, a group of Japanese tourists running after a bus, their feet scattering on the ground, then everything is soundless.

'What's wrong?' I hear Mike's voice, distantly, from beyond the other side of my shock. Memories rush over me, as though it had all been yesterday. As though nothing had happened since. There never was a since. Never a Mike or an Aimee.

Never a life. The man I'm convinced is Patrick is stepping off the curb, raising an arm to flag down a taxi, and in a flash this moment will be gone. Time seems to slow right down, giving me ample chance to do something. But do what? I can't speak or move. I'm a strange mix of wildly excited and ill.

I can only see him side-on, and it's enough for me to doubt again. The face is heavier. The profile isn't quite... If only he'd take off those glasses.

Mike takes hold of my arm. 'What on earth's wrong with you?'

Patrick is bending now, talking through a taxi driver's window. I even recognise the shape of his head.

'Celine?' Mike says again. I hear the concern in his voice; his fingers grip me tightly.

Is Mike trembling, or is it me? What I do now is going to be one of those pivotal moments that change everything. I know this, and all my instincts say *Let it go*.

All but one.

Patrick — if it's Patrick — is climbing into the back of a taxi, and I am now in such a heightened state of panic that I start trotting toward the taxi, hearing Mike call after me, bemusement and slight annoyance in his voice. But I've taken those few steps; the damage is already done. As the taxi starts pulling away, I find myself, inconceivably, starting to run after it.

Then two buses hurtle past, and I can't see the taxi anymore but still my legs have a will of their own. When I'm able to see around the buses, there is now more than one taxi, and I don't know which one he's in. But on I go. I'm a high-speed train about to wreck itself. All the while, my common sense is telling me this can't be Patrick, so what on earth am I doing chasing a stranger?

Then I have a stitch in my side, and a painful airlock in my chest. It crosses my mind that I might be having a heart attack.

The buses and taxis are converging at a traffic light, and I have to stop because my body is giving me no other choice.

I flop forward, my breath coming in gulps, thoughts piling on top of each other: I've just seen Patrick. Or was it him? The face wasn't quite… Maybe this man wasn't as tall.

But it *was* him. I know it was.

I picture him in a cab now, somewhere gone. Absolutely no chance of ever coming this close to him again. And I remember how I lost him the last time. I can still visualise him standing there, in the dim morning light of his cabin, with his bag packed. And me thinking, *You'll walk out of this door and I'll never see you again.* And as he left, my reproachful tone: 'Don't look back at me once you walk out of this door.' And he didn't. I listened to his feet walking away. With his every step, I was thinking, *Go after him, he's only at the tree, he's only at the road.* Then, *He'll only be on the bus, he'll still be at the airport.* Then, *He's somewhere in Hong Kong, he's still in Asia…*

Like the way I would write my address, when I was a child — placing where I lived; positioning my small and insignificant self in the broader context of where everything else was: Celine Walker, 22 Duke Street, Newcastle, England, United Kingdom, Europe, World, Earth.

Then I remember my behaviour. When I look down the street, Mike is standing exactly where I left him, as though he's cautioned himself from coming any closer. London returns to real time, but I continue to stand there helpless and inoperative. And I should be thinking only of how I can explain myself to him, but I am imagining the interior of a black cab with Patrick in it gazing out of the window, unaware that our lives have just synchronised again.

Why hadn't I just shouted his name?

I sit down on somebody's doorstep. And I want to stop the

tears for Mike's sake, but they come anyway. To think we'd been having such a lovely weekend. The earring-shopping; our really nice dinner out. The way we'd linked arms as we walked back to the hotel along the fairy-light-strung Thames Embankment. We chattered all night. Not the routine stuff of his work, my work, the state of the house, Aimee, but frivolous things, almost flirtatious: or it felt so; maybe it was the wine. Then in bed, his tender kisses down my throat; his hands gripping my bottom under my nightdress. The way he knows my body better than anyone else, yet fails to ever really excite me. And sometimes I'm able to pretend different, and sometimes I can't.

The coldness of the step penetrates my coat and jeans. All the good things about my life that I don't want to lose by losing Mike line up in my mind, urging me to remember that Mike is the one I'm with and the one I love. Not Patrick who has spent more time in my fantasies than he ever did in my life. But all I am is numb, defeated before I even try.

Next, I'm staring at Mike's slightly scuffed brown Clarks as my tears turn cold on my cheeks. When my eyes travel up his body and finally reach his pale face, I can see him waiting for an explanation. Dismay and disappointment gather around him, like a man just realising that there's something about his wife he doesn't know. Or maybe he does. Maybe there are things he knows, or suspects, and wishes he didn't. The weights and measures of a marriage; we know things but we choose not to think about them. We choose to bury our heads in the sand.

Mike says only one thing. 'That was him, wasn't it?'

# One

The mail rustles through the box and falls softly on the carpet. I leave my morning coffee and the newspaper and walk down our short passageway to the front hall.

There's the usual stuff: bills, flyers, the odd shares certificate for Mike that still comes to this address even though he moved out eight months ago. But it's the letter-sized white envelope with the solicitor's return address on the front that stops the casual flicking of my hand.

I walk back into our kitchen, conscious that the rain, which has been spitting on and off all morning, is now lashing on the window like a rushed and eerie whisper through a dream. That stealthy rain that is so common in April, sweeping across the wild and exposed Northumberland moors where we live, in a small rural hamlet, some twenty miles west of Newcastle Upon Tyne, about four hundred miles north of London. The kitchen has suddenly gone dark. I switch on the light and find myself just standing there looking out of the window, at my reflection, as though gazing through a ghost. The letter dangles from my limp hand, its contents on a slow parasail through my mind.

Beyond our crumbling stone wall, the wispy mauves and taupe and moss green of the rolling moorland are blanketed by a grey, slow-swirling mist that is probably in for the day. Our cherry tree has dropped its blossoms all over the grass. They lie there like confetti long after a wedding. I pull out a chair from under the kitchen table and sit there before rereading the letter.

The words are all there, saying what words on a decree absolute are supposed to say, but I can't quite believe them. I stare at them for so long that they merge and fuzz, and tears burn in my eyes. As four or five of them drop onto the page, I want — irrationally — for them to have the effect of a magic eraser. But when I look again, the words are still there, telling me the same thing.

We had split up before. I can't even remember why now: something petty and pointless, no doubt. Mike made a transparently unconvincing production of moving out with a tie hanging out of his suitcase, and putting himself up on the couch of a mate from work for five nights. By the Friday he was home, because a) his back was killing him, b) he realised he wasn't the one who was unhappy: I was, so if anybody should leave, it should be me, and c) we'd planned to go camping in Scotland that weekend and he'd been looking forward to it for ages. But this time when he left, he'd already rented another house. He didn't want us making up our minds and changing them again because we were too afraid of life without the anchor of each other, too afraid of the 'over' in case it was worse than staying together. But somehow, through all the business of him going, I still imagined him coming back.

My phone rings, shocking me for a second, and my first thought is that maybe it's him. The kitchen table that doubles as my work desk is covered in papers, magazines, client files, questionnaires, surveys, research findings, my empty cereal bowl, old coffee cups, a chocolate wrapper from a Mars bar. I find the phone just before it stops ringing. A name on my call display. But it's not his name.

The rain rushes at the window again. I'm cold even though the fire's on in the living room and it heats the entire main floor of our small, detached, two-storey stone cottage. My gaze goes to the photo of Mike and me on the shelf above the kitchen table. It was taken five years ago at a wedding: my first client's. Mike's hair, ever the same *Fonz* style. His straight, almost too perfect teeth, and kind, shyly sexy smile. I am head and shoulders taller than him even minus the hat. But it's still a good picture of us. Since he left, I've not once thought of taking it down.

I've noticed something lately though. No matter where I stand, those eyes are watching me. Like they're doing now. They've got this uncanny ability to change when the mood demands it. Sometimes they're smiling, if Aimee and I are locking horns. But other times, like now, they are full of pent-up sadness, as though he is choked with words he cannot say, recognising the frustrating limitations of the fact that he's just in a photograph.

My phone rings again. Someone is persistent. I answer with a flat 'Hello,' still unable to drag my eyes from Mike's seeing only, the untidying and untying of two lives, and the barrel of neutrality and pointlessness that I'm now staring down, at my future. It takes me a moment or two to realise that it's Kim, one of my clients. I run a company called The Love Market, a professional matchmaking service to upper-income executives across the North of England. I met Kim three months ago in her Newcastle Quayside office. She runs one of the largest public relations agencies in the country. The friendly smile and instant enquiry about where I'd bought my leopard-print boots made us bond instantly, in a way that only women can do over something as trivial as fashion. The broken capillaries at the base of her nose somehow mar her pretty, otherwise-flawless face, with its bottomless blue eyes. The faint neurosis when she suddenly cut me off mid-sentence, picked up the phone, and demanded her secretary come in to dust her desk. 'Allergies,' she told me. So that explained the nose. But perhaps not the Devil Wears Prada attitude.

Kim has been on three dates with David Hall, a widowed property developer who responded to my advertisement on the bulletin board of an exclusive golf and country club. I had hoped that three dates was a sign that everything was going quite well. 'I was hoping you might have a minute, Celine,' she says. 'Something really awful has just happened to me.'

Kim's dramatic personality type likes to leave you with a cliff-hanger. This has a way of ensuring that I can't say, *No, Kim, I do not have a minute, particularly as something terrible has happened to you.*

In Kim's case, I'm not too worried about how awful her awful is. After all, this is the person who refused to go on a date with a man because his last name was Schmink. A renowned heart surgeon would have been The One, if he'd only had shoulders and wasn't 'just a pair of arms pinned on either side of his throat.' And then there was handsome, easygoing Frank. What was his crime? Well, didn't he just order dessert for himself when she told him she didn't want any?

'What happened, Kim?' I tell myself I have to sound more concerned. Knowing my luck, this could indeed be the one time I've love-matched a client with Jeffrey Dahmer II, or someone who keeps albums of teenage girls in his night-table drawer. But the main reason is that Kim pays me two thousand pounds per year to match her with ten to twelve men. I take this responsibility seriously and wouldn't want any of my clients at The Love Market thinking I don't have their best interests at heart.

'Celine, I'm just so shocked and disgusted. It was horrible!'

I am guessing it's an issue of a deviant sexual preference, or an odd-looking private part. One thing I have discovered in this business: women will always clinically dissect their sexual encounters with their dates. Whereas my male clients never talk about their dates disrobed, and I've never yet heard a man say that the sex wasn't good enough. I pinch the bridge of my nose and try not to sound as if moments ago I was crying. 'Why don't you tell me all about it right from the beginning, Kim?' I say.

She launches into how the salmon was overcooked at dinner, and then about a film. 'We couldn't agree on which one to see, so we ended up going to see one that neither of us wanted to see, just to make it fair, which, of course was a complete and utter disaster, because if there's one thing I can't stand it's anything to do with aliens…' Now I get fifteen minutes on the plot of the film that neither of them wanted to go and see.

As she chatters on, I stare out at the garden again. It looks so barren in the rain. The empty planter boxes. The vegetable patch that probably won't get tended to now that Mike's gone. I'll never wake up beside him again, never attend a single one of his tedious office Christmas parties, try to match another pair of his socks, follow him into the toilet, argue over visiting his mother, grumble about the predictability of our lives, or why I don't think we're happy. *Never* is such a final word. The rain slides down the window like tears. I realise I've let my hand with the phone in it drop. Kim's voice is rattling on from its new place by my knee. When I bring it back to my ear, she's still going on about aliens. 'Kim,' I interrupt her. 'I thought you were telling me about David.'

'I'm getting there!' she growls. 'I'm just trying to set the scene. But as you're obviously in some sort of hurry…if you must know, we went back to his very nice Newcastle loft, and we were on his very nice couch, and one thing was leading to another. I had tugged down his jeans…' She sighs a traumatized sigh. 'Oh, it was awful!'

The Apollo rocket will come back from the moon before she finally spits it out. 'Go on then. Tell me.'

'It was just…it was just there. His raw, exposed…' She searches for the word, then dramatically says, 'Willie.' She tuts. 'The man doesn't wear underpants!'

'Oh!' I say, momentarily taken aback.

'Oh?' She sounds stern. 'Is that it?'

'Well, have you thought that maybe he was just behind on his washing?'

'But they weren't in the washing. And I checked his drawers. None there either. His entire flat is an underpant-free zone.'

'So, hang on a second. You were in his bedroom? Does this mean you slept with him?'

'Does it sound like I was attracted to him, after that?' Her tone has *imbecile* written all over it. 'I had a quick mooch when he got up from the couch to go to the toilet. To clean himself — who knows what they have to do.'

I try to force away the rather distasteful picture of David doing unsavoury things in the bathroom, and of Kim ferreting in his dirty laundry. While I'm always intrigued by what makes people tick, and the blend of part-science part-instinct that goes with matching two human beings — a bit like pairing wine with food — I never bargained for how this job would take over my life. I am called upon, whenever my clients need me, to be a psychologist, babysitter, best friend, life coach, stylist, punching bag, hatchet man, walking dictionary of everything… I'm always contemplating ways to charge them a retainer for the hours I generally spend just listening to them talk, which they seem to think comes free with the service, but I've never quite worked out how to do that. I've got to get onto it. I could be rich.

'He's a freeballer,' I tell her. 'They're not as rare a breed as you might think. Freeballers feel cleaner and healthier without underwear. Often it's because they've had air-flow problems in the past, so their doctors have encouraged them to give this a try. Freeballers aren't a known sociopathic group, so we're really quite safe with him. And — I know you'll disagree — but you actually can't make a judgment about anyone by their underwear status. And wearing underwear does not guarantee that you are a cleaner person. Just ask any woman who has ever done an old man's laundry.'

Molly, Mike's old black and tan tabby cat, comes into the kitchen to eat her food, and rubs up against my bare leg. I reach down and stroke her warm and bony body.

'I'm sorry — are you saying that I shouldn't find it disgusting, Celine?' She sounds hurt, and a little angry, as though I have crossed enemy lines. 'I mean, wouldn't you? He wears his jeans, even his Armani suit, next to his bare bottom. How often do you think he washes his jeans, or gets his suit dry-cleaned?' Her tone implies I obviously have suspicious hygiene habits myself.

I look at Mike's picture again. His eyes seem to be smiling. And I know he'd get such a kick out of this, if I told him. Then it strikes me how he's not going to come home ever again and kiss me, and ask me how my day was. I'm not going to sit over dinner telling him about Kim and the underpants, and Aimee and the latest school drama, and vent all my small frustrations. And somewhere inside me it feels like a colossal tragedy that our marriage has come to this. All those assumptions we had that because we were together, we would stay together. As though the two were somehow interknit.

'I'm just not sure it constitutes a serious problem, that's all,' I tell Kim, hauling myself back from where my mind just wants to go: thinking about us. 'I mean, not if everything else is good about him. Remember the Seven Deadly Sins? David Hall doesn't commit a single one of them. He's not chronically late, or rude to waiters. He's got no scary divorce stories, or satanic kids, he doesn't have anger issues, isn't unduly attached to his parents, and he didn't suggest splitting the bill on your first date. I'd say we shouldn't write him off just yet.'

'I don't know…'

'Try to remember what's out there. You know that David is one of the few men who can handle a successful, independent woman, and he isn't looking for someone thirty years younger.' A subtle reminder to her that, at forty-five, Kim is not likely to attract a man her age. I don't need a study to prove that heavy objects fall faster than light ones, nor do I need one to tell me that most men in their late fifties want to try out their inner Ronnie Wood when it comes to finding new love again, and that doesn't bode well for women like Kim, or me, who don't need an older man for his money, and prefer the standard age difference of 2.2 years. It pains me to think she might be giving up on him this fast.

My words ring a note of panic in me about my own future. Who is out there for me? Am I so played-out and jaundiced now that I can't energize myself to go down this same path with another man? Am I going to be that once-burned person — the very type I've counselled when they have wanted to join The Love Market? I'm not even sure I know what ingredients are supposed to go into this recipe for the perfect feelings you should feel for someone before you marry them. Before someone will accuse you of going into it for the wrong reasons.

I remember Mike's words in one of our last fights: 'If all I am is a safety blanket for you then this is just a marriage of convenience.'

'Can't you just give him another chance?' I plead, on David Hall's behalf. The photo is watching me again, as if it knows a few things about second chances. 'Shall we give it another try?' I can hear Mike saying, after every time we'd fought and talked about whether we should break up: sending up these trial balloons. Testing the waters of each other, to see if the other one was reaching the limits of their tolerance. I can't look at him, and yet I can't stop looking at him. I get up and turn the frame face down, thinking, *Okay, now all I have to do is erase his face from my head.*

'I don't know,' Kim says. 'Honestly, I'm not sure I can be attracted to him after this.'

'Look,' I tell her, brightly. 'Why don't you tactfully present him with a pair of underpants, and tell him you'd find him really sexy if he put them on?'

'Or, I have a better idea,' she says. 'You could have a talk with him. Tell him Kim says the underpants are going to be the deal breaker.'

I picture Kim as the Mafia Don, and me, her 'made guy.'

'After all, I do pay you,' she says.

With types like Kim, retaliation to irksome comments is no-win. You have to appeal to the higher power that controls them: their ego. Sweet talk them round to your way. 'I'm well aware you pay me, Kim. And you know I'll do anything to help. But in this case, given it's about his nether regions, I just think it's going to be better coming from you. I'm sure if you gently tell him how much it bothers you, he'll have those boxers on as fast as you can say oh-baby!'

'Do you think?'

'I don't just think. I know,' I tell her.

'Let me give it some thought,' she says, sounding miffed that she didn't succeed in getting me to do her dirty work.

When we hang up, it strikes me what a change I've undergone. How conceited I used to be about being a married woman with a child. I was lucky enough to have been lured into this false sense of security that you have when you are attached legally, and in other ways, to another human being. Where you can say and do virtually anything to them, and they will tolerate you and try to understand you, and put it down to you just being you — for some greater goal that even they don't clearly understand. It somehow put me above the petty criticisms that the single confer upon their dates. I had deeper, more justifiably petty things to find fault with. Back then, that seemed to signal that my life was in good shape.

I look at Mike's picture again.

It was clearly a very warped way of measuring success.

# Two

My seventy-five-year-old father is teaching my twelve-year-old daughter to draw — art being the only subject she seems to do okay in these days. Aimee has reached that age where she no longer believes what her report cards used to say to encourage her when her marks were lagging behind those of her friends: 'Aimee has not yet reached her full potential.' If trying hard were everything, Aimee would be a genius. Yet the best she ever hits are Bs. Gymnastics is the only thing she has consistently excelled at. Back in the autumn, though, a month after her dad moved out, Aimee fell off her bike. She was dodging a deer that had stalked out from behind trees along a country road. She broke her right arm and her leg in two places and had to miss six weeks of school. For Aimee, the bigger catastrophe was that she missed out on competing in the under 16s regional gymnastics championship that she'd trained so hard for.

I go over to the settee to where she's sitting, and drop a kiss on the top of her silky brown hair with its one tiny plastic clutch clip keeping back the fringe that she's trying to grow out. 'Hi, sweets.'

'Hi, Mum,' she says, flatly, and waggles her fingers in a wave, too absorbed by her 'Girls Aloud' DVD to look up.

I go back into the kitchen. My dad is seated at my messy work table. I do a double take on his face, as it seems frozen into a strangely guilt-ridden and electrified smile. My eyes go to the 8" x 10" manila envelope over which he has, quite possessively, laid both his hands. I go to pick it up, and he clings on, until we are playing tug of war. 'What's this?' I say, when I manage to get it off him and take out the photograph that's inside.

'Sandra Mansell, thirty-six, from Jesmond. Do you think she'd be interested in modelling for me? She has very good bones.'

I look at the photo of my buxom spa-owner client, and now, back at my father's bright red face that has broken a small sweat. 'I'm sure Sandra wouldn't want a man of your tender years getting his jollies from her picture,' I scold him, playfully tut-tutting, and I take it away from him. I put it back in the envelope.

'You never know,' he chuckles. 'She might.' Then he salutes the envelope and says, 'So long, Sandra. You're a real man magnet. It was wild while it lasted.'

I try not to let him see the smile that breaks out on my face, and I go and hang up my drenched coat behind the back door. 'Do you want to stay for dinner, Dad?' I set about emptying shopping bags onto my countertop. But he's still off in space with a shifty smile on his face, thinking about Sandra.

Being the daughter of a diminutive, dirty old man has been the cross I've borne to lesser and greater degrees nearly all of my life. When I was Aimee's age, my father left my mother and me for a young woman. Not because he no longer loved us, but because he loved this Marie more. He tried to explain to me that if my mother hadn't loved him so much, he might have loved this Marie less. And even though he loved me more than he loved any of them, he still had to leave us for her.

I was already confused. All I knew was the bottom line: I had lost my dad. And because my mother was so stung by life, in a way I had lost her too. Even more confusing was that my mother never looked like she loved my dad too much, not by the way he would do something that would harden her against him for weeks. And even when she'd forgiven him it was still there: the hesitant return to trust; the anticipation of another transgression later.

So this was what love was, I used to think. The slow unbeguiling. The sad thing was that in having my mother as his wife, my father already had what many men wish for: a much younger woman. They had met when she was a pretty nineteen-year-old art student at London's Royal College, and my dad was a forty-year-old Royal Academician who picked her up in a silver Jaguar, when he could barely afford to pay his rent. Five months later they were married, and after nine more, out came me. But parenthood was the fall to earth they weren't ready for. So my father moved us to France to live like the culturally superior expats he saw us as being. Hence the French name that I adapted by removing the accent on the first 'e' because all the kids in school used to poke fun at me. Somehow my father sold enough paintings and managed to pay the rent on a small flat in Paris. As one of life's blusterers, my father got by trading on the image he had invented for himself, of the suave older artist with his beautiful young wife and muse. And the baby. I always imagine I was paraded like a rather 'in' accessory, but when no one was there to admire me, they flung me in the cupboard with the handbags and shoes. Then it was time for me to go to school. My dad's creativity went through a dry patch, and they had no choice but to drag themselves back to Newcastle. Then his 'I can't paint' spell turned into a self-centred trip that lasted forever, and my mother became chronically depressed.

Apparently Anthony, as I came to call him over the years —
my token step in the direction of fully disowning him — needed
a posse of new and naïve women. All he would ever say, when
we had a very stiff attempt at ending the cold war between us
when I was in my mid-twenties, was that my mother didn't fulfil
her end of the bargain. Which means, I think, that she became
a bit too much of a real person for him. But I always sensed that
they divorced because when the mesmerism of each other wore
off, I wasn't enough to make them feel like they had something
worth sticking for.

'Did you say you are staying for dinner?' I re-ask him.
Sometimes it's hard to forget, and difficult to forgive, but time
has a way of ensuring you become bored with your own battle.
Plus I am powerfully aware that my father is an old man now,
and there comes a time in all our lives when we have to start
making amends before we exit this life with one too many
regrets on our conscience.

'Not tonight. I have plans,' he says, coyly.

'Plans?' I look at the deep furrows in his brow, and his hair.
My father has fantastic hair: the thickest, cleanest, most undu-
lating, most ski-slope white tresses. Then there's the black and
shiny pencil moustache, perfectly centred between his top lip
and the base of his nose, which looks like it has been skilfully
applied with boot polish. My dad is dapper, and handsome —
'for a little fellow' as he calls himself.

'Where did you meet this one then?' I ask.

'At the Grope a Grandma night at the old town hall.' When
he sees me smile he says, 'At an exhibition at the Laing, actually.'

'She's an artist?'

'Would meeting her at a gallery assume she'd have to be?'
My dad speaks posh for a council-housing-estate boy, always
sounding his 'ings.' Winning a scholarship to the oldest and

most esteemed art school in England was one of those flukes of fate that somehow validated his belief that he was too good for where he came from, and therefore made his fall greater when he had to come back.

'How old is she?' I ask him. My father used to love showing off his girlfriends — each one younger and more beautiful than the next — but now we never lay eyes on them. 'You sure she exists?' I asked of his last one. 'She exists,' he said. 'She just hasn't yet had her coming out at the debutante's ball.'

'Which means she's about seventy-five, right?' I teased. And he grimaced. 'Don't be ridiculous. I've never gone out with someone my age, and I'm not about to start now.'

Despite the fact that my dad is theoretically past it, he has lost none of his old ability to beguile women. Despite what he's thinking or feeling, my dad can turn it on for the ladies, at any time. It's a work of art watching him in action. How he'll laud the often-invisible minutiae of their beauty, as his hand finds its way to the curve of their lower back, so they are never in any doubt about the masculinity that wrestles in his trousers. But it's the way he talks about his passion for my mother, and his era as a painter in Paris that makes people recognise that men like my father don't come around every day. And not only do they deserve you humouring their stories about their life, you do so willingly, for the chance that something they say will change the way you look at your own.

'How is it relevant how old *Anthea* is?' he plays with me.

'Oh God! Anthea!' I have a chuckle. I'm picturing a thirty-year-old wannabe co-host of *Dancing with the Stars*, and he knows I am.

When he was young, my father took himself way too seriously; now he uses our mutual ability to find him slightly funny as something that brings us closer.

'Anyway, how is The Love Market these days?' he asks, with scoffing emphasis on my company's name. A romantic like my father finds it morally indefensible that anyone would actually pay someone to find them a partner. I look over and see him peering at a report from the University of St Andrews on 'Face Values Applied to Love Game' — the latest research on what people believe your face says about your attitudes to sexual commitments. My bedtime reading.

'It's doing well. Thanks for asking.'

'And how are *you*?' he exaggeratedly lets the paper float out of his hands, making sure I see, to emphasise his scathing regard for it.

I stop clanking things on the bench. What is it about an innocent inquiry about your well-being that makes you realise you're actually not doing well at all? 'I'm all right, Dad.'

'That doesn't sound very convincing.'

I shrug. Even though we've been largely absent from one another's life, my father still has a way of knowing things without my having to tell him.

'Remember what Gwyneth Paltrow said. The best way to mend a broken heart is time and girlfriends. And from my experience it has always worked,' he says.

I smile at his joke. 'Why's your heart broken this time?'

'I wasn't talking about me. I was talking about you.'

I scan the table for my decree absolute. 'Have you been reading my letters?'

'No. Would I? But if you leave things lying around they become public property.' Then he adds, 'But this is a sad day.' Because my dad always liked Mike.

We meet eyes, and in that moment, all the things I want to say line up for me to speak them, only I can't speak them, and he knows I can't. So he stands up, because he knows we're not going to have a big heart-to-heart. And inwardly, we will use the fact that Aimee is right here as the excuse to keep this uncrossable emotional bridge between us. He slips his raincoat on over his button-down-collared shirt — my father is always dapper, turned out like a lovable little pimp, as my half-sister Jacqui will say — then he goes and kisses 'his favourite grand-daughter.' Aimee will usually remind him, disdainfully, that she's his only granddaughter. Although, lately, Aimee seems to act as though she considers everything and everyone to be beneath her, not just her granddad and his tired jokes.

'I better be off, diddle-doff,' he says. '*Anthea* will be waiting for me.' He shoots me a prankish smile.

I go over to him and give him a quick cheek-kiss, wishing I could cuddle him, but how do you suddenly start being huggy when you never really have? What you do is you hug your daughter all the more, when she'll let you, to give her what you never had. 'Don't do anything you shouldn't do,' I tell him, affectionately, just glad that he's alive and he's got this much spirit left in him, and hoping I'm half as frisky as he is in my old age.

'Oh, I'll try,' he says, with a wink.

# Three

'What's wrong?' I ask Aimee, as we sit in an empty Italian restaurant called The Godfather, down a Newcastle City Centre side street, at Monday lunchtime. Three bored Italian waiters stand watching our every move, while the Gypsy Kings sing 'Bamboleo.'

I kept her off school today. Not that I make a habit of encouraging my daughter to play hooky. But sometimes they call it retail therapy for a reason. And I know from experience that satisfying Aimee's addiction to shoes once in a while has healing powers that all the mothering in the world can't compete with. 'It's about your dad and me, isn't it?' I ask the top of her head as she stares for a disproportionately long time at the four lunch specials on the menu. And she could be me, twenty-four years ago. Although my mother never took me out for my favourite food and asked me how I was doing.

She shakes her head. I look at her shiny mane of hair, the porcelain skin like my mother's, her lowered gaze and the heavy Garbo-esque sweep of her eyelids. My daughter, who turns herself out like a rebellious street urchin, is in her new style habit of wearing a short-sleeved T-shirt over the top of a long-sleeved one, shortie, pleated denim skirts, and colourful chequered tights — sometimes poking holes in them. 'If you want to talk about it, we can.' The waiter swoops, brandishing a notepad. We both order the lasagne.

And then she says the words that cut me open. 'Why don't you love him anymore?'

I close my eyes, and it's a moment or two before I can look at her again. 'I do love him, Aimee. Probably as much as you do. But the love between a husband and a wife is different. It's not quite as unconditional as the love your dad and I have for you.' In the way she looks at me now, I can tell that explanations are just fancy word games to her. She's asserting that one selfish right we both know she has: to have us be a family. And I know that because I've been there.

'Aimee, I have never stopped loving your dad. I'm just trying to learn how to live without him and it's a very strange place to be. I may have to figure it out as we go along. Other than loving you very much, that might be the best I can offer you right now. It might be all I have.'

Nothing. I can't read her. I sometimes want to beg her to cry, scream, anything. Not this. This flatness. She used to be such an expressive child. Then Mike left, she fell, and a part of her has stayed fallen. 'We tried, Aimee, that's what I'm trying to say. We tried to make our marriage work. But sometimes you realise it shouldn't require all that effort.'

The Gypsy Kings are singing 'Volare' now, and the waiter sets down garlic bread that we didn't ask for, angling for a flirtatious glance. Aimee stares at the top of the table. I can almost see her young little mind grappling its way around adult truths.

But am I lying to both of us? Now that my daughter is the very thing I hated being — a fixture moved back and forth between two parents and no longer part of a mathematical set determined precisely by what's in it — did we try hard enough?

'*We didn't really split up,*' Mike said, shortly after we split up the first time. '*We were just taking a little break from each other.*' He rubbed the tear off my cheek with his thumb. 'I'll never part with you,' he said, as though I was his favourite record from his prized seventies collection. I can still feel the way his thumb stretched the skin under my eyes.

I never had to ask myself if Mike only came back for Aimee. In Mike's mind I knew he'd never really left.

'I hate this dumb song,' Aimee says. The waiters are leaning up against the nearby wall, watching us, in competition for our attention. 'Who are they?' she asks. 'Dumb, Dumber, and Dumbest?'

I have a small chuckle at her childish cruelty. Looking at her, it's like living my life over again, analysing myself. 'We could go shopping after this for something for you to wear to Rachel's party.'

She lifts a sheet of bubbling mozzarella with her fork, her long T-shirt sleeve coming to knuckle-level. 'I'll get third-degree mouth ulcers if I eat this,' she says, peering at the steam coming off it. Then she adds, 'Why? It's not like I'm going.'

I set my fork down. 'Since when?'

'Since she didn't invite me.' She meets my eyes. 'But I'm not upset or anything.'

'Why didn't she invite you? Did you ask her?'

She rolls her eyes. 'How would it be better if I knew?'

I try to find an answer for that, but as often happens, my daughter outsmarts me. What she lacks in school marks, she makes up for in her ability to cut through the chaff and tell it like it is. 'You're not distancing yourself from her because she won the gymnastics championship and you resent her for it, are you?'

She drops her jaw now, and rolls her eyes again. I regret asking her. But something in her expression... I am not convinced.

'You had a fall, Aimee. Yes it was bad, but imagine how worse it could have been if you'd hit your head. Your bones are young and will heal and be good as new. You will win other competitions.' I know that my 'You can still lose the battle and win the war' line isn't all that much consolation, but it's the best I've got right now.

I look at her fingers seized around her fork. They are long and gangly and pale and perfectly tapered, with their pearly painted nails. I have adored them from the moment I first laid eyes on them. Sometimes I think I've watched Aimee grow through her hands. I'm like a fortune teller, only I don't read palms, and I only see the present. If only I could see what was even a short distance ahead for all of us. That might have been a gift worth having.

'Her mum said that marriages only break up because one person has met someone else.'

It's me doing the jaw-dropping now. 'Aimee! You shouldn't listen to things like that! Yes, people sometimes do fall in love with others. But in our case neither one of us was looking to meet someone else, Aimee. We never were.'

We eat the rest of our food in silence. When we're done, I glance over and accidentally catch the waiter's eye, which seems to make his day.

'You've got yourself a boyfriend,' Aimee says.

'And hands off, he's all mine.' I catch a hint of a smile. 'Listen, we're going to pay up and shop till we drop. And we'll plan our own party. How about that?' I pull out my money to pay the bill. The waiter is on me in a split second, gagging for some more eye contact.

'Who'll be left to invite?' she says, pulling a smile. 'They'll all be at Rachel's.'

'Don't worry,' I rub the top of her head. 'We'll think of somebody. Even if we have to pay people to come, just for show.'

She tuts at me now. But it's a happier tut. And right now, that feels like a major achievement on my part. 'Can we get out of this dumb restaurant now?' she asks.

'Gladly,' I tell her.

# Four

'I was reading an article the other day,' I tell my half-sister Jacqui while we're out running and attempting to get fit for summer. 'It was about how memories of your first love can ruin your future relationships. It said that if you had a passionate first relationship and allow that to become your benchmark, it becomes inevitable that future partnerships will seem boring and a big disappointment. It said ideally we would all wake up and have skipped our first relationship and be in our second one.' I am panting hard. My legs don't seem to want to work and my heart has gone out in sympathy.

'I'd happily have skipped mine,' she says. 'Remember Darren who wore the T-shirt that said I LUV LAXATIVES?'

I grin. 'Did he really?' I ask her. 'Love laxatives?'

She chuckles, and then says, 'So I take it you've been thinking about Patrick again.'

The mention of his name after all this time is like a groggy regaining of consciousness to a life almost forgotten. 'I wasn't. No. But of course now I'm going to. Thanks.'

'Divorce is like a death, Celine. You have to grieve the marriage but you have to move on too. There's no point in moping. It means a marriage is over, not a life.'

'Who said I'm moping, Jacqui?' My pace slows. 'And of

41

course I know my life isn't over! But it's only been a week. They say it takes two years to get over a divorce.'

'That's only when they've walked out on you when you're three months pregnant. Or they've been displaying their willies on the Internet. When you're the one that wasn't happy, life begins the minute he's down the garden path. In theory, I suppose.'

'I don't believe that. Not for one minute. Even if I wanted to run out and get someone else, I feel a bit like discounted goods now.'

She scowls at me. 'That's a thing to say!'

'It's true. It's not exactly an attribute, is it: telling someone you're divorced.'

It's stopped raining so I take off my nylon jacket and wrap it around my hips as we run, enjoying the April air on my bare arms. 'Do you think that's why I've never exactly cracked up, Jacq? Because I was so convinced it was what I wanted?' I nip my dripping nose. The worst I've done when he first left was spill the milk when I was putting it on my cereal, because I was distracted by a moment of extreme missing him. 'I mean, I've never totally lost the plot, have I? Never walked around Hexham market in my dressing gown, stockpiled Prozac in the garage, backed my car into a small person who I mistook for a street lamp… What's wrong with me?'

Jacqui's striking almond eyes latch onto mine. Even though we're not real sisters — Jacqui being the daughter of my mother's second husband — our thoughts and fears definitely seem to spring from the same well. We've even been told we look alike. Similar height — I'm an inch taller and we have similar body types — slim enough, but prone to packing on ten pounds after two weeks of pigging out. At thirty-six, I'm already going grey and colour my long hair a dark chestnut brown, whereas Jacqui, two years my junior, has naturally mousey hair, highlights it blonde, and wears it in a bob. When my mum married Len, his kids — Jacqui and Chris — had lost their mother to cancer. Somehow there we were, a miscellany of identities put together under one roof: a five-piece family in a doll's house. I just thought that Len was a pervert, Chris a lame-brain, and Jacqui was always there, trying to be my friend. Maybe I'd not have resented her if she didn't seem to have my mother's approval in a way that I never did, even if it was just my mother sucking up to Len — who was there, earned good money, and wasn't my father. That is, until he started going out in Chris's shirts and coming home covered in love-bites, then ran off with a nurse, and became exactly like my father. Then Jacqui, Chris, and I had a bit more in common. We all had absentee dads, and in a way we were all motherless: theirs had died, and mine was there in body but little else. Chris now lives near Hull with his high-maintenance girlfriend, and once in a while he'll phone and we'll end up talking for four hours, and then he disappears for two years. And Jacqui is the human equivalent of my ligaments, always holding me in place to prevent dislocation.

'You don't have to have a public breakdown to prove to the world that you carry pain,' she says.

I shake my head, feeling the tears build. 'It's just odd thinking of him being out there living a life without me. Him with someone else. Or me, with somebody who doesn't share any of my history, who isn't Aimee's father. Who never actually stood there and shared that joy and amazement when she was born. How do you suddenly not have someone in your life anymore when for thirteen years they literally were your life?'

Our pace slows a little more, until we come to a walk. Jacqui looks at me, with that expression in her eyes, of someone who will always want to protect me from my worst self. 'This isn't because you want him back, is it?'

'I can't be that messed up, can I?'

'It's got definite Taylor-Burton elements to it. But where's the law that says you can't get back together again if you've made a mistake?'

I lean over and pant, realising that as I've not been running in about two months I seem to have become seriously unfit. 'Yes, but we were never Liz Taylor and Richard Burton, were we?' Jacqui will always confer romance on everything, and I've become so cynical that I don't know whether she's right to want to, or she's mad to try to. 'They had something indestructible that destroyed them. We were empty vessels who wanted the other to fill them.'

'How do you know he's not divorced and out there thinking about you?' she asks.

I stand up straight again. 'Are we talking about Patrick again by any chance?' My sister is like a dog with a bone over this topic. After I told her about him all those years ago, Jacqui was the only one who seemed to fall under the spell of him, the way I had. She was the only one who didn't judge him, or me, when I told her what the problem was with Patrick. I could say things about him and she knew. As though she too had been his lover at one time. Plus she was the only one who ever tried to drill me with good advice about how to forget him. Which couldn't have been brilliant because it clearly never worked.

We walk now, Jacqui strides it out employing both legs and arms, always convinced she has to shed a few more pounds than she really does. 'I don't know anything about him, or what he's doing. Do I?'

'But the point is, you still wonder.'

'Thanks,' I tell her. 'For being in my head.' I peer at her strikingly pretty face. 'But actually, I don't. Not anymore.'

'Have you Googled him lately?'

'I don't do things like that.'

'Why not? You did it before.'

She forgets nothing. 'Once. Ages ago.'

'But didn't you look him up after you thought you saw him in London?'

I tut. 'Okay, twice then. And it wasn't him. We've been through this a million times.'

'All because he was wearing sunglasses and you needed to see his eyes to be convinced. And you rang the hotel and they told you there was no guest by that name.' Sometimes we will find ourselves talking about Patrick as though he wasn't old news.

I remember how I snuck away from Mike to use the payphone, how my heart hammered as I dialled that number. How I was worried Mike was going to know just by my face. I was outside myself watching myself do it, disapproving but unable to stop myself. If it was Patrick I had to know. And I would have to cope with whatever act of insanity I would commit when I found out. The fact that I was even contemplating a reckless act of insanity of course spoke volumes to me about my marriage, which depressed me for days. And that was a side effect I tried to hide, but Mike had to see it, and know.

'Everybody wonders about somebody, Jacqui. It's called the politics of disenchantment. But — I even researched this once — most reunions with old flames don't work out. Not unless it was a war separation or something on that scale. The moral is, you have to live the life you're living. Not some parallel life that you wish you could live.'

She pretends to play the violin. 'Nice words. I've got some

too. Life is short. Botox is just round the corner. You have to grab your happiness by the horns. Maybe seeing him three years ago meant you were on some parallel cosmic track. Maybe it meant you weren't supposed to forget him.'

'Well, I'm sure he's forgotten me. I mean it's not as though he's ever come looking for me in all these years, has he?'

'Who knows? Maybe he really wanted to. Or maybe he did and you were nowhere to be found. If only you'd been a modern gal who keeps her own name in case old boyfriends try to look her up.'

I laugh.

'Seriously,' she says. 'You're thirty-six and gorgeous. You're a good person, a great mother — even if Aimee doesn't think so at the moment — and whatever you felt deep down, you were a good wife. So it's guaranteed that you're going to find another man. But there's still this unfinished business in you. And even if he lives in another country, even if you've not spoken to him in fifteen years…who's to say that there's absolutely no way it can ever happen? What have you got to lose by looking him up? Really? When you think about it, Celine — nothing.'

I give her a sweaty hug. 'You talk a load of pipe dreams, but I love you nevertheless.'

I go home and Google 'breaking up'. How did I ever exist before I used the Internet to find out how I'm feeling? There is so much written on divorce. All the distasteful puns by men about ex-wives taking them to the cleaners. Quotes from Zsa Zsa Gabor to Margaret Atwood. There's 'Wikihow' to cope with going solo again. Apparently God has a lot to say on the subject too. And best of all, there's the jargon that sounds impressive, by the so-called relationship experts, but no one has a clue what it means. My favourite being:

'*When you and that person have changed to any extent, it is necessary to let go of the relationship, so that each of you can fulfil your life path.*'

Life path. Wasn't I on a life path? If I wasn't, then what was it? If I wasn't already fulfilling it, then what the hell was I doing?

'*Refusing to let go of the painful past will serve as a roadblock to love.*' Yes, and you'll become like my mother: one of those stung-by-life people who can't exactly love themselves either.

'*Letting go of your old self and letting the new you emerge can be frightening. But by taking a leap of faith into the unknown, it might reveal what you are truly capable of becoming.*'

The new me, and a leap of faith into the unknown?

I think about this for a while, not minding this one, actually. Didn't the old me used to be such a daring girl? I dove headlong into life, and the thrill of it was fantastic. Then marriage made everything feel a little too certain for my comfort level.

I click off there, and think of Jacqui egging me on to do this.

Then I type in Patrick's name.

# Five

There are countless articles on him. Many of which I've seen before, because, of course I've Googled him way more than I've ever admitted, which always felt like a form of infidelity in itself. Would I have liked Mike looking up the same ex-girlfriend? Would I have been able to convince myself that it was enough that it was me he'd married? But then again, perhaps infidelity is not the worst thing that can happen to a marriage; it's giving up.

I digest everything on him like it's new to me. Wikipedia references. Career profiles. Something about him winning an Emmy for his coverage of Hong Kong being returned to China. A fascinating interview with him in *Frontline* magazine. But it's the image results that spellbind me. So many of them I have seen before, when I combed over them to answer that one question: was it him I'd seen in London?

There's a new one on. He's wearing a khaki combat jacket, and is posing against a parched mountainous backdrop of some foreign war zone. It looks like it's probably recent. It's his most 'close-up' shot on here. The face is older: shockingly so; the cheeks fuller and softer with age, a flush of a suntan across the bridge of his prominent nose. His once fair hair is greying, and there is a sadness and seriousness that never used to be there in his eyes. 'Wikipedia' tells me his birthday — which I already knew. Patrick is forty-three now. 'Journalisted' catalogues every article he's written on wars. And yet, I can't find anything very telling about his personal life. Nor is he on Facebook, or I might have drummed up the nerve to add him as a friend.

Just purely to see if there is some, I type in the words 'Patrick Shale, contact information,' and hold my breath. But all that comes up is the name of a literary and talent agent — Sheckle and Land — who, it seems, represents him. I try again, 'Patrick Shale, email,' not expecting the result to be any different.

But hang on…

There is a Patrick Shale, with an email address, who lectures in the journalism school of a place called Ryerson University, in Toronto.

It has to be him.

# Six

I have to go down to Manchester for a Fake Date. To meet a potential client — a lawyer who was referred to me by one of my female clients, the sparkly and infectious Trish Buckham. Trish is a highly successful lawyer herself, even though you'd never know it by her micro-minis, funky hairstyle, and foul mouth. She has been on a couple of coffee-meets, because she prefers the quick-exit strategy, rather than the way I normally like it to happen — in a restaurant, where you're forced to get to know your match for the time it takes to consume a civilised meal. She never sounds over the moon when I ring her about a possible match. So sometimes I wonder if her heart really is in meeting someone, or if she's doing it just to convince herself — or others — that she's trying.

It's usual for clients to refer friends to me, but it's almost always people I've already successfully matched, who will refer a friend, usually of the same sex. So this is a bit different. Before taking on new clients, I will meet the women for lunch, as well as talk to them a lot on the phone. I always make the men meet me in a restaurant for dinner, in a fake-date situation so I can see them the way a female date would see them, and iron out their kinks before I put them on The Love Market.

Manchester is a bit out of my net, but Trish all but begged me to help her friend.

My train's at twenty past ten, so I drop Aimee off at school at ten to nine, then plan to run a few errands around town before heading to the station. Just as I'm pulling out of the school drop-off area, I see Rachel's mum's shiny white Range Rover pulling in behind me. I put the car in park, wait until she has waved off Rachel, and then I get out of my car just as she is about to pull off.

'Sorry,' I tell her, when she gets out. 'I didn't mean to flag you off the road like a policeman, Sandi!' We exchange a bit of friendly chatter and I try not to imagine her cozying up in bed with her husband and them talking about me and Mike and assuming one of us must have had an affair. I tell her that Aimee is sad she hasn't been invited to Rachel's party, when every other girl in her class has.

As she listens, nothing moves except for her blonde hair blowing around her face in the early April wind. Then her expression hardens. 'I'm sorry, Celine, I wasn't really aware… They don't really tell you things anymore, do they? They think they're so independent now.' She blushes, avoids my eyes, and holds onto her hair to stop it blowing — something I think she wants me to know is irritating her — so I know it's going to be a short conversation. 'You know, it's not really up to me to tell her who to be friends with.' She tries a smile, her hand up by her ear, her Rolex gleaming from under her jacket's sleeve. 'They go through phases, don't they?'

I feel my spine elongating and try not to come off as though I'm growing myself to doff her on top of the head with my cheap handbag. 'You know, Sandi, Aimee's been very down since her fall and everything. Not being able to compete for the gymnastics trophy after the months of hard work she put in—'

'It wasn't Rachel's fault she had an accident! Aimee didn't have to make her feel so bad for winning!'

'I was going to say, it absolutely devastated her.' But this outburst stuns me for a moment or two. Then I say, 'I'm sorry, I didn't know that. I thought Aimee rang and congratulated Rachel?'

'She did. But Rachel could tell she didn't really mean it.'

Rage pounds in me. 'Well...Sandi, if she wasn't squealing with excitement for Rachel it's because she was just so gutted!' Can't she see? Has she absolutely no idea? She has a child herself!

Sandi gives me a withering look. 'Well, you have to teach her that it's no way to behave.'

I open my mouth to say: Well maybe you could try asking Rachel to imagine how she would feel if her parents had just split up, then she falls off her bloody bike and is laid up with broken limbs. Then she can't compete in the one competition that she practically lived for.

The words are bursting out of me, but instead I look at her Hermès scarf neatly fastened around her neck, and remember that in life you can't expect everyone to behave and think and feel as you. So I say, 'You're right. And you know, if you and Rachel think it's fair to invite every girl in the class except Aimee, well, if you can live with that, then I suppose I'll have to.'

Our hard stares last two beats of my rattling heart, then Sandi Bradshaw says a snooty 'Good heavens!' and starts walking back to her car. Then she gets into her supercharged petrol-guzzler and drives off.

I got into the matchmaking business mainly as a hobby when Aimee was little. Going back to my job as a recruitment consultant after my maternity leave, while Mike worked nights and looked after Aimee during the day, wasn't really working out. I was spending so much time at work and travelling the twenty miles to and from Newcastle that I rarely saw my daughter, and Mike never had time to sleep.

I had loved my recruiting job initially. With my degree in Human Resources, and my own flair, I was good at the business development side of attracting new clients, the relationship-building. But best of all I loved searching the market for suitable candidates, the interviewing, and the psychology of evaluating their personality tests — seeing how they might react in certain situations and using it to determine if they were the right fit with a certain corporate culture. I loved the whole exploration of who a person really was, compared to how they saw themselves — and saving them from ending up in jobs they weren't suited to. Then, in my mid-twenties, two things happened around the same time. I had recently headhunted an account-ant called Sharon Gillespie for a new position that was being developed in credit control for an international retailer based in Gateshead. It was the only case I'd been involved in where the fit was wrong. But I had gotten to know Sharon quite well as she'd tried and failed to settle into her new role, and I also knew that she was single and wanting to meet someone. I had an inkling she might get on well with another client of mine, who also worked in the financial sector and was having a career crisis of his own. They were similarly educated, similarly attrac-tive, and both quietly spoken. I introduced them, and love bloomed. Two years later they were married — Mike and I attended their wedding — and Sharon ended up returning to the job I had headhunted her away from.

Around that time, I read an article on how Internet dating was set to go mega. So I started to put my mind to a business idea. After a lot more research into the market for personal introductions, I reasoned that I could apply my existing skills of people-fitting while offering a high-end matchmaking service, the likes of which wasn't really being done in the North East of England. Mike and I had already decided I should leave my job and stay home until Aimee was school age. So I decided to run some ads in the right magazines, to treat it more like a hobby at first and see what happened. I came up with a name — The Love Market, which felt like an obvious choice — bought a Mac computer and designed my own website, all this while Aimee took naps or played beside me. After the first six months I had eleven clients and growing. After the first three years I was successfully matching more than fifty per cent. Now, I have a manageable portfolio of eighty: fifty women to thirty men, and a success rate of seventy per cent. Is it a bad life? Well, sometimes it's frustrating. But it can be entertaining and rewarding. Occasionally it puts me on a such a high that renews my faith in the concept of their being 'the right one' for all of us. That's more than you can say for most jobs.

James Halton Daly is everything that Trish said he is. I can tell this the moment I catch the handsome sight of him at the table. When he looks up from the menu, he sees me striding toward him. He stands to greet me, beams an honest, warm smile, and gives me the quick and shameless once-over.

It strikes me that I've never been on a fake date since Mike walked out, which makes this feel more like a test-run than a business-meet.

The Instant First Impression. Hair: blond and shaggy, like a Wheaten Terrier's. Handsome, in a Sebastian Flyte meets Hugh Grant way. I already know he went to one of the top public schools in England, then Oxford (where he met Trish), and now at thirty-eight, he's a partner at a top Manchester law firm. A charming, likeable toff. 'A' for style. The tweed blazer with the turned-up collar. The pink, striped dress shirt, open at the neck, and the dark jeans with the turned-up cuffs.

'We could forget that I'm about to hire you to find me a girl-friend, and you could be my girlfriend,' he says.

'I'm taken.'

'Are you?' he lays a hand on his heart. 'Well, I imagine it must be one of the leading credentials of being a matchmaker, right?'

*You'd think.*

'How do you become a matchmaker, anyway?' he asks, as I sit down. 'I mean I thought you'd have to live in New York and look like Cher.'

I tell him how I wish I looked like Cher. Then I tell him how I got started, and what it is about the business that gives me a buzz. He seems fascinated. We chat easily. He is shamelessly checking me out, but I'm flattered. I like his boldness. I like the thick silver ring he wears on his left index finger and the way he corrects the waiter by reminding him he should be taking the lady's order first.

I finally get him onto the topic of women.

'Well, the last ten I went out with—'

'Ten?'

'Well, obviously not all together. Over a period of…' He pulls a thinking face, '…a year and a half maybe, went from bad to catastrophic. There was, in no specific order: the smoker, the inferiority complex, the one that was more interested in my friends, she who thinks all lawyers get murderers off, Jen who was obsessed with tango dancing, then there was Miss Religious, Miss Missing Front Tooth, the one that was only fourteen years older than her daughter, then Frannie Fat Fingers—' he recoils, squeamishly '—and then the one who compulsively checked her mobile for messages.'

'Whoosh! That's quite a list of fatal flaws. Especially the compulsive checker of messages.' I tease him, sipping on the Kir Royale he insisted I have.

'It seems that every single woman in her late thirties has issues. Desperation issues, confidence issues, ex-issues, chips on the shoulder…' He shrugs.

'Fat fingers and chips aside though, what is it that you're looking for?'

He seems to think about this, lolling back in his chair, totally at ease. 'Well, an independent, free-minded brunette, who doesn't take life or herself too seriously. Who likes to travel, be spontaneous, is perhaps unsure if she wants kids. She'd be a fabulous mother if she had them, but she'd feel just as complete in an exciting, child-free marriage.'

'Don't you want kids?'

He looks at me candidly. 'I don't know yet. I've not met any-one yet that I could see as the mother of my children.' He looks up at the ceiling. 'Oh, and I don't want any golden retrievers.'

I dip some French bread into the poached egg and bacon appetizer on frisée lettuce that the waiter has just set down. 'What's a golden retriever?'

'Blonde. Beautiful but generic-looking. Always needs brush-ing and combing. Eager to please but suffers from separation anxiety. Destructive when she gets bored.' He chinks his spoon off the edge of his escargots dish.

'Plus, I don't want a lawyer.'

'Why not?' I glance him over, totally taken with his confi-dence and charm.

He leans across the table to whisper. 'Generally, I don't find them very interesting.'

I study him. 'What about Trish?'

'Trish?' he frowns. 'Well, Trish is definitely not your typical lawyer. But she's a mate. I'm hardly going to have a romantic relationship with a mate, am I?'

'Aren't you? Why not?'

'I don't know,' he narrows his eyes, as though he thinks I'm testing him. 'Did she tell you, by the way, that she and I are in competition? We're curious to see which one of us is going to find our soulmate first.'

'Are you? No, actually, she never mentioned that.'

He nods, studying me now. 'So what were you asking? Oh, yes, if I was going to have a romantic relationship with, say, Trish for the sake of argument, then I wouldn't be here, would I? Hiring you?' He leans across at me. 'No, frankly, I don't want a lawyer for practical reasons more than anything. The balance of work and home life. I just don't think lawyers get the concept of balance very well.'

'So you don't want any woman who has a demanding career?' They never do. Even though most of them don't want intellectual dingbats either, or women with no interests or ambition.

'Not true. I'd love a woman who had an absolutely fascinating headache of a career. I just want it to be different to the headaches I have in mine. And I want her to work to live, not the other way round. You can't have two people doing that in any one household. And if we ever did want kids…'

'You'd want her to stay home to take care of them.'

'Politically incorrect. But true.' He pops the last of his six escargots into his mouth and then quickly adds, 'But only if she wanted to. I'd prefer if they didn't get brought up like I did, by a parade of nannies.' He watches me put my napkin on my side plate. 'I'm in the bin now, aren't I? Did Trish warn you you'd go off me this fast?'

'Not at all,' I smile. 'If I put you in the bin, then I don't know what that would mean I'd have to do with some of my other clients. Cremate them maybe, and then bin their ashes?'

He laughs. 'That bad, eh?'

'Actually, no. I'm just joking. I have lovely clients.'

'So what's with this personality profile thing you had me fill in?' he asks over his steak frites, and my Roquefort-stuffed free-range chicken breast. We have talked about his university days, his travels, his social life, and his last proper relationship that lasted six years. 'Can you really match a person with another person based on their answers to those particular forty questions?'

'You mean, as opposed to any other forty questions?' I find flirting with him quite easy and have found my mind wandering a few times to how good in bed I think he might be. And I'm guessing, with that roguish, confident way he has, that he might be a ten. 'Actually, you'd be quite surprised. If a woman answers that a mate's physical attractiveness is extremely important, then I'm not going to set her up with a six-stone jockey with a third eye, am I?'

'Do you have a three-eyed jockey on your books?'

'I used to have a two-eyed one.'

'Did you match him?'

'Eventually, yes.'

'Hang on,' he wags a finger, then reaches down and digs in his briefcase. 'Question, what was it? Thirty-two?' He pulls out the questionnaire I emailed him. 'Ah yes. Love it! IS YOUR BEDROOM MESSY?' He turns serious-faced. 'I mean, if I say yes it is — which, yes, it always is actually — does that mean you'll match me with an equally messy person so we'll live in complete chaos forever? Or are you going to pick a neat freak? That way she'll get so frustrated with my mess that our marriage will become a constant nag-fest?'

I'm about to answer, when he says, 'Or, this one: DO YOU ENJOY A GOOD JOKE? I mean, I'm just curious, is there anyone who will say "No, personally I bloody loathe a good joke — despicable things, good jokes"?' And what about, HOW OFTEN DO YOU GET ANGRY? ONCE A YEAR? ONCE A MONTH? ONCE A WEEK? A FEW TIMES A DAY? Are we talking angry as in ready to singlehandedly open fire on a care home of snoozing senior citizens? Or your more garden variety anger, of "That wanker just cut me off in the passing lane"?'

He's wearing me out. 'Are you done mocking my questionnaire?' I chuckle.

'Yes,' he says. 'I mean, I could go on if you like.'

'Actually, I never used to have any sort of psychometric evaluation—'

'You call this a psychometric evaluation?' His eyes are a mischievous twinkle. 'Oops, sorry, go on.'

I push a rosemary-basted potato into my mouth and try not to grin at his knack for making me look ridiculous. 'What I mean is, I used to just go on instinct. You know — do they look right together? Do I sense a similar outlook, views, values, humour? But so many of my clients expected to fill in a personality profile, because other dating services have one. Personally, I think it's people who are looking to pass themselves off as somebody they're not. You don't have to fill it out if you don't want to.'

'Now if I say I want to, you're going to think it's because I'm dying to lie about myself.'

'It's okay, I've got you sussed already as it is.'

His eyes are flirting all the way to bed. And if this wasn't a professional relationship, he'd already have me there. 'Did Trish fill it out?'

I think back. 'No. As a matter of fact, she didn't.'

He drops it onto the floor by his briefcase, sits back, looks at me, and beams. 'Fancy sharing a dessert?'

I conclude, after our date, that, of the four main masculine personality types (thinker; doer; ideas man; dreamer) James is the classic thinker: the type that forty-one per cent of women are drawn to. Thinkers will immediately command attention when they walk into a room. Thinkers are logical and challenging; they're the managing directors of every big business you've heard of. Communicative, emotional women are attracted to them because they represent stability and security.

All that, and he's sexy as hell. I'm going to enjoy finding the lucky lady who will think this guy's fantastic.

Admittedly, I do.

A high has to be followed by a low. On the train home, Kim of missing underpants fame rings me.

'It's no good, Celine. I went out with him again last night. I picked a very low-key restaurant and I just came out with it and asked him if he was wearing any underwear.'

'What? Kim, that's not exactly how we planned to broach the subject.' I attempt to whisper, cowering in my seat and trying not to look at my travel companion — a businessman opposite who is glaring at me around his copy of the *Financial Times*. I accidentally got booked into a quiet car and should not be using my mobile.

'Well, he said it's completely unreasonable of me to tell him how to dress!'

'Well, in a way he has a point, doesn't he? I thought we were trying the subtle approach? That we were picking the right moment to say how much it would turn you on to see him in a sexy pair of briefs?'

The man across from me has lost all interest in his paper.

'I know. But I'm an out-with-it person! I can't bear pussy-footing around. It's such a time-waste.'

'But he may have felt ambushed.'

'Over underpants?'

'Over the set-up. You. Him. In a restaurant. Grilling him on whether he was wearing underwear. It probably really embarrassed him.'

'I was the one who was embarrassed!'

'Well, what would you like me to do, Kim?' I ask her. 'If the knickers are the deal breaker, which I'm sensing they are?'

'Find me someone else,' she says.

I pointedly switch off my phone and smile at my now rather stupefied-looking travelling companion. No wedding ring. Should I give him my card?

# *Seven*

'Who's that dude you've been Googling?' Aimee looks up from her history book. I was quizzing her on Peter the Great for her test tomorrow.

My hand freezes on the door handle. 'Which du— I mean, person, are we talking about?'

'Patrick Shale.'

'Since when do you check my Internet history?' I clamp a hand on my hip.

'Since you check mine.'

'That's different. You're twelve. There are a lot of perverts out there.'

She rolls her eyes, as though she has met a few. 'So who is he, this Patrick? Is he your new boyfriend?'

'Boyfriend? No! He's just someone I used to know years ago. A Canadian whom I met when I travelled in Asia.'

I see the rare interest, and tinge of scepticism, in her eyes. 'When did you ever go to Asia?'

'When I was twenty-one. Right after I finished Uni, I went travelling around the world.'

'You never told me you went round the world before.'

I think about this. 'I suppose it never came up.'

'So you had a boyfriend centuries ago, and now you're back in touch with him again?'

I laugh a little. 'Well! It was hardly centuries. And he wasn't really my boyfriend. And I'm not in touch with him. I might have Googled him when I had nothing to do, but that's all.'

She frowns. 'Why was he not really your boyfriend?'

I remember the mysteriously covert world that adults move in. My mother never gave me an 'in.' I was like a dog sitting waiting for table scraps of knowledge about her interior life. But they never came.

I go over and sit on her bed, disturbing Molly, who meows and then resettles herself in the side of Aimee's legs, and starts purring.

'He was a Canadian foreign journalist working as Asia Correspondent for the Associated Press, based in Hong Kong. He was my first true love.' She pretends to go on reading, which amuses me. 'Patrick was intense, argumentative, energetic, devastatingly attractive. He was the most exciting man I'd ever met in my life, at that point, and I was lost the minute we looked at one another.'

She puts her book down now, turns onto her side with her back to me and pulls up the duvet, leaving an ear peeking out for more of the story.

'There's a village in the mountains of Vietnam, called Sa Pa. And the story had it that many years ago, a girl and a boy from rival tribes met here, in the market square, and fell in love. But their parents forbade them from marrying. So the lovers made a pact that for the rest of their lives they would meet every year in the same square. And it started a bit of a tradition. It became known as The Love Market—'

'That's the name of your company!'

'Yes,' I smile. 'The way it worked, families would bring their daughters to The Love Market. They were probably the same age as you. And the young boys would come looking for a wife.'

'Wife? At my age?'

'Yep. If you lived there, Aimee, you'd probably be married with ten oxen, a couple of dozen buffalo, and seven kids by now.'

I see her ear move up. Could that be a smile?

'The Love Market,' she repeats.

'Well, it was really a marriage market though. We go to our local market to buy food; these people went to find a wife.'

'That's very twisted.'

'Actually, it wasn't. It was charming. The boy made up a love song and sang it into the darkness. And somewhere in the crowd, a girl sang her own words back to him. Soon they'd be singing in perfect harmony—'

'I'm going to barf. What did they sing about?'

'I don't know. It's not like they sang in English just for me!' Her ear moves again. A definite smile.

'Anyway, the two lovers would then disappear into the forest for three days. And when they next emerged, that basically meant that—'

'They'd had sex?'

I still cannot get used to hearing the word *sex* come out of my daughter's mouth.

'Well, okay, yes, they probably had. But over there, Aimee, once you'd had sex with a boy that was it for you; you got him for life. The girl would go off to live with the boy's family. Her parents would lose a daughter, and another family would gain another pair of hands to work the land.'

'Drastic,' she says. 'I am SO glad I don't live there.'

'No! It was romantic!'

'Ergh. Which part?'

'Perhaps you had to be there.'

'Or not, as the case may be, thank you. I am SO NOT EVER going there.'

I smile at her as she shudders. 'It wasn't just young lovers though. Many of the people were there because they were married to somebody else, but their hearts belonged to another. I remember Patrick telling me that people came to the market to find what they had lost, or what they'd never had.'

She turns slightly again, and looks at me, a little intrigued. 'In my case, someone I met in Asia had told me about The Love Market. I always felt like I had to go there on my own. Something about it appealed to my romantic heart.'

'What happened?'

'Well, Patrick was staying in one of the tribal settlements, in a primitive wood hut, the typical place you'd imagine a foreign newsman roughing it in. And I was staying in a fairly Westernised, sanitary little two-star hotel.'

And it was a swift, wordless passage from hello into bed. I beam a picture of him to mind, and all the old feelings come with it. Patrick was tense and intense, and had trouble relaxing. He couldn't seem to stop overthinking everything — that confidence that bordered on arrogance but never quite crossed the line. He could be demanding and quite cutting. But I loved that about him because it said he was comfortable with me so quickly. He had a glamorous career. I had a degree in Human Resources and no career plan. We were opposites, yet none of that mattered.

'Go on. It's just about getting interesting. Did you have sex with him on the first date?'

'Aimee! You're twelve. I'm not talking about my sex life with you.'

'But did you?'

'No. You never ever have sex on a first date, with anybody.'

'So after how many dates is it okay to have sex with some-one?'

I think for a while. 'Ten.'

Her jaw drops. 'Go on then, get back to what you were say-ing about Patrick.'

'Well, there's not much more to say. We just clicked. We only had four days together but it wouldn't have mattered one way or the other: there was this tremendous connection between us.'

'Only four days! What happened then?'

'Well, Patrick had to leave.' It feels so odd being plunged back into the memory.

'Where did he go?'

'He had to go back to Hong Kong. And he had to go back to his life.'

I don't tell her that he was married. That he'd just gotten married that year. That my impression was that he'd somehow found himself in his marriage a bit by accident. Meeting me seemed to confirm a doubt in him that was already there.

She looks as though I've lost her again.

'I remember thinking I'd never get over him. That this was what having your heart broken was about. And then I met your dad.'

And Mike was FedEx to forgetting. He was so easy compared to Patrick. And much as I loved him for his guilelessness and his gentleness, it wasn't a rip-me-open sort of love. But I'd already decided I didn't want that ever again. 'And obviously I fell in love with your dad...'

Aimee falls silent for a moment or two and then says, 'Do you wish you'd been married to Patrick rather than to Dad?' Her voice sounds sleepy now, and I love her so much in this artless little second where her attention is slipping.

'No. But you never forget your first love. That's just the way life is. So when you meet yours one day, recognise him for what he is: someone you will probably think of many times over the course of your life.'

'Did you always want to set people up after that?'

'Not consciously. But maybe my choices in life that came after were all secretly leading me to it. Who knows?'

She seems to think about this. 'Maybe I could go into The Love Market business with you when I grow up. I hardly think I'm going to have to know all about Peter the Great to know about a few men and a few women.'

'Maybe,' I tell her. She yawns and reaches to stroke Molly. I trace a finger over the part of her ear that's curled over like a dry leaf.

'Maybe you can tell me more about it tomorrow.' She moves her head just slightly, to look at me. 'Oh, and, erm, Rachel invited me to the party.'

'Did she?' I ask, a little surprised. 'And you're going to go?'

'Of course,' she says. 'Why wouldn't I?'

When I walk out of her room, I go straight into mine, to my jewellery box. From underneath a tangle of beads and baubles, I pull out the folded piece of paper he sent me, and read.

# Eight

From the top of Ham Rong Mountain, a grey mist hovers over the village of Sa Pa, North Vietnam, like an exhalation of breath on a cold day. The red-roofed settlements of hill tribe life sparkle through the mist like a handful of rubies beneath a transparent, floating scarf. Little stirs across the never-ending paddy fields from this great height, just a feeling in you, that you are somehow standing alone at the moment when a part of you grows up, something inside you changes forever.

I don't know why I've come here, or why I now feel a part of me will always be unable to leave. I don't really believe in the concept of one true love. Or that there is one person in this world that is meant for us, and we either find them or we find something inferior. But I do believe that the more unusual the way you meet somebody, the higher significance you'd give it.

For the Red Dao tribe, easily identified by the red coin headdresses worn by the women, marriage is a commodity that can be bartered for in the price of a song. The Saturday night ritual of the Sa Pa Love Market isn't what it used to be, before it fascinated tour operators and travellers world-wide — bringing me there and bringing her there. And now hundreds are drawn here, to The Love Market. The Red Dao are private people. Few will accept your American dollars in exchange for your right to take their photograph. On Saturday nights, Red Dao hill tribe youths of both sexes gather in a weekly courting ritual. The males strut around doing a sort of tribal version of Harry Connick, Jr, in the hope of attracting a pretty young female. The songs are rarely romantic. What does any fifteen-year-old boy know about romance? Mostly it's a bragging rite chronicling the boy's physical prowess, or his strong work ethic and ability to be head of a family. But it's well known that the men can usually be found sleeping off opium in the shade of a lethargic water buffalo, while it is the women who do the work. But in the Red Dao culture, everyone is meant to find a mate, so on that one Saturday night at the Love Market, when they walk off into the sunset with a faith in each other that's built on nothing more than a melody sung in harmony, you can't help but wish that finding a soulmate was as simple as that in your own village square.

It definitely wasn't as simple as that for me. I met her there. She was drawn there for reasons not unlike my own. I won't give her a name. By not giving her a name, I am pretending now that she never really existed. I won't say I fell in love. That would complicate things more than they already are. If a marriage is wrong, you can end it. But only a noble coward soldiers on. Best to ruin three lives rather than have two people be happy. Because, as I've said, I don't believe that there is one person for us, and we either find them or we don't.

I didn't have to sing to her. Fortunately Western mating practices conspired and I didn't have to work that hard.

*Being a journalist, you'd think the most natural thing for me to do would be to have taken her photograph. But I had a sophisticated camera I'd bought in Hong Kong and I hadn't quite figured out how to work it. All the photos I took of her came out in shadow. But that shadow follows me now wherever I go. Maybe one day it won't.*

Six months after I returned to England, this came in the post. He didn't even write a letter, just put: A *piece I wrote on spec for* National Geographic, *which they rejected.*

Years later, Mike found it when we were spring cleaning. We ended up having a huge argument, probably because I got so defensive about why I'd kept it. I remember tearing it up in front of him, and throwing it in the bin, out of anger, not capitulation, to prove something more to myself really, than to him. Then I went to bed devastated that I'd destroyed something that had been so meaningful to me. I felt like I was relinquishing a part of myself to Mike that he had no right to own, and what's more, he hadn't even asked me to; I'd done it, to spite someone — probably myself.

A while later he came into the room, holding out a piece of paper. It was Patrick's crumpled letter. He'd dug it out of the bin and taped it back up.

'I don't want you to think you can't keep something because I'm going to feel threatened by it,' he said. 'Because I'm not.'

I should have said throw it away. Instead, taking it from him seemed like an acknowledgment of Mike's insufficiency and my conflict. He looked at me for a while as though establishing a truce. Then he got into bed. It was clearly just one of many glitches to me, which he was used to now. I lifted my head off the pillow and looked at him lying on his back staring at the ceiling. He turned his face toward me, smiled. Then he leaned over and kissed my cheek. It was over, for him. Our marriage wasn't going to end over a letter.

But in a strange way, it did.

# Nine

'Special delivery.' I am surprised to find Mike standing at my door, with Aimee.

I am half-dressed to go out with Jacqui for a drink. Mike was going to pick up Aimee and take her back to his place because he gets her every second weekend.

'I don't understand…' Aimee slinks past me into the house, leaving Mike and me facing one another on our doorstep. It must be so odd to have to knock at the door of your old home, and not be able to just walk in.

Since Mike left, I can only imagine that our relationship has been as civilised as breakups get. Mike is fair. I am fair. And we both have Aimee's best interests at heart. Because of Mike's night-owl hours at the radio station, and Aimee being in school all day, he doesn't get to see her as much as he'd like. We made a deal that, in addition to every second weekend, he can see her as much as is convenient for everyone during the week. He just gives us a little bit of warning so we don't trample each other's plans.

'She's fine. She just wanted me to come and get her. Said she'd had enough. Then she said she wanted to come home. Sorry to sabotage your night out on the town.'

'It wasn't really a night on the town,' I say. 'Only a drink down at the pub.'

He leans casually against the door frame. We hold gazes. It's so odd to find him standing here on the threshold of his up-until-recent life. It's like one of us is visiting the other in prison, and even if we both put our palms against the glass it still wouldn't feel like we were touching. A boundary has gone up because we've moved from the intimate thing of being married to the hostile thing of being divorced. Or we're supposed to be hostile, but neither of us can even manage to get that right.

He continues to stand there, in no hurry to leave, looking at me as though he's drinking every bit of me in, instead of just seeing a face he knows as well as his own. And in an attempt to look everywhere but into his sad eyes, I see him more objectively than normal: as Mike this human being who I happen to know quite well, yet he's once or twice removed from me, as though we're an impossible form of related strangers. He's wearing a jacket I've not seen before. A dark brown leather three-quarter-length thing that, because he's short, comes almost to his knees, instead of, probably to his bum, where it should. Mike has always had a distinctive style. There's something 1970s about his over-sized jackets, his skinny jeans, winklepicker shoes, and the prematurely grey Fonz hair. Rather than not being a follower of fashion, Mike is his own fashion. He's comfortable with himself. And there was always something very attractive about that.

Mike looks me over. My form-fitting black dress with the capped sleeves. My hair swept up and secured with a chunky tortoiseshell clip, bits straggling around my face. I had made an effort to look excited-to-be-single. For a moment, staring at my unusually over-made-up face in the mirror, I thought I'd pulled it off.

He shrugs the one shoulder that's not leaning against the

door frame. 'I'll have her next Saturday if you want to change your plans and go out then instead.'

'It's okay,' I tell him. Then, 'Why do you suppose she didn't just want to go back to yours?'

'It's not home, is it?' he says, and holds my eyes.

'She did rubbish on her history test,' I change the subject. 'I even helped her study for it.'

'Maybe that was the problem,' he jokes.

I smile. 'I was thinking maybe we need to get her a private tutor. Just for the main subjects.'

'I think maybe we should back off pressuring her. She's only twelve. Don't you think she's had enough to deal with these past few months?'

I nod. 'You're probably right.'

I've missed our conversations. Even our arguments had a certain comfort value, and I miss them too. Not that we had many, Mike tending to be more passive aggressive than full-on confrontational. 'You look really nice, by the way. You got your hair cut? How was your business trip?'

My hand goes to the straggly bits of hair around my face. My divorce cut, as Jacqui calls it. 'It was only down to Manchester. I left Aimee in good hands. She loves Jacqui staying with her.'

'I know. Why do you sound like you're apologising?'

'I'm not. I'm only saying…' What am I saying?

'I took them both out for a pizza. Did Jacqui tell you?'

He must see my surprise. 'No! Actually.' Why does it bother me that he went out with my sister? A divorce shouldn't mean families have to take sides, yet Jacqui's my sister and I don't really want to share her with my ex-husband. 'You're allowed to take people out. You don't have to give me reports.' I realise I'm being childish about him inviting Jacqui.

He looks down at my feet, diverting a potential argument

perhaps. 'You've only got three toes done,' he says, of my nail polish.

'And they're smudged and have bits of carpet sticking to them,' I smile. My heart wasn't really into going out; I was just fighting my inner tendency to be a hermit on weekends.

'I think they look great. For three toes.' This is Mike. Always tries to make you feel good about yourself.

He continues to stare at them, as though my feet are an emotional stop sign he's trying to get past but can't. I think of my unprovoked outbursts about why I wasn't happy. My feeling that marriage had become some kind of stopping place, some destination we'd reached only to find that I'd hoped for more when I got there. The strange thing is, what did I ever think it was that he stopped me from being, doing, that I want to run out and be and do now?

When he finally looks up, he stares somewhat unseeingly into my eyes and it's as if he's just quickly reread his *Coles Notes* on the section that deals with how you learn not to care. 'Anyway, while I have you here…' he says. He briefly looks past me into our house and his face is a snapshot of sadness and regret. I can hardly bear to look. 'Before you shut the door on me—'

'—I wasn't going to shut the door on you.'

'Yes you were.'

'I wasn't. Why would I do that, Mike?' It hurts me he'd think this.

'Because, finally, you can.'

I don't answer this. He moves closer, his eyes going fleetingly to my mouth. 'I've given a lot of thought to this business of being alone, and I have a proposition for you.'

'I don't like the idea of any of your propositions.'

'You won't. No. But I'm going to make you an offer you can't refuse.'

'You're going to put a horse's head in my bed? I suppose I deserve it.'

'Actually, that was going to be my last resort.'

We smile at my lame attempt at a joke. I've missed his smile; its kindness draws you like a moth to light. 'What I mean is, given that we are now officially divorced, and given that I for one am ready to take some giant step to move my life forward, I thought you might be able to help me out.'

'Doing?'

'I want to employ you. To help me meet somebody else. My soulmate.'

He scrutinises my presumably stunned-looking face. 'It makes sense. You know me better than anyone. You'd know who would be good for me, probably better than I would. And I'm obviously going to pay you. I'm not asking for favours.' His eyes settle where they've been buzzing, at the base of my throat.

Mike always looks at me in shades of many conflicting emotions. But I always sensed that while I might have doubted him, he never doubted me. Another thing — Mike never looks at you as though he's seen it all before. I've never been made to feel that he'd fancy me more if I put lipstick on for him, or had bigger boobs. I know this is rare, from many of my SADs (Sane Attractive Divorcees, who are grounded, healthy, normal, and just want a second chance at happiness), as opposed to the SAFs (Spinster Attractive Females who have never been married, and are getting more desperate and more inflexible the older they become). Mike may not be a six-foot, wheeling dealing hulk of testosterone, but he knows how to appreciate a woman. Which makes me picture him appreciating someone else.

'No way.'

'Hear me out.'

'No. I'm not doing it.' I fold my arms under my breasts.

He extracts his eyes from my throat. 'I'm an opportunity for you to make another two thousand pounds. I'll be a good client. I want the full service, though. The fake date. The whole works. Just like I was any client. Just because you were married to me you can't hold it against me. No assumed prior knowledge.'

'You don't meet the MIS.'

'What's the MIS?'

'You know what it is.' Minimum Income Standard of sixty thousand pounds that the men have to meet to qualify.

He wags a finger in front of my face. 'No prior knowledge, remember?'

'Okay. Mike, you're not well off enough.'

He shrugs. 'So this is the one time when you can bend the rules a bit. And I'm not asking you to set me up with Angelina Jolie. One of your dodgiest eights will be fine.'

Mike knows that the women have to at least rank an eight on the attractiveness scale. Because research still shows that men are into looks, and women are into money. I hate saying it. I'd hoped we'd all somehow got sensible over time. But we haven't.

'I don't need a pin-up. After all, I'm more into personalities than I am looks. I mean, I was married to a gorgeous woman and see what happened there.'

We hold eyes, in the aftershock that follows such a remark. 'I'm not doing it, Mike.'

'Will you at least think about it?'

'No. And I can't believe you're even suggesting it. What normal person would do this?'

'But we know you're not normal,' he barbs, in his passive-aggressive way that's meant to hurt you, but he can't quite pull the punch. 'And who cares what others think? Most people don't have an ex in the business, do they? And you're so good at what you do; why wouldn't I want to try to benefit from that? I could meet someone else still. Maybe even have another family — not that any other child would ever replace my first.'

'You know what? I've changed my mind. I am going to shut the door on you.'

He cocks his head, trying to win me over. 'Come on, Celine. Is it too much to want to see me happy? Do you hate me that much?'

'I don't hate you!' A pain blazes in me. 'Why would I hate you? I'm just...'

Puzzled. Why would he insist on the Fake Date?

'Mike... I hope this isn't some strategy to get me back.'

I regret saying it the instant it's out. All the good humour slides right off his face. Then his gaze travels quickly up and down me. 'You know what, Celine? Even in my darkest moments — because I still get them, far more than I would wish — I would never want to go back to being married to you.'

We stare at one another while my humiliation takes a bow before leaving the stage. I go to close the door now. He gently puts his hand out to stop me. 'Just tell me you'll think about it.'

I look off to the side of his head, through a spring of tears. 'Move your foot or I'll slam this and break all your toes,' I bluff.

Tense moments tick, and I get a quick flashback to one of our last fights. Mike usually has a personality like a sea before the storm, but he'd occasionally lose his rag — something that usually came off more funny than threatening. That time, he pelted a shoe at me across the room. It missed me, but hit the Lladró figurine of a little boy that Mike's mother had given us. Mike knew I'd always hated it, even though he'd loved it. It seemed poignant that he'd broken it. As though, by fighting, we had succeeded on some darker level, in breaking him rather than just an ornament.

Mike studies me closely, and then he moves his foot. Finally, I am able to close the door. I lean up against it, my breathing racking me. I don't fully breathe out, until I hear the scrunch of gravel under his feet as he walks away.

And I realise one true thing. The thought just floats up from whatever place it comes from. No one will love me like Mike loved me. And that much I know. I know without anyone having to wag their index finger in front of my face and tell me.

# Ten

Aimee sits by the window, swinging a flared indigo denim leg over the chair arm, in the powder blue satin top we just bought her. 'Why didn't he come in?' she asks.

'I...I don't know,' I shrug, still feeling somehow traumatized by our encounter. 'I suppose I didn't exactly invite him.'

She stares at me. 'What does an orgasm feel like?' When she sees my face she says, 'If you don't want to tell me, I'll ask somebody else. Granddad. Or Rachel's mum.'

We face each other in a narrowed-eye standoff.

'Like a sneeze,' I tell her, trying to be offhand about it. 'A-choo! Only not with your nose.'

She twirls a long piece of newly blonde hair around a finger. Jacqui just took her to the salon as a treat. She got soft golden highlights put in. It's nice. Makes her look very grown up. 'Would it be completely inappropriate of me if I asked you why you want to know this?'

'I kissed Rachel's boyfriend.'

I frown. 'I didn't know she had one. Where?'

'On the mouth, of course.'

'I mean, where in the house? I'm assuming you'd go somewhere where Rachel couldn't see.' *A bedroom? With pants off? I'll kill him.*

80

'Outside. No one saw.'

'You don't kiss a friend's boyfriend, Aimee. It's one of the big no-no's of life. Are you still jealous because she won a competition? Surely not…'

'He wanted to do other things.'

*He's dead. And I'm never letting her out of my sight again.*

'And you? What did you want?' I ask her, feeling burnt out with my sudden inner, quiet panic. She stops playing with her hair, lets her leg just dangle now over the side of the chair. She does look stunning, and I see my daughter through a boy's eyes. She's sexy, which is a very odd thought to be having about your own child. 'I don't know,' she says.

'Is this why you suddenly wanted to come home?'

She shakes her head. 'No. Mr Bradshaw caught us kissing.'

'I thought you said no one saw.'

'Well, he did.'

'And?'

'He wanted to kiss me too.'

'That's not funny, Aimee.'

'It's not meant to be.'

'Pete Bradshaw would not want to kiss one of his daughter's friends in his house full of thirty teenagers, with his wife there!'

Off goes the wagging leg again. Aimee was defiant, even as a baby.

'You don't make up lies about people, Aimee. Somebody might take you seriously and that's a very dangerous game to be playing.'

'So I take it you're not going out boyfriend-shopping tonight then?' she asks.

I ignore that, and tell her I'm going to bed.

'I'm sorry,' she says, later when I look in her room. 'About the boyfriend-shopping.' She pulls a rueful smile.

'It's okay,' I tell her. I go in and sit on the edge of her bed. 'Are you all right?'

She puts her book down and looks at me, like she's grasping for the right way to say something, like someone trying to work her way around a speech impediment. 'It was just weird having Dad leave me at the door.'

'I'm so sorry… You wish he was coming home with you.'

One hand uncurls from her book and her thin fingers meander down the cat's belly. 'I don't know. Not if you don't.'

This show of unity touches me.

'It was just weird.'

I go to stroke Molly as well, and Aimee's and my fingers meet, briefly. 'I know,' I tell her. I remember how I had to share my dad with his new girlfriends, often getting dropped at the last minute for a better offer. Could I see Mike suddenly dropping visits? Neither of us has had to share him before.

'Mr Bradshaw never tried to kiss me. I made that up.'

'I know that too,' I whisper. 'Don't worry about it.'


My book on physiognomy is fascinating: the assessment of a person's character or personality from their face. But rather than make me sleepy, it's got me picturing all of my clients and comparing them against the theory. While I thought a big nose was a sign of a big something else, it's apparently an indicator of health and vitality. Big ears? More comfortable taking risks. A thinner top lip to the bottom one? Watch out, this person may be serially unfaithful. And a woman's eyebrows plucked into a tiny line, like my client Kim's, is a sign of suppressed rage. I get out of bed and pick up a mirror and look at my own face. Definitely not thin eyebrows. Disproportionately tiny ears. I go back to bed, but put the book away. Lay there looking at ceiling.

Still can't fall asleep. Now Ian Dury's 'Hit Me with Your Rhythm Stick' is playing on a never-ending loop in my head, so I decide I might as well check my email.

I've a bunch. The first four are from Kim. Speak of the devil. The first one is titled Urgent.

*Time is ticking. I haven't heard from you in a while. Do you have anybody else for me?*

The second is titled Urgent!!!

*On second thought, I'm not sure I can go through with any of this again. Will phone you early in the morning to talk — unless you're up now? I can't sleep.*

The third is titled IMPERATIVE you read this!!!

*I'm having serious second thoughts, Celine. I just don't think you and I are working out. I'm not even sure you even WANT to match me anymore.*

The fourth: Did you DIE?

*Sorry, I know you're going to think I'm overreacting but I have given this a lot of thought. I can't do this anymore. I've just had enough. Please prepare a refund for me.*

Oh dear.

No one's asked for a refund before! Of course it's all poetic justice; I usually charge the women half what I charge the men — mainly because they aren't such high earners. But in Kim's case I charged her the men's fee because I read in the *Newcastle Chronicle* that she was loaded.

But she's not getting a refund! Number one, I don't like to admit failure. Plus I've put time and thought into matching her, and every time she brushes through clients, writing them all off, I lose a bit of credibility with them. But also, I don't really believe the solution to her unhappy singlehood is to dump me. So by giving her a refund I am failing both myself and her. But if I reply now, knowing her, she'll be at the other end of the email, and then I'm never going to get to sleep. I'll wait until morning, until she's cooled off.

The next one I see is from Fran Kennedy. Fran married Allan, the man I'd matched her with, only, very sadly, Allan now has lung cancer and she often pours out her heart in an email. I open every one she sends me fearing the worst, but true to form in this one, Fran's spirits are high even though he's not doing well. I read it several times and then type a long reply. By the time I am done, I am sleepy. I'm just about to log out, when another email pops in.

When I see the name, I am so shocked that I lie there inhaling for about half a minute and nearly forget to breathe out.

The name is Patrick Shale.

# *Eleven*

Have I just had a painless heart attack?

There's no message header, so I scroll for the message, part of me thinking I must have fallen asleep and this is a dream.

But there's no message.

I log out, log back in again. Still a blank where the message should be. I close my eyes, take a breath, open them, and look again. I log off again, pull the plug from the socket, wait awhile, stick it back in again, and reboot.

Still no message.

Patrick has sent me a blank email. Why would he do that? And why would Patrick even email me at all, especially since Jacqui and I have been talking about him so much lately?

I smell a rat. A female rat that's voluptuous with a blonde bob, called Jacqui, and it works as an architect.

I scroll down again just to make sure I've not missed anything, and then what I see makes me squeal out loud. Underneath the 'nothing' that he has written, there is a small line of text that reads:

<On 26/4, Celine Lewis at CelineLewis@hotmail.com wrote>

Hang on. I wrote?

*I wrote?*

85

I scroll down to read what it is that I supposedly wrote, and there is... Nothing! What?

When I look up, Aimee is standing in my doorway, staring at me as though she's seeing an alien. 'You look weird,' she says. Her eyes instantly go to my laptop.

I realise my face is stuck in a just-been-terrified expression. 'Sorry...I...can't sleep.'

'I heard a noise.' She frowns at the laptop.

'I got up for the loo and stubbed my toe.'

'Can you stub it more quietly next time?'

'I'm sorry.' She looks at me now. 'Can I take you back to your room?'

'Why? Has it moved?'

I get off the bed and go and give her a quick kiss. 'Can I ask you a question though, before you go?'

'Hum?' She rubs her eyes, vigorously, with the knuckles of her index fingers, like she used to do when she was little.

'Aimee, you didn't look up Patrick on the Internet and send him an email, did you?'

Her eyes go from me to my laptop again and she blushes. 'No,' she finally says. 'Why would I do that?'

'Well, I don't know. Maybe because you knew I'd been Googling him. Maybe you found his email, intended to type something, got distracted, and the message accidentally got sent anyway?'

She looks at me like I'm raving. 'Mum? Are you sure you don't think that's a really strange question? Why would I want to email your old boyfriend?'

'I don't know, Aimee. You're right. Forget I asked.'

She nods and I watch her traipse back to her room, not plod-plodding her feet this time like a herd of pet elephants — something she has taken to doing lately. Right now she's too tired. Her nightshirt is stuck in her knickers, a milky white bottom cheek peeking out. 'Aimee,' I say, before she disappears into her room. 'You didn't tell Aunt Jacqui that I'd Googled him, did you? You know, the other day when she took you to get your hair cut?'

Jacqui would employ all her wiles to find his email, I'm sure. If she got the sudden urge to try to reunite us. Too much of a coincidence that the message was sent when I was in Manchester, when Jacqui was staying here with Aimee.

She turns, rubs her face again. 'No,' she says, tiresomely. 'Now can I go back to bed?'

I stare at his name for about ten minutes, and the blank space where he could have written something but didn't. Why reply at all if he didn't want to say anything?

Feeling he's even this tiny step back in my life is electrifying. That he's actually out there, alive, on the other side of this mind boggling piece of technology. I click on Reply. Then I suddenly overheat, my palms, feet, back, and chest breaking out into a hot flush. Now what? I stare at the blank screen and ponder a few scenarios, which all sound equally contrived, desperate, or just plain mad.

Then I find my fingers typing...

*Dear Patrick,*
*I have a very odd family who think it's funny to meddle in my personal life.*

Honest, at least. A start.

*The truth is, I don't know how either my sister or my daughter (not sure who is the culprit yet, but I will find out) found your email address, or why they went looking for it in the first place, or why they decided to send you a blank message. I'm sorry for this. I'm sure you were as surprised by it as I was in getting your reply. Sorry again.*
*All the best, Celine.*

I press Send.

# Twelve

*Dear Celine,*

*I'm not sorry to have received your email — quite the opposite. But yes, it did come as a surprise. And the main reason I emailed you back without writing anything was, to be truthful, because I really didn't know what to write after all these years. But other than having that lame excuse, it was a pretty dumb thing to do.*

*I looked you up when I got it, and I found your website, and I see you run an introductions service, and you called it The Love Market. You can't imagine how that touched me, or how it took me back. Although you probably won't believe this, I thought of you just recently. I was sorting through some boxes in my apartment and I came across the Dictaphone I used in Sa Pa. Remember? When I stood by the window and you sat there watching me?*

He means, when I sat on the end of the bed naked, and watched him by the window trying to work. But he couldn't concentrate on what it was he was saying, because he was too busy concentrating on me. 'You're distracting me,' he said, looking at me a few times until he finally gave up.

*I hope the last fifteen years of your life have been good
ones. I always imagined you would have married a great
guy, and ended up settling and having a good life in that village you loved to hate. Looks like you have a daughter
too… I am happy for you.*
   *Patrick*

The shades of green and grey and mauve moorland don't
change the longer you sit at the kitchen table and gaze out of
the window.

I am paralyzed by his email.

I'm so paralyzed that when the phone rings, I pick up without bothering to look at my call display, thinking it'll be Kim
on the case of her refund.

'Hi.' I hear a voice say. And then, after a pause, 'Do you
know who this is?'

The voice has an accent. I'm about to say 'No, but I don't
talk to telemarketers — or anyone ringing to tell me there's a
dead billionaire with no relatives who bears my last name.' But
all that comes out is a rather strangulated 'eu-oooh.'

Because I know who it is now.

Butterflies have colonized my stomach. 'Sorry,' he says,
amused.

Patrick says.

'I just saw your phone number on your website, and I
couldn't stop thinking about the idea of talking to you.'

Patrick's words in my ear.

Silence. Perhaps I've died.

'Are you still there?' he asks.

'I, erm…' —have to remove the hand from my mouth
because I'm biting my palm and it hurts.

'Good,' he says. 'It's amazing how easily you can find people when you suddenly go looking for them. But then you know that already.'

Mischief in that voice? 'I didn't go looking for you, Patrick.' Seems I've found my tongue. 'It was my sister who—'

'Can't you just say it was you?' he says, disarmingly. He always had the power to blindside me with his directness and his ability to place an innocent few words onto a charged, higher level.

'But it really wasn't!' I'm almost too stunned to have a sense of humour. The butterflies have turned to nausea. That wobbly stomach I'd get with just the memory of sex with him. It's back.

'You've changed,' he says after what seems like a very long silence. 'I mean that in a good way. I saw your picture on your website. I can't stop looking at it. In fact, I'm looking at it right now.' A definite smile in his voice. Patrick had a way of coming close to intimidating me with something very simple that he'd say, in the sexiest, yet most unnerving way, and it seems as if it's fifteen years ago all over again; nothing's changed. To think he's sitting there looking at my picture is wild.

It's the one Jacqui took in our garden. A medium close-up. My dark hair cut into flattering long layers, slightly falling in my eyes. My black and white stripy halter-top looking very glam with my two-week-old tan from our holiday to Cyprus.

We must have taken hundreds getting me to look — as she insisted — wise and insightful, like someone who you'd trust to make a sound decision about your personal life, yet a fun girl with her finger on the zeitgeist. 'Bloody cooperate!' she said. 'They want Jennifer Aniston–cum–Oprah Winfrey as their matchmaker, not Martha Stewart.'

'You suit being in your thirties, if that makes any sense. It's like the age that was meant for you.' He sounds as though my picture has touched him.

'Patrick, I...' I laugh, nervously. 'I'm sorry, I don't know what to say.'

'Just don't hang up on me, okay?'

I laugh again. 'Okay. But this is too weird that I am actually sitting here talking to you!'

'I know. Isn't it? I can't believe I'm talking to you either,' he says, quietly. Deliberately keeping his voice down?

'Where are you?' I ask him, lowering my voice to match his. 'I mean, what far-flung place?'

'Not that far-flung. Toronto. I'm based here now.'

'Oh. So you don't work overseas anymore then?'

'Well, yes and no. They pulled me out of the Middle East some months ago and I've been doing what they call parachute journalism since then. They literally drop me in wherever there's a story to be filed, whether that's the war in Iraq or the European Cup; it can be anywhere, or anything.'

'I often wondered where you'd be, you know. If any harm had come to you, even if you'd died. You know you hear in the news, so many journalists…' Why am I telling him I've thought he might be dead? But the truth is, whenever Mike and I were watching the news, and a foreign report came on, I always half-expected that one day I'd see Patrick's face. And I often wonder if Mike thought that too.

'It's okay. I've always been a pretty lucky guy. Although I might have come close a few times.' I can hear the smile in his voice. 'You needn't have worried, but I'm flattered and touched that you did.'

His voice is strange to me: the one thing about him I may have forgot. The drawn-out vowels and rounded 'o' of the Canadian accent striking my eardrum on a plane I'm not used to. His sibilants like a whisper around my face. Memories of our intimacy filling whatever blanks in me exist, because it was always there; beneath the sex and the closeness with Mike, I would be wanting in the worst way to feel more.

A dart, now, of the memory of how well we worked together.

'Are you still there?' he eventually asks.

I chuckle again, nervously. 'I'm still here I think!'

'You're shocked,' he says. 'Can I ask you one thing, though? You said your family likes to meddle in your personal life...'

Patrick never did beat about the bush.

'I'm divorced.'

Do I catch a draw of breath? 'Recently,' I add. 'I'm still not even used to the idea.'

'I'm sorry it didn't work,' he eventually says. I can almost hear his brain computing the new information. And I compute him computing me. And the incredulity is ever there, skipping away along with my heart, that this really is Patrick on the phone. Patrick has rung me.

'And you?' I venture.

'Same,' he says. 'Divorced. A long time ago.' Then after a while of me not speaking, 'Look, I'm sorry to have just called out of the blue. I never saw myself getting up the courage to call you, even though...'

'Even though what?'

'Well, I looked you up about three years ago on the Internet. I was thinking back, and wondering about you. But I couldn't find anything.'

Three years ago. When I thought I'd seen him in London. What did Jacqui jokingly say about us being on some parallel cosmic track?

'I changed my name when I got married.' I think of what Jacqui said about this too. She has a way of always being right.

'I thought that might be why. I still had your mother's address, where I sent that letter to, remember? I thought about trying to contact you through her. But I didn't know how she would feel about that. If you were married with a family… And after such a long time I didn't know if you'd even want to be found.'

'I'm sure it wouldn't have been a very good idea,' I say, once I've momentarily recovered from my surprise at hearing this, wanting, inexplicably, to shed a tear. Our timing has been all off.

'No. But it still didn't stop me wanting to.'

'You sound like the same Patrick.' I smile.

'I am the same Patrick,' he says.

I try to imagine what would have happened if he had sent a letter, via my mother. What I'd have done. What could I have done?

Finally, he says, 'Celine, all I can really say after all this time is it's fantastic to hear your voice. And what's weird is that now we're actually speaking it doesn't feel like fifteen years since we last did.'

'You're right. It really doesn't.'

'Can I tell you something? I feel I just want to say this. I mean, I hope you know this already, but when I left you that morning, I didn't just walk away and forget everything. I had to consciously block you out of my thoughts for a very long time. The truth is — and I know we all make mistakes but some of us make bigger ones, with bigger regrets and bigger consequences — I should never have let you go.'

It's only when we have rung off, and I process all that has just happened, that I realise my body is doing a cataclysmic tremble.

# *Thirteen*

Jacqui is stunned.

Either that, or she's a very good actress.

'What's he like?' she asks. I've met her down at Newcastle's Quayside, in her lunch break. She works as an architect for a firm in the City Centre. She sometimes bends the rules and takes an extremely long lunch break just for me: her reward, she says, for working such long hours, giving so much of her life in the pursuit of ambition. We sit on a bench in front of the law courts and a fancy hotel, staring across the Tyne River, finishing off a sandwich. From our position we can see all the way south over the city to the distinct and charming hodgepodge that is Newcastle architecture. Elegant grey stones converging with sixties slab blocks, modern lofts, half-timbered houses, and the world's only tilting bridge — the Winking Eye — that Jacqui raves about. It's too summerlike to rush. I could sit here with my face to the sun all afternoon.

'He sounds much the same, actually.'

Her eyes are gazing off across the water. I believe that Jacqui has always envisaged Patrick and me being reunited. Years ago, when I came home with my broken heart, she said that Patrick and I should have done our own 'affair to remember' and agreed to meet again in the Love Market ten years on — no matter what else might have been going on with our lives at that point. 'When are you going to speak to him again?' she asks.

I gaze at the lashings of mascara on her already superhumanly long eyelashes. 'I don't know. Maybe never. The conversation was quite brief really. Almost as though he rang out of some sense of — I don't know, politeness or duty. '

She gives me a scolding look. 'Duty? He probably just felt as strange as you did. Don't worry, he'll phone again.'

'How can you be so sure?'

She meets my eyes now. 'Celine, a man doesn't phone after fifteen years if he's not still thinking about you. If he's got no intentions of ever phoning again.'

A flutter of nerves hits my stomach just at the possibility of his phone call unlocking a door. 'But I can't start obsessing about him, Jacq! Not after all this time.'

She stares after a couple of nicely dressed businessmen who stroll past, immersed in conversation. 'But I thought you never stopped?'

In spite of myself I grin at her. 'Well, that's one way to put it. But if I'm to make any more money, Jacqui, or even maintain my current income level, I have to get focused. I have to find new ways of getting The Love Market out there. I need more clients. Word of mouth and local advertising is one thing, but it's not enough. I'm on my own now; I've a mortgage. I can't be daydreaming about my nonexistent love life and letting my real priorities fall by the wayside.'

She stares out across the water again, at the stunning glass building of the Sage Centre for Music, which, as an architect, is one of her favourites in the city. 'Can't you think about both?'

'No! I'm not that clever!'

We chuckle.

I peer at her through narrowed eyes. 'Why would you write nothing, by the way? That's the bit that intrigues me the most. I mean, I can understand you contacting him — I suppose — given the years you've spent dreaming of my love affair and making it your own. But I can't understand why you'd send a blank email! Who would do that?'

She laughs, exasperated, but she's blushing madly. 'I told you I didn't email him! I'm pleased you give me all this credit though. But I'm not that clever.'

'Ha ha!'

I have to smile at her. She looks voluptuously sexy in a short fitted black skirt and jacket, with her slim and shapely legs shown off in high heels. Jacqui has the kind of body that gets men tripping over their tongues when they pass her.

'I should have asked him if he has kids. It's almost as though, by not really asking him anything about himself, he might have thought I really couldn't have cared.'

'He won't think that. But this could be the reason for you ringing him back. You could just say, *'Now Patrick, while we're on the topic of you not being married anymore...'*

I playfully slap her.

'Come on. I have to go back to work soon,' she moans. We get up off the bench and start walking. Before she does go back to the office, she wants me to have a quick peek with her in a shop to help her find a dress for a work 'do.' And I know there's a reason why she wants to look extra lovely.

He told me from the outset that he'd only have four days. Then he was expected back in Hong Kong. He had a job, stories to file. This had already been an unscheduled side trip.

By the end of the second day, the countdown to him going was there between us. He was edgy. I tried not to be. I tried to make it okay that I was going to lose him. That I understood the deal.

'Fly there with me!' he said, on our last night. 'You'll love Hong Kong. I'll get you somewhere...a hotel.' I could see his brain wildly thinking through possibilities, taking the idea on board. He had a way of always looking like he was pacing the floor, even when he was sitting down. A relentless energy always made him appear to be in the grips of something.

'For how long?'

'For however long we want. We can work that out as we go along.'

'I'll just — what — live in a hotel?'

His mind was thinking ahead. He pulled himself back to my question. 'Until I... Well, yes. Or an apartment. Somewhere.'

'So you'll have your marriage, and I'll be what? Your mistress?' The idea was absurd yet freakishly plausible.

'Mistress? God no. I don't want a mistress!' He looked at me, in genuine exasperation now, as though the very word offended everything he stood for and believed in. It was a look I could close my eyes and see for years — that intensity of the man — even when I'd almost, frustratingly, forgotten the details of his face. 'Come up with something better,' he said. 'What the hell are we going to do, Celine?'

The idea of going with him and ending up being whatever I ended up being to him hammered there, along with my heart. It's not like I had anything to hurry back to England for. Yet in a way he was asking me to find him an 'out,' and part of me thought that if he really wanted to find one, he should be capable of doing it himself. But still, I didn't want us to end with a fight. Our brains rattled off in a million directions and then we just looked at one another, speechless, in acknowledgment of how impossible it all was. I couldn't stand to think that this was our last night and in the morning he would leave. He'd go back to his wife, and I'd be out there searching for the rest of my life, desperately trying to feel this again with somebody else, and probably failing.

'Can't you leave her?' I said, because it had to be said. Yet I knew that the question was unnecessary: Patrick was not going to leave his wife, this much was clear. And deep down, I didn't really think it fair that he did. She'd found him first. She'd trusted him to go off on his own, for his work, and was this how he was going to repay her? Yet, I wanted him. And if he'd said, *I'll leave her*, then I'm sure I'd have recovered from my guilt pretty easily. 'Tell her you've met someone and you've fallen in love.'

'I have fallen in love,' he said. 'I'm pretty sure about that. But I can't just walk in after having been away for only four days and tell her our marriage is finished, Celine, because I met you. I mean, you must see that. She gave up everything to follow me around the world. She's in a new country. We've barely been married two minutes!'

He'd said this earlier: about everything she'd given up, without being specific. And when I asked him more, he said he didn't want to spend our time together talking about her. And neither did I really.

But the more he said he couldn't do it, the more I thought that he could, and maybe he should. Or at the very least, maybe he should have given me a greater indication that it was a hard choice for him to make.

We went through the motions of eating and drinking rice wine. Then, when it came to having sex for the last time, neither one of us could bring ourselves to, so we just lay there, bare arm next to bare arm. In my side vision I could see the prominent bridge of his nose, his steady blinking. Patrick's mind always working.

'What are we going to do?' were his last words before we both went to sleep. But I'd given him the only answer I could think of.

Next morning, he wasn't there when I opened my eyes. I thought he'd snuck off while I was sleeping. I thought, *This is how I'll always remember you; as a person who sneaks off, without having the guts to say a proper goodbye, after everything we have been through.* And then I saw his bag.

He was standing outside. Very still. His long body, narrow back, legs a stride apart, his blondish, wavy hair. His dilemma was palpable. I could see it. I could feel it. I ached for him. And I knew then: that, as bad as it was for me, it was equally as bad for him. A low mist hung over everything, blanking out our view. Just me and him and this small, primitive place. He turned and looked at me, as if to say, 'I'm still here.'

Back inside, I watched him pack the rest of his stuff. I remember the quick sound of him zipping up his bag. That zip sounded like it belonged on the bag of a man who was dying to get the hell out of there. When he stood there with his bag in hand and looked at me, in the still dim early light I could almost feel his relief. In his mind he'd crossed his point of no return. He was on his way back home, to what felt familiar, and safe, and the right thing to do.

*You'll walk out of this door and I'll never see you again,* I thought, as I said the words, vaguely threatening, 'Don't look back at me once you walk out of this door...'

He stopped by the door, rested his head on his forearm, on the wooden frame. He didn't lift his face from his arm, stayed like this while, clearly, he went on wrestling with himself.

Then he said, 'I have to go,' as though telling himself, rather than me. Or, as though his better judgment was telling him.

And then he went.

'Where are you?' Jacqui asks me as we climb the steep bank of Grey Street that leads from the Quayside to the main clothes shops that are collected around Eldon Square shopping centre.

'Sorry, lost in thought… But I've been meaning to ask you, how is the office romance these days?' A workman leans his handsome face out of a van and wolf whistles at us, his eyes clamped on Jacqui's legs.

Christian Taylor is the new project manager at Jacqui's firm. He's a dead ringer for Brad Pitt — or so she tells me — and he always wears a navy Paul Smith suit with a navy shirt, which makes me wonder if he's spent all his money on that one outfit and he's now got nothing else to wear. And Jacqui has a little crush. This would be fine. People are allowed to have crushes on co-workers. But they're not supposed to have them when they're about to get engaged to their live-in boyfriend of five years.

'I have updates,' she says, excitedly. 'We had an incident in the lift.'

'Incident?'

She sees my face. 'No. Not that kind of incident. I wish! Just, well, we were both going down for lunch — not together, of course; I wish that too…but there were all these people in, all these bodies between us, and yet his eyes were fixed on me. And every time someone moved, blocking us, he'd peek around them, playfully, so he could see me again. So we could continue the eye-game. It was so hot. I just wanted to push people aside and ravish him.' She gazes at me with sparkling eyes. The look she always gets when she talks about Christian, yet one I've never seen when she talks or looks at Rich.

The bank is steep. I am winded. There is something about this fellow that I don't like, and I don't know why. It's not as though I've even laid eyes on him to formulate a proper impression. 'But what if he's like this with all the girls? Do you really want a man who every other woman wants? Imagine his ego.'

'Well, you can certainly smell the pharomones when he leaves the room.'

'I think the pharaohs are in tombs in Egypt probably smelling very dodgy in their own right, but it's the pheromones you're on about.'

She chortles and stops walking and turns to me, all aglow. 'Oh, Celine! Driving home, I sat through a full traffic light change. And I feel so bad for Rich. I mean I have this good man who wants to marry me, and I love him, in almost all the right ways. Then there's how much I badly want to kiss Christian, a complete unknown quantity, who flirts with me to the point where it's all I get up for on a morning. Rich is about to take me on holiday for my birthday and propose, yet I just want to be locked up in a photocopier room — just me and Christian's mouth. Those big succulent lips, the bottom one that looks a little bit split, like Angelina Jolie's.'

'You had me until you mentioned Angelina Jolie.' So many of my male clients cite Angelina as the type of woman they're looking for. It gets tiresome. Although I have as many women who want Daniel Craig. Everyone thinks that if they're paying for it, this entitles them to someone several degrees out of their league. 'But you'd probably want other parts than just his lips,' I tease.

'I wouldn't! For me, kissing has always been better than sex. A kiss has something ahead of it. Sex has nowhere else to go.'

She gazes at my face with that half-here, half-in-some-romantic-netherland expression in those eyes. 'I love that whole time before it actually happens, you know, when you're wondering which one of you is going to make that first move. I love that tantalizing anticipation of what he's going to kiss like. And that split second when his face moves in, right before you find out.' She looks up at the sky and inhales longingly, then smiles at me. 'I'm not the matchmaker in the family, but my theory is, a kiss can determine an awful lot about your compat-ibility. I think if you both like to do a lot of kissing, your relationship will survive the bumps in the road.' She is looking at me like a person who has walked out of a very romantic movie and realised her life doesn't measure up, only she's forgot it's not actually supposed to.

We resume walking. I remember kisses with Mike. There was niceness. There was certainly love. But there was never real fire.

'Well, as my dad once told me years ago, you don't have to marry someone just because they want to marry you,' I tell her.

'I know, but it's hard to walk away from someone who loves you. You worry that no one else will be along to love you in the same way.'

'Well, Jacq, people marry for all kinds of reasons. But you don't want that particular reason to be yours.'

Something dawns on me. 'Rich isn't unwell again, is he?' I have noticed that her usual sparkle has been missing for a while. I know that Rich has suffered from depression in the past, and it really got Jacqui down in the early days. But he changed his medication some time ago and seems fine now. Or, at least, she never brings it up anymore.

'No, he's fine,' she says flatly. 'It's not that. Not really. To coin a phrase, it's me, not him.'

'So what happens when he whisks you away and proposes?'

She meets me full on and her eyes suddenly fill with tears. 'I don't know. Part of me wants to stop the holiday, and stop the birthday so it won't happen. I'm dreading being on that precipice. Where whatever I say might be the wrong thing.'

'Well, I'm sure that even if you tell him you don't want to get married he'll just accept it, and you'll go on as is.'

'But it's not fair for me to make him compromise what he

wants, is it? And I'm just not sure it's what I want. Or that I want to marry anyone. Do I have to have a marriage contract dictating how I live the rest of my life? Just because everybody else seems to have one. Then we'll end up having a baby and I'll never get to do all the things I want to do.'

'Like?' We sit briefly on the steps of Grey's Monument, the tall pillar erected in memory of the former earl and British prime minister — the man who lent his name to an aromatic blend of tea.

'I don't know. But there are things. Just because I can't think of them right now doesn't mean I won't the second I know for sure that I'm not going to be able to do any of them.'

She takes a foot out of her stiletto, and wiggles her toes. There is a red groove across the top of her foot. 'Well, if Rich isn't the one, don't marry him. That's about the only advice I feel completely confident in giving you. That would be the unkindest thing you could do to him.'

'I'll take that as good advice coming from you,' she says.

She forces her shoe back on and we cross the road and head into Fenwick's department store, to scout out their designer floor for her party dress. 'Imagine if he came here,' she says. For a second I think she's talking about loverboy at work.

'Who?'

'Patrick, of course.' She heads straight to the Karen Millen section like a girl on a mission.

'Patrick is not going to come here! Now we're being ridiculous!'

She looks over her shoulder at me as she walks. 'How can you be so certain? It's wide open, Celine. Neither of you is married anymore. You at least have to email him.' It comes off as a plea.

'Leave me alone!' I playfully hide behind a mannequin.

'I will never leave you alone on this. I'm not going to have your divorce be all for nothing.'

I think about what an odd remark that was. And something else I always wonder about: in believing that Patrick would have been right for me, did that automatically make Mike wrong? Did I sabotage my marriage's chance for success by always mentally holding onto four days that I spent with someone else? 'Do you remember how I used to get rid of you as a kid, when you got on my nerves?' I ask her.

Jacqui's Achilles heel: I discovered it when we were watching the telly and an advert came on with a talking octopus trying to sell an anti-itch remedy. Jacqui took a screaming fit and locked herself in the loo for half an hour. I reckoned she couldn't be afraid of a box of anti-itch cream, so it had to have been the octopus. So I thought, what happens if I draw a picture of one, just as an experiment, and show it to her? I was quite a good drawer. Although I didn't have to be... For even a quick doodle of a hand with eight fingers was enough to send Jacqui into a spasm of screams. All I had to do was wag my pen when I saw her coming with her trying-to-befriend-me routine and she'd run for days and leave me in peace.

'I'm about to pull out a pen and paper.'

She laughs, holds up both hands. 'Okay. I won't try to meddle in your life ever again! But promise me you'll email him. Send him a picture of Aimee, or the cat. Anything. Or if you don't...' she flits off to another rack, 'I will.'

# Fourteen

James Halton Daly signs back my Love Market contract. I ring Trish to let her know. She squeals, laughing when I tell her about the fake date.

'What's with all the issues all the ex-dates have got? I'm thinking he's the one with issues. Issues issues.'

'But it's good that he's picky, isn't it? Once he's written them off, he doesn't mess around with them.'

'You like him, don't you?' I pull up a photo of him on my laptop. His aristocratic good looks. The charm that oozes out of him.

She's silent for a second. 'Of course! We're good mates. You know how we met, right? I told you? I was mates with his best friend Andy at Uni, who now lives in Newcastle. But since we graduated, whenever James comes up here to see Andy, he and I seem to spend more time together, because Andy's girlfriend always wants to be in tow and that pisses James off. So now, James will tend to phone me and make plans with me, and invite Andy, and if Andy brings his girl, then it's not so bad, since James has me to talk to.'

'He's very attractive, isn't he?' I ask her.

She falls silent and then laughs. 'God! I mean he is, in a way.

His personality. But do I personally fancy him?' She overlaughs. 'Don't you think he's a little bit, you know? Gay?'

I bring him up in my mind, sitting across from me at the table. 'He's a bit of a Ra Ra Rupert. I particularly liked the popped collar of his tweed jacket.'

She howls. 'Oh God, he didn't pop his collar?'

'He did. Anyway, enough of James. The real reason I called is that I have someone for you. A professional athlete. Football. Premier division. Retired. A knee injury.'

'So he'll be pissed off at life, and in chronic agony. My kind of man.'

'I don't think he's either of those things. He's cute, laid back, nice Irish accent… He's heading up an initiative to send under-privileged kids to football camps in the summer. And he says he's had it with WAG wannabes. He wants somebody interesting and he's more into hiking than nightclubs.'

'I'm in,' she says.

'But the catch is I want you to go on a real date with him.'

'But I don't do real dates. I told you.'

'But he's initially quite shy. I don't see him doing great in the "hit and run" coffee shop atmosphere.'

'I'll bear that in mind and won't hold it against him.'

When we ring off I stare for a moment or two at James's signed contract. *Find me someone as sexy as you, and you might be in for a bonus,* he scribbled on a yellow Post-it note.

Cheeky!

We have a spell of peaceful living. And then we have a flood.

Aimee is standing there with a towel around her, dark blue varnished toenails sinking into the rug. Water is climbing steadily up the side of the bathtub. 'Turn the tap off!' I screech.

'Duh! I've tried that.'

She's pulled out the plug but the water won't drain. 'It's all your hair clogging it! I've told you about washing your hair in the bath.'

'Sorry,' she says. 'I'll wash it in the sink and clog up the sink next time.'

I realise we need to switch off the stop tap.

'You'll have to ring your dad,' I tell her.

Pause. Glower. 'Why can't you ring him?'

'Aimee, you'll understand why I can't ring him when you're grown up. Now please, can you ring him and without telling him why you need the information, just casually ask him where the main water stop tap is?'

She tuts like I'm certifiable. Meanwhile, I start ladling water from the bathtub to the toilet with a bucket. 'Go on!' I scream at her.

'The bath's overflowing and Mum doesn't know where the stop tap is,' I hear her say to her dad. Then a withering look in my direction. An outstretched hand, with the phone in it. 'He wants to talk to you.'

I grab the phone off her. 'Yes, Mike.'

'Have you given any more thought to my proposition?'

'Your...? Can we talk about that later?'

'No,' he says. 'I think we should talk about it now.'

'And if I haven't?'

Pause. 'Better get your wellies out then.'

I glance at Aimee. 'Hang on. You mean, if I say no I'm not doing it, then you're not going to tell me where the tap is?'

'Yep.'

I open my mouth, as Aimee rolls her eyes and walks out of the bathroom.

'Mike,' I say, patiently. 'I'm going to ask you this nicely. Please tell me where the stop tap is, before we flood our house.'

'Are you agreeing to find me a girlfriend?'

We have about two inches of room left before the water will be spilling on the floor. 'Fine!'

'Great. It's in the cupboard under the stairs. You go in there every day to get your shoes. It's got a red handle.'

# Fifteen

On Saturday night, Aimee is staying with Mike, and I turn down a chance to go out for drinks with a female client, deciding instead to phone Patrick.

I'm just creeping around the phone, as though it's a sleeping wild beast, and thinking, Oh God, I can't do this! I haven't a clue what the hell I'll say! What if he's home with a girlfriend? What if I look desperate? — when it rings.

I recognise the unusual number on my call display, and die a small death. When I recover, I pick it up and say, 'I was just going to phone you!'

'No you weren't,' he teases.

I beam. 'No, really, I was. I'm totally serious.'

'So I've got you where I want you, have I? As keen to talk to me as I am to talk to you.'

I light up now, and plonk down in a chair, throwing my legs over the side. 'I might have to learn to be less of a sure bet, then.'

'No,' he says. 'Don't do that. Please. Just be who you are.'

Silence now, while I recover from that comment. While I try to picture him sitting across the Atlantic, having got up the courage to call me again.

'Tell me about your life,' he says.

I laugh. 'What?'

'Anything you like. Tell me about a day in the life of Celine Walker, from northern England?' He calls me by my maiden name.

I fidget and have no idea what to say. 'Well…for example, today I went running. Well, no, I mean, I woke up early, had breakfast with my daughter, then Mike — my ex-husband — picked her up and I went running through Tyne Valley park with my sister. Then we had lunch. Then I came home…' I wonder if he's died of boredom. 'I rang my father to see how he was doing. Did two loads of laundry. Opened a bottle of wine and now I'm sitting here. Talking to you.'

I hear him moving around.

'I know. It's so thrilling, you're speechless.'

'No. I'm just enjoying listening to you.'

'I didn't think you'd ring again,' I tell him.

'Come on,' he says. 'I don't believe that. You must have known I would.'

I am tongue-tied. I get up and go over to my laptop, and after a few clicks, have pulled up that latest picture of him. 'And you?' I say, gazing at his face. 'What did you do today?'

He sounds like he's moving papers around. 'Well, I marked some assignments — I've been teaching a course at a local university. Then I spent a lot of time on the Internet,' he says. 'Booking a flight. I have to go away for business. Research, I suppose you would say.'

'I suppose you travel a lot.'

'I do. Yes.'

'That's interesting. I can't begin to imagine your life, and actually, it doesn't sound interesting, it sounds exhausting! Where are you off to this time? Anywhere nice?'

He stops shuffling things. 'Well, that's the reason for my call actually. Other than the fact that since I last phoned you I've thought of nothing else except talking to you again and hearing your voice. I'm actually phoning because in two weeks' time I'm going to be in London.'

I freeze. Then I laugh, disbelievingly. 'London?'

'Yes,' he says. 'And I'm wondering if you would feel like meeting me?'

# Sixteen

I agree to meet Mike at Karma, one of the newer, funkier 'it' restaurants in Newcastle where I now come to do all my fake dates because it's fun, unthreatening, serves great food, and you can actually hear your dining partner talk.

The young host, a handsome lad in his early twenties, who is often the one who seats me, is at the door when I come in. As soon as he sees me, for some odd reason, he blushes the colour of a Valentine's Day heart. He can't seem to meet my eyes, burbles out some incoherent words, grabs two menus and walks me to Mike's booth, tripping over his feet, and looking out of the corner of his eye at my mine, in my skyscraper black stilettos.

Mike stands up — eyes going to my shoes too — and I am taken back to our first date. Mike still that mix of ill-at-ease and disarmed. He might even be wearing the same pair of jeans.

We'd been out together three times before the 'proper date.' The first time, we were feeling out the possibility of going either the romance route or into friendship noman's land. The second, I drank too much wine and told him all about Patrick. On our third, we were in a very noisy Quayside bar. Mike talked close to my ear, and I was so busy trying to hear him that I was oblivious to any whiff of sexual tension that might have been there. But then I started to note the way his eyes would stray from my face to my breasts, and he'd blush. As though he was trying very hard not to look at my body, and was inwardly kicking himself for failing. I stopped caring about what he was saying, and was more interested in the way that his lips moved as he spoke. A smile would sometimes be on the brink, not quite making itself available to me, but tantalizing me with its sexy potential. Then I was homing in on the satisfying sensory things about him: the cleanness of his breath, free from anything unpleasantly foody, or artificially pepperminty; his fair, soft skin, and his general overall pleasing masculine smell. A hint of aftershave? Maybe. Or it could have been nice soap. Even his unusual personal style was becoming attractive. I remember trying to engage his eyes in a way that might transmit my thoughts, but I didn't seem to be having much luck. By the time we left the bar, I decided I probably wasn't going to see him again; he was being too wishy-washy. But when I got home, I lay there for ages trying to rewrite the night, to make it so he'd just been a little bit more decisive; maybe he'd kissed me. And, unfairly, trying to rewrite him a bit too. If he donated those winklepickers to a charity shop, and I took him to Toni and Guy...

He rang the next morning and asked if I'd like to go for a quick lunch. There was something desperately unsatisfying about it as we sat in an Italian restaurant hurrying down a pizza that took an age to arrive. I dropped him off at the BBC building because finally he got around to telling me that his car had broken down, and I wondered if this had been the only reason he'd rang — because he wanted a lift. But in a parking spot outside he said: 'Would it be all right if I kissed you? I've spent all this time kicking myself for not doing it last night.'

I leaned in, somewhat relieved. His cold lips met mine, and

it was nice. His thumb was stroking along the tops of my collarbones and it all felt very...

Like we had company.

I opened one eye to see the BBC security guard's face on the other side of the windshield. I attempted to tell Mike to stop, but Mike somehow took my moaning as encouragement, and revved up his kissing. His hand went to swiftly unbutton my blouse. It had found its way into my bra before he must have sensed something was wrong. And that's when he saw our intruder. Mike removed his fingers from my nipple, which was now there for anyone to have a look. The security guard smiled. Mike smiled. Mike got out of the car. And I skidded off before the car door was even shut.

After that I never heard from him for two weeks. When I could stand the suspense and the cold shoulder no longer, I decided to ring him. 'I'm phoning to tell you that I don't think this is going to work,' I said.

'Is this Celine by any chance?' he said.

'Yes, Mike. This is Celine.'

'I understand,' he said. 'I seem to cock everything up every time we go out, and you're still in love with someone else. And maybe you always will be, or maybe you won't. I don't want to rush you. We can either pick it up in your own good time. Or we can still be friends, and you've got my word that I'll not put pressure on you. Or, of course, you can choose to never see me again. That too. Which is what I'd probably pick. If I were you.'

'Mike, about our kiss.'

'Celine, please, if it's okay with you, can we forget about the car episode if you don't mind?'

'Forget about it?'

'I'd rather not be reminded.'

'But it's over. I'm sure if he told anyone you were feeling up your girlfriend in your lunch hour in the parking space no one would believe him anyway.'

'You might be surprised,' he said. 'I think quite a few believed it with no trouble.'

'Huh?'

'The thing was, it got captured on the security cameras. Then the entire staff of the BBC ended up with it as their screen saver. I'm never going to live it down.'

'Nice to meet you,' he says now, looking me over the way he always did: appreciatively. I wonder if he catches the nostalgia in my face. He stands up as the waiter pulls out a chair for me.

'Nice to meet me?' Oh yes. I forgot. *You have to treat me like we were never married.*

As I look at him, a thought just blindsides me: if only this was our first date. If we could rewrite thirteen years of whatever it was we got so wrong. If only there was a magic wand they gave you on your wedding day, so you could undo every subsequent argument, every petty resentment, every tear you caused, every lashed-out, hurtful comment that you didn't even mean.

He is analysing me, cautiously optimistic. 'Mike… This is mad.'

'I know,' he says. 'But it's for a good cause. Please stay.'

I am aware of the heat of curiosity from other diners. Mike often attracts attention: the nonconformist look that makes him interesting to others. I sit down at our booth, and immediately bury myself in a purple, leather-backed menu.

By the servers' station, the young host and a young male waiter are exchanging smirks, their eyes directed over here. When they catch me looking, they quickly glance away. They have me sussed. Nobody, not even a reasonably attractive, thirty-something female, goes on this many dates with different men. I'm obviously a high-class tart. 'What are you smiling at?' Mike asks me.

'Nothing,' I tell him.

Mike now pretends to study the menu but his eyes keep bobbing up to fix on me. He's made an effort to dress nicely. A new-looking white shirt, a few buttons undone and showing his grey chest hair. A grey blazer that's the same shade as his hair. The drainpipe jeans. Tan winklepickers.

'You're analysing me and wondering what you ever saw in me.'

'No I'm not! Why would I do that? This is the first time I've met you, remember?' I narrow my eyes at him and try not to react to the clear amusement in his.

'Somebody once said you should never criticise your husband's faults, because if he didn't have any, he might have found somebody better than you.'

I launch a smile. His eyes twinkle at mine now. I go back to perusing the menu again, even though I come here so often I know it off by heart. 'I understand you work in radio,' I humour him.

'Yes,' he quietly charms me. 'I'm the producer of the Jackie Zane show, on Blaze FM.'

'I never listen to it.'

'So that's a conversation stopper right there then.'

'No it's not. It sounds like an interesting job. Do you like it?'

He pretends to think. 'Put it this way, I've done it for twenty years, so I certainly don't dislike it. It's been good to me, so I've been loyal back.'

It's true. Mike never cared if he got promoted, made more money, never seemed to mind that he always worked the graveyard shift. When we were happy, I'd admire his ability to be so content. Then when we were getting on each other's nerves, I'd want to hold it up as evidence of a personal handicap or demerit on his character.

My friend the mischievous waiter arrives and reaches over to make room on the table for a basket of bread. 'Besides, the lifestyle would be hard to give up,' Mike says. 'You know, exotic travel. Penthouses in five cities. The company Ferrari. The chance to eat at a fine restaurant like this, and meet a woman as beautiful as you, who would have otherwise been way out of my league.'

The waiter places the bread down and a smile has set on his face, like a little boy caught with his finger in the pie. Mike asks him for two gin and tonics. 'Absolutely, sir,' he says, and backs up, looking possessed by an alien.

Mike frowns. 'What's his problem? And why's he calling me sir?'

I grin, relaxing into the groove of the light piano jazz, and the wholesomeness of Mike's company that is so familiar to me. 'You know, Mike, we could always skip this fake date part, and just talk about Aimee or something? If you like.'

'Is there something wrong with Aimee?'

'No.'

'Then we can't skip this part.' The waiter is back surprisingly fast with the drinks, cheeks the colour of two plums. Mike continues, 'I'm paying for the full service, remember? That was the deal. Everything that you normally do with a Jim I want done to me. The whole works. No crack or crevice unexplored.'

The waiter freezes momentarily, and then tactfully backs up half a dozen steps, turns, and wonders how fast he can return to his friend.

'That's actually a very nice dress,' Mike's eyes go down the front of me, as he quickly strums his fingers on the table in time to the music.

'You don't have to compliment me.'

'I'm not. It is. It's a good colour on you, with your hair. Red's not normally a colour you wear.'

I unnecessarily look down at myself. 'I got it in the sale.'

'Was it marked down because it was too bright for everybody else?'

'Ha ha.'

His eyes meander over the top half of my body, making me nervous. I snap the menu closed, cross my arms. 'Here's the thing, Mike, about your proposition: I'm not sure I have anyone I can set you up with.'

'Really? I'm having the liver and onions.' Mike snaps his menu closed too. 'So tell me about the person you're going to set me up with.'

Isn't he listening? 'I'm saying, I don't have anyone in mind.' But even if I did, that's not how I work. They have to trust that I'll match them right, not just with somebody they like the sound of, or the look of. I never let them know too much in advance about their dates. That way, I'm doing what they pay me for, not just selling them a catalogue. It also forces them to break old habits. In matters of lust and love, people are usually repeat offenders, attracted to the same qualities that have failed them in the past. But there's another more selfish reason why I don't give too much away: I only promise them one date a month so they'll know I take what I do very seriously. If they want a numbers game, there are plenty of online services for that. But the main reason I can't let them pick and choose is because I don't have a huge client bank. If they wrote everybody off the second I described them, I'd soon be out of business.

'And another thing,' I tell him. 'Nobody said you're in. I actually don't let everybody in who wants me, you know. I'm very picky who I do this with.'

The waiter is hovering there with his pad, disbelieving his own good fortune.

'God, he creeps up on you like baldness, doesn't he?' Mike says after the lad manages to take down our order. 'He's as red as a week on the Costa Brava. I think you might have got yourself an admirer.'

'I think it's you. I think he's after your car.'

He scowls. 'My car? Oh! My Ferrari you mean.' He laughs.

'You'd actually suit a Ferrari, you know.'

'But then I'd be a case of "small bloke, big vehicle" and you know what they say that means.'

'As I was telling you,' I beam at him, 'you have to pass this fake date first, before I can agree to take you on.'

'Why do I feel I'm already screwed?'

'I don't know, Mike. If that's how you feel, then why are you here?'

We hold eyes. 'I want to fall in love. I miss being in love,' he says. His reproachful gaze cruises over my face. And it strikes me, when he looks at me like this, how much regret is still there. And I want to find somewhere to look other than at his sad, still-loving eyes. I want to. But I am failing miserably.

'Cute versus sexy?' I tap my pen on my notepad waiting for his answer. We've finished off the wine. Mike has been entertaining me with some of the radio station sexual politics stories that I have, admittedly, missed. I note that the upbeat jazz has been replaced with Katie Melua's 'Nine Million Bicycles,' one of her songs that Aimee and I really like. I can hear Aimee's little voice droning along to it. 'I have to have these answers for my personal profile. If you don't want to—'

'No, ask away. What was the question?' He was off listening to the song too. 'Oh yeah… Cute is sexy, isn't it? Did you fix the bath tap?'

'I called someone in to do it, yes.'

'To fix a tap? I'd have done it.'

'It's done.' My eyes go back to my notepad. 'Your definition of thin?'

'Kate Moss. I still don't know why you'd pay somebody to fix a tap. How much did he charge?'

'Thirty pounds. Who is a lucky person?'

He tuts. 'The tap man, I'd say. Easy money for some.' He sighs. 'Brad Pitt's a lucky person if you want to know.' He starts whistling, sits far back in the chair, stretching his arms across the back.

'What's hot?'

'Somebody who argues passionately but knows when to stop. Somebody who laughs a lot, and isn't always searching for things they don't even know if they really want.'

'What makes you laugh a lot?'

'Not a lot these days.'

Am I being hypersensitive? 'What would you have liked to be if you weren't who you are?' I press on.

'Virtually anything that's not a married human being. A dog. Geese are good too. A walking stick. A postage stamp, then I'd get to travel.'

No, I'm not being hypersensitive. Mike is sticking it to me in this ever so slightly passive-aggressive way he has. 'You're not batting high on the compatibility score. I did once have a woman who wanted to be a walking stick, but my geriatric clients were all fighting for her.'

'You haven't really started taking on geriatrics, have you?' he asks. His spot of sullenness has passed.

'No. Not yet. But we're all getting older. We'll all be on my books in thirty years, if we don't get taken soon.'

'Do you want to be taken soon?'

His gaze confronts me. I have to look far across the room, to not see it, and to struggle to keep the tears back. 'I don't know. I don't think so.'

'That's a shame.' He sits far back in the chair, with his legs spread, like a man subconsciously trying to maximise the space he takes up to assert his status, as he does when he's into you. Or, in this case, perhaps just because he's more comfortable this way. 'You deserve to be taken. To be swept off your feet.'

Another Katie song now. Seems like we're getting the whole Katie CD. It's too mellow for the occasion, and for some reason makes me feel very sad. 'Maybe I don't. Maybe I once was and I didn't even know it.'

'Meaning?' he says.

I look down at the top of the table and feel his eyes burning into the top of my head. The waiter comes and saves the moment by asking if we want dessert.

'Why don't you go and find him?' Mike asks, when he goes again. Mike's magnanimous capacity to care for me, that makes him selflessly detached at the oddest moments.

The restaurant has cleared out, Newcastle folk now having moved on to a bar or a club. We've been here a long time. Time always used to just disappear when I was with Mike, that's how little he bored me. 'Find who, Mike? And why do you care so much that I find anybody? Can't you just be a normal divorced, bitter, resentful sod of an ex-husband?'

He shrugs. 'Find anybody. Someone who is a vast improvement on what you had.'

'But that would be difficult in many ways.'

'You know, you almost sound like you mean that.'

I have to drop my eyes from his. 'I'm sorry,' I tell him, my voice rasping.

He cocks his head. 'What for?'

'Everything left unsaid.'

We sit like this for a while, wordlessly, as Katie sings 'The Closest Thing to Crazy.' Then he says, 'The things we painfully find out long after it stops mattering: just because you're in love doesn't mean you're going to be happy. And just because you're not in love, doesn't mean you're going to be any worse off.'

We study each other until my eyes smart from the raw burn of his gaze.

'You and your fake dates,' he says, not bitterly, and I look away through a cast of tears. 'You know, I always imagined that while you were out there dining with your Jims you were secretly hoping for an opportunity to jump ship.'

I look at him, sadly. He always used to call the men 'the Jims.' 'With a belief in me like that, is it any wonder that we're divorced?'

'Why are we divorced?' he quickly asks. 'I mean, I know, but I don't know.'

I look at him now and he holds my eyes so grippingly that I am deadlocked there.

I think of him saying to me, 'I can't be with you when there is not a doubt in me that I am somehow holding you back.' I had wanted to ask him, From what? It seemed he knew, maybe more than I ever did.

'Don't do this, Mike,' I stare at a spot far across the room again. I can feel him staring at me, his eyes soaking me up.

We sit in silence until the bill comes. The lad watches while Mike puts down the money, says a grudging 'Thanks.' Mike never was a great tipper. I can almost read the young lad's thoughts: *You greedy Ferrari-driving bastard.*

As we walk out, Katie Melua is singing 'My Aphrodisiac Is You.' I reckon we couldn't have picked a better time to leave.

When I get home, Jacqui, who has been minding Aimee, looks up from reading a book, cross-ankled, on my couch.

'That bad?' she studies my face.

I flop down in the armchair. 'I should never have agreed to do it.'

'Do it and call off the debt.'

'I don't feel there is a debt.'

'Yes you do.'

'Yes I do.' I pick up the cat and cuddle her.

Jacqui studies me for a long while, and then says, 'Do you want the good news, or the better news?'

'Both. Please.'

'Patrick rang.'

I blink. 'What's the better news?'

'There isn't any. That's it.' She smiles. 'Actually, he was phoning from his hotel in London.'

'London,' I say to myself, but out loud.

'Are you going to go?' she asks.

# Seventeen

My father has an appointment at the dentist's. He has to get his upper wisdom teeth removed and asked me if I'd go with him. When he's on the phone I say to him, 'Dad, do you think that it's ever a good idea to go back? That if you have something that was almost perfect once with somebody, you can ever recapture it?'

'What has this got to do with my teeth?' he asks.

'Not a lot. But I was jus—'

'Love is love,' he interrupts me. 'If the person's state of mind hasn't drastically changed, then those feelings never change. Whether it's a good idea to go back is another question.'

Then he surprises me by saying, 'You obviously divorced him for a reason.'

'I don't understand,' I tell him in the car. 'If you've had your wisdom teeth for most of your life, what's the big rush to get them out now?'

He sits beside me in his navy blazer with the brass buttons, the red handkerchief peeking out of the breast pocket. He looks paler than normal, his hands clenched into fists on his thighs.

'Are you getting back together with Mike?' he says.

I glare at him. 'No!'

'Well you should,' he says. 'That is, if you love the man. If you don't, well, obviously that's a very different matter.' Then he looks out of the window. 'They're far back, so they're hard to brush. And besides, the rest of the teeth are crowded, so once they're gone, the top teeth will finally have room to stretch out.'

We shoot each other one suspicious glance, and then he directs his gaze out of the window again and seems to refuse to look at me.

I sit reading a well-worn magazine while he's in the chair. There is a whirring of dental instrument noises, and the dentist's pleasant and reassuring voice from time to time. A radio quietly plays chart hits. The receptionist makes dinner plans on the phone with her boyfriend.

And then, after about an hour, my father reappears with the dentist — a tall, serious-faced but not unattractive man — walking him out.

'All right?' I stand up, as my dad manoeuvres toward the reception desk, mopping saliva from his chin with his red hankie.

'He'll be fine,' the dentist smiles at me. He has a nice voice, and manner. I tell him, 'Thanks.'

The receptionist confirms he knows which mouth rinses he has to do and tells him she'll ring him in a day or two to see how he's getting along.

We leave. My dad still hasn't spoken.

'Are you sore, Dad?' I lay a hand on his arm.

From behind his hankie, he mumbles oral hieroglyphics.

'Go on then, give me a little look.' I reach to pull away his hand.

He swipes me away, mumbling a mouthful of invective. And

it's only then that I catch a glimpse. His greying, peglike teeth have gone, and a set of skittlelike creations, the colour of double-churn butter, have mysteriously appeared in their place.

'Say cheese,' I coax him, as we wait for the lift. I'm dying for another glimpse. Has my dad really got dentures?

He turns his head away, like a dog whose mouth you are trying to remove a bone from.

'Go on. Please. Cheese.'

He turns his head away more. His hands are still clasped into fists by his sides; his small shoulders square and rigid.

'Hah can hawk,' he says.

'What was that?'

'Hi said, hi can-t hawk,' he repeats himself, slowly.

We walk in silence, given that I think he's just told me that he can't talk, to the car. Driving home, I steal glances at him when I hear the sound of tiny chomping noises coming from him.

'Heep your eyes on the hoad,' he growls.

# Eighteen

I met Jennifer Platt a few weeks back when I was posting an ad for The Love Market on the bulletin board of an exclusive Jesmond tennis club. Jennifer works there part-time while she tries to get a home business off the ground making gourmet meals for National Express East Coast — the North East to London train line. What struck me about her was the fact that here was a pretty lady with a brain and ambition who seemed to be the real thing. She said she would never have considered going to an introductions service before if she hadn't met me personally first. I've agreed to take her on and waive my fee, mainly because I know she's not well off, and I can think of a few men who are going to be interested in her. She's got virtually everything (minus the hair colour) that the modern man goes for. Yes, the textbook male client, as written up in the *Daily Mail*, wants a five-foot-eight-inch blue-eyed blonde, who is an extremely fit size twelve, who rents rather than owns her own flat, and makes less than twenty-five grand a year. I just want them to occasionally surprise me.

We meet in Deb's Tea House in Jesmond, near where she lives.

The first thing she says to me is, 'I'm nervous about getting back out there. It's been so long. I was married for eight years. I don't know how I'm going to cope with someone else's sexual preferences, navigate someone else's body. What if I'm no good?'

Haven't I spent nights wondering the same thing? Dreading stripping off for someone new? Having to adjust to a new pace? Third-date pressure — or is it second now? Wondering if there are new sexual positions that have rendered what Mike, Patrick, and I have done passé.

I can see that Jennifer's temperature has risen just by talking about this so I instantly rule out two of the men that first came to mind for her because their sexual personalities might be a bit too intimidating for her.

'Don't ever think in terms of you being inadequate, Jennifer. No man who is lucky enough to be in that position with someone as lovely as you is going to be worrying about your skills or adequacy.'

Wish I could take my own advice.

She smiles. 'That's very kind of you, thanks.'

'But why not just forget about joining The Love Market for now, and just go out there and have some no-strings fun first. Have you thought about that?'

She's shaking her head before I'm finished. 'I think you can have fun in a committed relationship. I want someone who is going to be around once I've gotten to know him.'

'If I wasn't a woman I'd want to go out with you myself.'

She laughs. I snap a photo of her for my records. 'So tell me, Jennifer, what are you really looking for in a man?' Sometimes they think I'm testing them, given that I generally ask them this on the phone and then in more detail when we meet. And occasionally I am. Like asking them their age. If you quickly follow the question with, "What year were you born in?' and they hesitate, you discover one universal truth: that people generally aren't as quick with numbers — or lies — as they might have thought.

'You know, I've never had a particular vision. It always bothers me when friends say oh he has to be six feet tall, and have all his hair. I mean, it takes more than height and hair to make someone attractive.'

I nod. 'You're brilliant! Maybe you should work for me?'

She blushes. 'Really, he doesn't have to be any one particular thing. Except honest and kind. I like finding qualities that are attractive in people that aren't necessarily the glaringly obvious things.' She scowls. 'Does that make sense?'

'Perfect. And it's a brilliant answer. I wish all my clients were like you! Do you have a single sister or any friends?' I am half-serious. Referrals are fail-safe. They are how I get eighty per cent of my clients. Nice people usually have nice people in their lives.

She beams, sips her tea, a silver signet ring on her right-hand middle finger. There is something faintly old-fashioned in her gentleness and good manners, although nothing mumsy, by the looks of the petite curviness that seems hidden under her clothes.

'If I did match you with a high earner, how would you see your life changing?' I never ask this in the first conversation or, for some, it becomes all about the money. And then that tends to influence how they market themselves to me from then on. More up-sell, less honesty. I am all for impression management. I encourage it on those early dates. Beyond dress and the visual appearance, I urge them to manage their general behaviour, to come off pleasant and assertive, to watch their body language, conceal anxieties and show openness. I beg them to be economical with their life stories and past mistakes and downplay any negatives that might result in them being written off. But I don't like them holding back and managing me.

She seems to think about this. 'You know, I'm not sure. I think in the fundamental ways I'd not want to change my life. I'm not sure I'd continue to work at the tennis club. I mean, I don't even know why they gave me the job. I can't even play!' She blushes again. 'No, I'd probably want to invest a bit of money in setting up my kitchen with a commercial-sized oven, then I'd be more able to handle the big contract when I get it. *If* I get it, of course.'

I tell her that I'm sure she's going to get her contract.

When I reach for the bill, she insists on buying our tea.

# Nineteen

Patrick is staying at the Cadogan Hotel. When I phone him back and he tells me this, a chill flutters up my spine.

'I always stay there,' he says, when I quiz him. 'Why do you ask?'

I tell him that I was in London three years ago and I thought I saw him, coming out of that very hotel. 'We were there for our tenth anniversary. It was in November.'

'November '07?' he repeats. Then after a moment: 'I was in London then. I was on my way back from Baghdad to Toronto, then Cyclone Sidr hit Bangladesh. They decided to send me there to cover it. That was…wait a minute…around the 16th when it happened.'

'My anniversary was the 24th. I saw you the day before. We'd just got off a bus. You were coming out of the hotel. You flagged a taxi.' I am almost breathless with tension.

'Yes. I was back the week after the 16th. It would have been then, for sure.'

'Patrick, I phoned the hotel! They said they had no guest by that name.'

'We rarely travel under our own names. For security reasons.' He sounds confounded. 'So you got off a bus with your husband,

131

in the middle of London, and you saw me, of all people, get into a taxi...'

I can't tell him how I belted after him. How, if I hadn't seen him, maybe I wouldn't even be divorced now. I think Mike could handle knowing that he was always surer about me than I was about him. Yes our marriage had fissures, but that could have easily been all they were. But that day in London Mike saw that Patrick was clearly more than a fissure. He was a regret. He was a "what might have been".

'If only I'd seen you,' Patrick says.

We have agreed that I am to get the 9:55 train to King's Cross and he's going to meet me on the platform.

That is, if I ever get there.

On Wednesday morning Aimee has a very bad headache. When it's still bothering her on Thursday, I phone Mike in a state. 'Do you think I should take her to the hospital?' I ask him, catching him still in bed as it's only 9 a.m. and he would have been at work until the wee small hours.

'For a headache?'

'She looks really awful. And she's just lying in bed. She's so lethargic, Mike. There's something wrong. I'm sure there is.'

Pause, while I know Mike is second-guessing himself. 'Well, maybe you should take her.' I hear him shuffling around, probably looking for his jeans to pull on, his shoes from under the bed. Sometimes I get the oddest feeling that Mike and I aren't really divorced — something has just taken him away, but he'll be home. 'Do you want me to come as well?' He doesn't wait for my answer. 'Hang on, give me twenty minutes to get some clothes on and I'll pick you both up.'

I'm instantly relieved, even though, technically, I've given up the right to lean on him. 'What if it's connected to her fall, Mike? A blood clot or something?'

'Celine!' he sighs. 'Just get her ready. She's not having a bloody stroke, all right?'

When I hang up, Aimee is standing in the doorway of my bedroom, looking a mite more pleased.

We're at the hospital forever. Waiting. For the doctor. For another doctor. For a head scan. For them to read the results. For them to talk, examine her, look over her medical reports, say little and leave us in suspense, walking in and out of rooms, running shoes squeaking on the polished floor. Aimee sits slumped against Mike, with her head under his arm, once in a while sending me a look that's laden with blame and designed in some way to make me jealous.

The verdict: everything's fine. Their words don't sink in. I had prepared myself for worse. Now we don't have worse, I am feeling suspicious. 'Are you positive it's not connected to her fall?' I ask. I remember the doctors saying at the time that it was a miracle she hadn't hit her head because unbeknown to me she had gone out without her helmet on. 'What would have suddenly brought this on?' I ask. They want to know if she has been unusually stressed about anything. Mike and I look at one another. Mike tells them about how we have gone through a divorce, in addition to the fact that she seems to be struggling in school a lot, and lost out in competing in a competition that had meant the world to her. Aimee sits stock-still, with that posture of someone being talked about. The doctor gives her some pills. 'Come on,' Mike says to us. 'Let's go home.'

'Can we go eat together?' Aimee asks, once we're in Mike's car. 'The three of us.' When I glance round at her she is suddenly looking a little brighter.

The restaurant used to be one of our regulars. I've never come back here since we split up, and I wonder if Mike's been back, but I can't bring myself to ask. Knowing he had would hurt, making me think that Mike doesn't attach the same sentimentality to our old routines and has managed to continue on where we left off, taking ownership of what was once ours.

It's full for a Thursday night. Mike goes to the bar and gets Aimee a lemonade, and two glasses of red wine for us. He walks back to our corner table slowly, carrying all three drinks carefully stacked in a triangle up by his chest. 'Should we help him?' I ask Aimee, and he looks up and catches us watching him warily.

'You thought I was going to drop them, didn't you?' He sets them down carefully on our small table. 'Faithless buggers.'

Aimee chuckles.

At the carvery station the chef loads us up with slices of roast turkey, and we help ourselves to the accoutrements. 'Take some veg, Aimee,' Mike tells her.

'I have,' she says. 'Potato.' She walks back to the table, clomping her feet 'like a herd of pet elephants' as I will always tell her.

I slide some of my veg onto her plate. She tucks into her meat with a remarkably good appetite for somebody who just had us all so worried.

'So you're getting an early train?' Mike asks, just as I am thinking of something Jacqui said: that I'm lucky that Mike and I have managed to remain friends. But have we really? Aimee is the glue that still sticks us together. I had convinced myself it was a mutual breakup. Considering that I was the heartbreaker by never being fully present in the marriage, Mike ought to hate me. And for all I know, maybe he does. This is the thing with Mike: you can never really tell what's going on in his head. He has a remarkable ability to act as though nothing much of any concern is.

It's only when he mentions the word *train* that I remember

I'm supposed to be going to London in the morning. I told him I was going down for a work conference.

'She's fine,' he says. 'Your work's important. Go.' He looks at Aimee now as he pushes the last bit of potato into his mouth. 'Can't you eat at least some of those vegetables?' he says to her, somewhat uncharacteristic in his firmness, but she's absorbed in whatever it is she's doodling. 'Hey, Aimee! I said why don't you try to eat some of those carrots?'

She glances at him now, disdainfully, and then pointedly picks up a carrot and directs it into her mouth. Mike shakes his head at me. Then he lays an arm across Aimee's shoulders and pulls her in for a kiss, eyes planted on mine. *You can't change who you are, and what you feel,*' he said, when we were splitting up. *'Maybe you once thought you could.'*

'You go to London and do your thing and we're going to have a very good time, aren't we Aims?'

"Yeah," she says, subdued.

Patrick is there waiting for me. I see him the second I step off the train. He is at the far end of the platform. In the instant after I see him, he is smiling and holds up his hand in a wave, and I just know.

Then he is cutting an urgent path through the crowd. He is beaming, his eyes seeking out my face, as a sea of people bob in-between us.

I am rooted to the spot. Then he is right here. The idea that this really is him is on a slow burn inside of me.

He laughs a little. My hand cups my mouth now. He removes it, and holds it, briefly.

It staggers me how much older he looks, now that I am no longer staring at him in a picture on the Internet. The face is fuller, even though he doesn't really seem heavier in his body.

The hair is still wavy, the same dark blond. But it's the lines around his eyes. Patterns of them, like cracks in china.

His arms go around me, he plants kisses all over my face and neck. Then his arms strap me to him. And I am aware of only one thing: of fitting, of belonging with him, of a click of something between us, an instant falling into place of all the pieces.

And I feel like dropping into tears — at the shock yes — but at something far more indelible and tragic than shock. At the loss of his boyishness, and the years I could have had to love him that I never had.

I wasn't quite expecting this sort of greeting. 'You're really here!' I say, in disbelief of him all over again.

His hands fall away from me for a second, as though in astonishment, and then he grasps my upper arms and gives me the smallest shake. 'It's you,' he says. 'It really is.'

'You're wearing the jacket,' I pull away from him, as much as he will let me because he seems to want to go on squeezing me. 'The same one you had on when I saw you—' I can't finish. I am choked by the power a coat could have over me.

He looks down at his casual olive-coloured jacket, still smiling. 'Oh, this old thing? I've had this years. You'll find I don't actually own many clothes... How are you?' he asks quickly, dismissing the importance of his jacket. 'I was worried you might not show.' I try to answer him, but he kisses me again, full and purposefully on the mouth.

Patrick always was spontaneous.

'Don't answer that,' he says. 'I don't want to hear that you may have considered not coming.'

He stops me from speaking again, with a kiss. So here we are on the King's Cross platform, as people move around us,

looking at us: a real-life, black and white Marc Trautmann photograph. The ticket man leans out of the train door and whistles
overtop an announcement of a train arrival.

I have to laugh. Because, really, I don't know what I was
expecting…us being stiff with one another. Me feeling out of
my depth. Him looking at me and us both somehow being disappointed. Anything, but not this easiness, this falling away of
all the years in-between then and now. He takes my small suitcase from me, 'Come on, let's get out of here, to eat, or get a
drink or something. All right?' He puts an arm around my
shoulders and pulls me into him. 'I can't believe I'm touching
you,' he says.

I am struck again by his face — that oddly charming nose,
and how dark his eyes are against the pallor of his skin and how
attractive a contrast I find it. Just like all those years ago.

'I can't believe I'm looking at you,' he says, hardly taking his
eyes off me as we walk. And when he smiles, the years fall away,
and he looks young again. Into the soft London sunshine,
Patrick directs us to the taxi line. 'I've changed my mind,' he
says, his hand moving to my waist where I feel the urgent press
of his fingers. 'Forget eating for now. I think we should go back
to the hotel. You drop off your bag, and then we decide what
we want to do. How does that sound? Or is that far too intense
for a first encounter after all these years?' He beams at me, gazes
at me with intent, intense warmth, and pleasure.

I laugh. 'Well…' I burn with an odd embarrassment.

He plants a firm kiss on my mouth again. Then his hand on
my back propels me up the taxi line. As he leans in and tells
the taxi driver where we would like to go, all I can think is, I
know this is really happening, because I'm bearing witness to

it, but it still feels neither credible nor possible. I have to be catching myself in a moment of schizophrenia. A smile breaks out of me while I shake my head. He turns, catching me.

I don't see much during the ride to the hotel because I am too busy looking at him. Amazed by the proximity of him all over again. It strikes me as more than a little significant that the last time I came to London was the time I saw him, and part of me never wanted to come back again, even though Jacqui was always trying to drag me down here for weekend breaks. Astonishing really, the avenues of pure agony that have gouged so deeply in me, where this man is concerned.

He sets my suitcase down behind the door in the dimly lit room that feels more soundless than quiet, and I am tugging off his jacket by the time he stands up. We don't speak as our faces move in on each other, eyes locked until we can look at each other no more.

Now, just the flourish of his jacket falling to the floor, feet scuffing along a carpet to a bed, two bodies landing as one. I open my legs and arms so we are quickly spread on each other like starfish. The unusual sensation of someone heavier than Mike on top of me. He is taller, broader, different altogether than Mike. The whiff of unfamiliar deodorant as he quickly peels off his T-shirt, static crackling. My hands slide up the sides of his body where I used to be able to walk my fingers up his ribs. The soft padding on top of the muscle. My nose in his hair. The scent of his shampoo as he lowers his head to blaze moist kisses down my neck.

Familiarizing myself with Patrick's body after all these years is like going away on holiday and sleeping in a strange bed. That first night of finding out how a new pillow fits, a new duvet settles around you. The texture of new sheets, a fabric softener you're not used to. The sad realisation somewhere that you're more comfortable in this bed than you ever were in yours at home.

Patrick's eyes lock into mine as he slides his hands down the back of my jeans, lifting my bottom. His nose up and down my neck, stopping in places, absorbing the smell and feel and taste of me. I am his strange bed.

I tug at his belt as he reaches for the button of my jeans. Then I'm lifting my bottom again for him, as he struggles to get them off, my little white knickers coming down with the effort. The sexy peel-down of clothes against skin. All this frustrated by the fact that he now has to contend with the fiddley buckles of my sandals. A snicker from me, while he pulls at shoes, brushing his lips along the insides of my knees and looking up at the view of my crotch. 'Success,' he says, flinging the shoes behind him; one of them bounces off a piece of furniture. I tug his jeans over his hips. Then he takes the soles of my feet in the palms of his hands, as though his hands are stirrups, clam-shelling my legs, opening them to put himself in them, then closing them around his back.

I have missed how we work.

As the tears run down my cheeks as he enters me, he just kisses them away, as though I don't have to tell him why they're there. I remember how occasionally I would be emotional as Mike made love to me, but for different reasons. As I clasp onto him, and more tears run down, he dries them up, dotting kisses here, dotting kisses here and there.

We are quick. And if we hadn't slept together before, one of us might have worried about this. He groans when he comes, then he groans when I do, staying inside me, his fingers paused now between my legs, where he has been touching me, to make it happen for me, just like he remembers how.

Our hearts hammer as we pant there for a while. I wonder what I've felt like to him. I move my hands to the top of his head, clasping his head between my hands, with his nose pressed into my forehead, thinking I hope he likes the woman over the girl.

I read a study about the elusive thing of physical attraction. Somewhere in our early lives we are supposed to imprint in our minds our idea of the perfect face for us. We don't realise we've done it, or even remember what it was that influenced our preference, but when we see it again later, we know. I thought it a very lovely idea.

I am kissing the perfect face.

# Twenty

He thinks we should eat at a bistro in the neighbourhood. We're both hungry. I know this when I go to put my clothes back on again and feel off balance standing up.

'Did we really just do that?' I say, hopping around, trying to locate my underwear.

'We did, didn't we?' he plays along.

Again, I don't know what I'd imagined. Us having to acclimatize ourselves to one another first, perhaps.

We dress without bothering to shower, and gaze at each other all the way downstairs in the lift, in a rapt study of each other's faces.

It's a nice late May afternoon. A gentle thrum of traffic and a red bus marked South Kensington move past us in the watery yellow sunshine. Patrick's fingers lace through mine. 'Did I feel different?' I ask him. 'Was my body a lot different?'

He looks at me, pretends to think. 'Ummmm... You were— how shall I say...'

I nudge him. 'Stop choosing your words carefully!'

He laughs. 'I was going to say you were just as into it as you were when we first met, and I definitely don't have doubts about the chemistry still being there. And your body...I think your body's fabulous.' He pulls me into him and glues a kiss on my cheek.

'More fabulous than it was when I was twenty-one?'

'More fabulous.'

I can't resist a big grin. 'Well, that's a good ego boost, even if I don't believe you.'

'Believe me,' he says, whispering into the side of my face, into my hair.

I chuckle. 'We should have waited, and got to know each other a little more first.'

He frowns. 'That was us getting to know each other.'

The neighbourhood is a-bustle. People reading newspapers outside cafés, a model-like young woman climbing into a black taxi holding a fluffy white dog, a navy blue Bentley inching out of an ivy-walled, cobbled drive.

Patrick takes it all in. 'You know, a few years ago I got the chance to work for CNN's London bureau,' he says, looking momentarily nostalgic. 'I regret not taking it in a way. I've always loved big cities.'

We decide on the restaurant on the corner. A French name. Wooden tables and seats. Prints of the *Folies-Bergère* on its two longest walls. We gravitate to a window table, scan a menu, and I order a Croque Monsieur with frites and Patrick orders a steak sandwich. I secretly observe him without actually looking at him. And, by the way he looks off to the side of me, in a kind of vacant concentration, I think he's mastered the same skill. I find I can let my eyes settle in a space five or so degrees to the left of him, then have them slide to the right, circling him as though in some bizarre animal kingdom mating dance, catching every movement of him. And I know when his eyes are doing the same dance around me.

With his long legs and broad shoulders, he looks big and bulky and formidable, as though the chair and table are somehow too small for him. It's an optical illusion, after being so used to seeing Mike sitting across from me.

'When did you leave Asia?' I ask him.

'In 1997. After Hong Kong was handed over to the Chinese. Then I was sent to cover the war in Kosovo. I was based on the Albanian border for most of the time, covering the refugee crisis. Then it was the terrorist attacks on the World Trade Center, and then the War in Afghanistan. I've been in the Middle East pretty well ever since. Up until six months ago, as I told you.' The waiter puts down some wine, and Patrick pours us each a glass.

'And your marriage?' I ask, feeling brave.

He meets my eyes. 'Over before I left Hong Kong.'

So Patrick split up with his wife not all that long after we'd met. I wonder if he contemplated contacting me then. Knowing our timing, if he had, I would probably have just got married to Mike.

Now that we have opened a door into personal territory, I feel safe venturing in.

'And you never remarried?' I ask him, and see his expression falter slightly. One thing that hasn't changed about him: Patrick's tension is palpable, even when he's trying to look relaxed. I can feel the energy of his mind working overtime and wonder if it ever stops.

'Not with my life. Divorce is like a tropical disease among foreign correspondents. It eventually gets everybody.'

'But hasn't that been lonely though? Haven't you missed having someone?'

He briefly looks out of the window. 'No. The job kinda becomes your love life. Relationships are things that end up becoming like work.'

'What happened to her? To Anya?' I always remembered her name because it sounded so glamorous, and I imagined she was, too.

The food comes out quickly, and we start eating. 'She moved back to Toronto. Married a doctor. She has a family now. Still works in the business.'

'Business?'

'Anya was a journalist. Did I never tell you that?'

I am stunned. 'No.'

He wags the foot that is laid across his opposite knee. 'Yes, of course, she was. I can't believe I never told you that. I met her at Carleton journalism school. We both worked in small towns for a while and then landed back in Toronto at the same time. Then I applied for a job with the Associated Press. I didn't tell her. By this time we were living together. I never thought I'd get it. But then I did.' He looks at me briefly before gazing distantly out of the window at the people walking by. 'She was shocked, of course. She'd just landed a good job at the *Toronto Star*. It was shitty timing. But we had to make a decision. My opportunity was the bigger career move. We both knew that I couldn't *not* take it. So we decided to get married and go together.'

'That's very strange,' my gaze goes up and down him. Why didn't he tell me any of this then? 'I always imagined her as not really having a career. Maybe because you said so little about her. Maybe I just assumed there wasn't much to say.'

'No,' his eyes scope around my face now. 'Anya was extremely ambitious. One of the smartest, most driven people I knew. I think that's what attracted me — everybody — to her, really.' He shakes his head, shrugs. 'There was every opportunity for her to have a great career in China, freelancing. You have to understand, when you're both out there trying to figure out a whole new culture, a new language, you're as likely to get a good story in the grocery store as you are sitting at your desk in the bureau. In fact, more likely. And it wasn't just me telling her that. There were many two-journalist couples with the bureau. Some of them were our friends, doing exactly what we could have been doing. But it was as if she turned resentful that I was going out to work every day, and she was left to her own devices. She seemed to think she was somehow subjugated to me, which was ridiculous. She kept going on about what she'd given up for me.'

'So when you met me—' He looks suddenly tired, his jet lag catching up.

'We'd barely been out there three months. I was learning on my feet how to file daily news reports for the most influential news-gathering operation in the world, wondering how the hell I was going to survive the challenge, and doubting whether we had done the right thing in getting married.' He looks at me frankly, shakes his head in some lingering exasperation. 'It had been my idea for us to get married. Essentially I'd dragged her out there. She was clearly depressed. I felt responsible. I thought I had to at least try to make our marriage work, to make something worthwhile for her.'

'Worthwhile?' I pull my cardigan across my shoulders. 'But you don't stay married to someone as an incentive for them to be happy.'

His trouble-laden eyes hold mine. 'No. You don't, do you? But I was young and I was in one of those "save everybody and save myself" grooves, you know. It kind of came with the territory of the job. I was coping, or surviving. I wasn't really thinking.'

I can feel him studying me, as I look distantly out of the window, across the road, through the traffic sliding by, thinking of all that he is telling me, and of how he has just made love to me and I can still feel that pull toward him that was always there. 'Why didn't you tell me any of this back then? You should have, Patrick. I was so gutted by losing you. I deserved at least to know what the reasons were.'

He wipes his mouth with his napkin. 'I'm sorry. I didn't handle it right. I wasn't handling a lot of things right back then. A part of me couldn't bring myself to talk to you about her because I didn't even fully know my own mind.'

We stare at one another. And I can tell that, whatever highs he might have had in his career, this is not a happy face. I am not looking at someone who is content with his life. 'We didn't know each other, did we?' he says. 'It was four days. And while you can learn a lot about someone in that time, you usually don't go making life-altering decisions on the strength of it.'

His words ground me. He's absolutely right, of course.

'If I'd told you exactly how I felt, you'd have encouraged me to leave her. And you'd have probably been right to. But I had to decide that on my own. I wanted to make sure it was about me and her. Not me, you, and her. It wouldn't have felt fair for me to do that to her.'

I nod slowly. We finish eating. 'I wouldn't mind some fresh air,' I tell him.

He pays the bill and we leave. He takes hold of my hand as we walk down the high street. 'If you'd been forgettable I'd have forgotten you.' He squeezes my hand. 'If I wasn't still curious about you, I'd not have found myself flying the Atlantic, with hardly a minute's thought put into the decision, just for the chance to see you again.'

A flock of birds flap their wings in my stomach. 'But you came here for business.'

He kisses my cheek. 'There was no business. Just this business.'

We intend to walk as far as Hyde Park but end up walking back to the hotel instead. Where he makes love to me again.

'So tell me about this crazy job of yours,' he says, after, propping his head up with an arm and lying on his side, looking at me.

I brighten. 'It's not crazy! I don't know why men always think what I do for a living is funny.'

'I don't think it's funny. The journalist in me just wonders how you made the leap from meeting me fifteen years ago in the famously romantic Love Market, and having a disastrously failed, albeit very intense relationship, and then you go home and decide to go into the matchmaking business. I mean, it would make more sense if ours had been a love affair that hadn't ended so badly.'

My eyes can't stop consuming him, and I'm shocked again how attractive he still is. 'It really didn't have anything to do with meeting you,' I tell him. 'It was just a fluke.'

I tell him the story of how my company came to be, and about some of my clients, while he traces a finger over my collar-bones and up and down my throat. Then he picks up one of my hands and stares at it, gently turning it over in his, as though he's fascinated by it.

'It must seem unbelievably superficial after what you do for a living.'

'Yes,' he says, shocking me, and I laugh.

'Oh well, at least you're honest.'

'No. I'm joking. It's not superficial at all. Being responsible for somebody's happiness and the biggest personal decision they will make in their lives is hardly something to be taken lightly.' He kisses the dip in my throat. 'I think I'd rather have my job than yours. Any day.'

The same serious expression that I remember. The nose that I loved: long and fine-boned, with quite the pronounced bridge that gave his face a certain appealing, aristocratic imperfection. The type of nose that means a person is intelligent and engaging, and routine work is not their specialty. The intense dark eyes — if you were going to search him for flaws — just the tiniest little bit too close together, but perhaps noticeable only to someone who was a student of facial biometrics. He gazes at me as though he's getting a fix from my face. Then his uber-intense expression launches into a smile, and an unforgotten longing fills me.

'Do you want to go out for a walk?' he asks.

'No,' I say. 'Why would I want to go for a walk?'

We make love again. When I get up and go to the toilet, I stare at my flushed face in the mirror. Then when I come back in the bedroom, he has pulled on a T-shirt and is propped up with a pillow, quite at home. Trying to look relaxed, but failing spectacularly.

And I stand still in the doorway, and all I can think is this: I could have been married to him all these years. We could have been on holiday and this could be the most natural thing in the world, me coming out of the bathroom and him lying here on our bed.

When we do eventually go out for a walk, my mobile rings. It's Kim. I had sent her on a date with Ralph Caswell, a fifty-one-year-old divorced dentist. If I don't pick up, she'll ring back until I do.

'Everything was going fine, until he came back from the toilet,' she says.

Oh no. I glance at Patrick and widen my eyes.

'It wasn't until he'd sat down again, and put his napkin back

148

on his knee that I saw it. It was suspended there, between his nose hairs like an anaemic spider in a web. It actually glistened, like a bead of dew.'

I put my head in a hand.

'It was moving in and out with his breathing. Like it had a mind and a central nervous system of its own. I spent the entire meal riveted to it, waiting for the moment when it was going to fall into his food.'

'Kim,' I say, my walk slowing now, and Patrick looking at me. 'Look, I'm in London right now, but I'm coming back. So let's meet. Let's sit down, have a glass of wine and a chat.'

'About my refund?'

'That. And about how things are going in general.'

'They're not going very well, are they? I'd rather talk about my refund.'

'I know. I realise. And I promise you that if after we've chatted, and you still want a refund, I will give it to you.'

'Can I have that in writing?' she says.

I look at Patrick and smile. 'I think I'd rather have your job too,' I say.

# Twenty-One

In the morning we walk down Queen's Gate all the way to High Street Kensington, and have coffee at Café Nero, before moving on to Kensington Palace gardens. I tell him about Aimee, the accident, the divorce, and how with every decision I've ever made in my life, I've spent far too long second-guessing whether I've done the right thing. It's a wonder I ever manage to run a business, especially in my line of work.

'They've offered me a job in Toronto, with a television network, anchoring the nightly news,' he says. 'They've given me twenty days to sign the contract.'

'Wow. That sounds very glamorous. You're going to be on the TV every day? What's to decide? Don't you want it?'

'I should. Since I pulled out of the Middle East, I've been back in Toronto kind of spinning my wheels, doing a bit of lecturing at college, waiting for assignmetns but not getting the same fulfilment from the work anymore. Before that I spent the last six years in one of the deadliest spots in the world for the foreign press, so if I'm going to leave, the time is now and this couldn't be a better opportunity. The network wants young blood. Someone who can interview and ask all the tough questions. They think I'm it.'

'That's fantastic,' I study him. 'Isn't it?'

'Maybe. For some. But I'm not sure I know how to be on the other side. My entire career has been standing there in the hotspots of conflict. I've spent my life reporting breaking news and trying to find a way to add the context, thriving on the pure adrenalin of it. I've been part of a team of people, Celine — reporters, TV crews, photographers, not just those from the AP but from bureaus all over the world, back in the heyday, before the bureaus started falling like dominos. These people's idea of relaxing is jamming into a high-risk bar in Baghdad to talk shop, debrief, bounce around ideas that might help us all broaden our understanding of the complex stories we were immersed in. This has been my life. I don't know how to have a home, in a city, how to go into an office, sit in a chair and speak into a camera day after day after day. Even though, yes, they'd be paying me three times my salary to do it. And I'm probably going to live to see out my old age.'

'But surely your life's more important than some adrenalin rush?'

'Try telling an alcoholic that his liver is more important than his vodka.' He smiles distantly, bringing his eyes back to mine. 'Anyway, enough about that. Tell me about Mike,' he says. 'I know you've told me some things, but, I guess... I'm sorry, maybe it's wrong for me to ask.'

I think for a while. 'He's the most decent, most guileless man in the world. He's a great father, and he was a good husband. And he deserved to be married to someone who had no doubts.' I look at him.

He holds my eyes. And then he kisses me, affectionately, on the cheek. 'You and I wouldn't have had doubts,' he says. 'If I'd been able to marry you back then.'

We stand admiring Kensington Palace through its black and gold gates. We watch the dogs playing off-lead, one of them friskily trampling over ornamental flowerbeds, and the couples out walking, enjoying their park on this beautiful May day. We gaze at each other, the way two people do who are quite fascinated with each other and have no one they have to hide it from.

'What are we going to do?' he asks me, abruptly. There's that same urgency he had back in Sa Pa, in his hut, right before he was leaving to go back to his wife.

'I honestly don't know.' I knew this would come up. I had just had a moment where I'd caught myself being aware that I'm too happy. 'A part of me always believed that if I ever did meet you again, you could never live up to my fantasies. You know, when you want something, and you obsess about it, you make it more than it really is? So this is all rather shocking, that you actually are living up to them.'

He drags me out of the path of a family of geese who seem to be on a mission to peck my feet. Patrick thinks it funny.

'What we need is some perspective on this,' he says. 'A reality check. The fact is, neither of us is married.' He releases my hand and puts his arm around me. 'So theoretically, anything is possible. You live in the North East of England, and I live, for now anyway, in Toronto. Admittedly, a small but fixable problem.'

'Fixable how?'

'I haven't got to that part yet. I'm at the perspective stage, not the clarity stage. But what I always find is you never have one without the other, so I'm just waiting for the solution to hit me.'

'What I think is going to happen is, you're going to go home to your beautiful Canada, accept your fabulous job, and become an overnight sex symbol for the entire female Canadian population. And I—'

I can't say the words *I'll never see you again* because they're going to kill me, and, besides, I don't want to give him ideas.

'—we'll email, keep in touch, see each other when you pass through London.'

'No,' he says, stopping on sun-dappled ground under the canopy of a huge plane tree, and facing me, gripping me by the shoulders. 'That won't do for me.'

'Hang on, I was going to add "until it gradually fizzles out."'

He pulls me into him as he leans back against the tree. 'It's not going to fizzle out. I made a bad decision years ago. I'm not going to make another one.' He rests his chin on the top of my head. 'I'm not sure what I can promise you right this very second, because as I said, I don't have an instant solution, but I can promise you that. Occasionally getting together while we're both living different lives won't do for me.' He looks at me in complete seriousness. 'It's either all or nothing. That's just the way I am.'

He pops a kiss on my cheek. 'So which is it going to be?' he says.

# Twenty-Two

Back at the hotel, I check my email, and try phoning Aimee to make sure everything's all right, but she's not answering her mobile so I just leave a message, repeating that I'll be home tomorrow night.

I have several emails. The first is from Kim, wanting to get together to talk, 'So I can get this over with and get my refund.' I told her I was in London! Gosh! The second is from Jacqui, asking 'How is it going?' I reply saying, 'Fantastic! Just as it was…'

Then there's a message from Sandra Mansell, my quiet-spoken spa-owner client, whose photo my dad had a thing for. It just came in about twenty minutes ago.

> *Dear Celine,*
>
> *Had a lovely time last night. Although it was NOT what I expected! Your father is an extremely adorable, charismatic man, and SO interesting! If only he were forty years younger! Please thank him again for a lovely evening. I was very flattered.*
>
> *Sandra*

Father?

Evening?

Flattered?

What is she on about? I quickly type back telling her I am in London, and add, *I'm sorry, Sandra, I have absolutely no idea what you are talking about! I am about to ring my father now, to find out.*

Then I ring my father.

Of course I know he won't pick up when he sees it's me. So I do Kim's trick of hanging up and then ringing again, until I've annoyed him enough.

'Hey,' he starts singing, 'did I happen to meet the most beautiful girl in the world? And if I did, was she called Sandra? Sandra...'

'Anthony!' I growl. 'What on earth is going on? How did you end up spending the evening with one of my clients?'

'Not the entire evening. Though it wasn't through lack of trying. Just dinner.'

'You took her to dinner?'

'I did, yes.'

I have to sit down. 'How?'

'Well, she didn't exactly go out with me. She went out with a six-foot-tall, thirty-eight-year-old paediatrician from Jesmond, who has never been married, wants children, likes foreign holidays, country walks, and fine dining.'

It takes a moment for the penny to drop — which it does, as soon as I hear his dirty chuckle.

'Hang on, you set this up? You pretended you were one of my clients?' I'm so stunned I think I must be still asleep and having a nightmare. 'But how?'

'Well, I didn't exactly set it up. It was your trusty assistant, Freddy, who phoned her and told her about the date.'

'My who? Who is Freddy?'

'Nice fellow. A little long in the tooth to be still working at his age. But he has an instinct for a match made in heaven.'

'Hang on, you're saying that YOU posed as the assistant I don't have, and then you rang a client and set yourself up with her?' Patrick is just coming out of the shower.

'She's thinking of sitting for me. I told her that the planes of her face make her the ideal model.'

'Oh, God help me!' I hold onto my head. I bet he wasn't looking at her face. 'I don't believe this. How many others have you done this with, Dad?'

'None,' he says, disdainfully. 'But now you're giving me ideas.'

When I hang up, I fly off another email to Sandra.

*I am so sorry! I am so embarrassed!!! I can't believe he'd do something like that! I don't even know how he got your contact information!!!!! This is terrible! Please accept my apology!!!! Will have much more 'appropriate' match for you as soon as I return!! Promise! And will kill my father!*

Then I reread it, delete all the exclamation marks, and send.

When I come back upstairs from breakfast and check messages again, Sandra has written:

*Had a wonderful time with your lovely father!!! No need at all to be embarrassed! As I said, he was utterly charming, and knowing someone would go to those lengths to meet me really gives me hope!*

Well, I suppose that's one way of looking at it, yes.

# Twenty-Three

We agree that Patrick is going to come up North.

I am to go on ahead today — Sunday — as planned. Then Patrick will take the train up on Wednesday. I will check him into the Station Hotel in Newcastle. And I will try to wangle as much time with him as I can get, before he has to go back down to London the following Sunday, for his Monday morning flight. I've decided, after a good deal of thought, that I'm not going to tell Jacqui. Patrick and I will have too little time together as it is, without my having to parade him before everybody. Plus we still don't know where any of this is going — perhaps there will never be any need for him to meet my family. But most of all I don't want Aimee or Mike knowing about him. It would hurt and confuse Aimee. And it's impossible for me to imagine how Mike is going to feel if he knows that Patrick is back in my life — only perhaps, that his marriage had been a sham.

We go to King's Cross Station and get Patrick a train ticket, and he waves me off on the platform.

While I'm on the train I sit in a daydream for a while and then force myself to do a bit of work, mainly to catch up, because I've fallen so far behind this last week or so. I email Trish to make sure she's going to show up for her coffee date with Liam Docherty, the ex-footballer. She cancelled on him the first time. Then I spend a bit of time poring over my mental filing cabinet of ladies to try to find someone for Trish's James Halton Daly. He emailed me this two days ago:

*'Know that Rome wasn't built in day, but am fossilising waiting for the list of lovelies you are setting me up with…?'*

Something niggles me about James. He's right; I haven't exactly jumped to line him up with dates. There really is no reason why. I think I just have to try harder. I pull up his digital photo so I can stare at it and rack my brains.

I have Petra, another client who owns a spa in a posh end of Newcastle, and is very attractive in a high-maintenance way. Perhaps too? Then I have Elaine Thompson, who owns a travel agency. She's worldly, interesting, but five years older than James. A bunch of others just wouldn't be on his intellectual level. I could see him getting really turned off by Lorraine McNaughty's lack of self-confidence and by Julia Forrest's talk-ativeness and her very strong and sometimes incoherent Northern accent. Diane Bookington isn't a bad one. I reread her profile, and the notes I made on her. She works in marketing for the Northern Sinfonia, is certainly attractive, well-educated, dignified… I stare at her photo now, and then go back to James's. They'd certainly look fine together. I can't think of a reason *not* to match them.

Well, only one that keeps floating around in my head…

Monday is a powerhouse day: I frantically check stuff off the to-do list so I can clear up time for Patrick. The day starts with Aimee stomping around the kitchen in the new cork-heeled shoes that her dad bought for her, grunting incoherent replies when I ask her how her weekend was.

Next, I do something I've never done. I finally return

Jacqui's millionth phone call and I lie to her. I tell her that Patrick was fantastic, but I'm not sure all the old feelings are still there, for either of us. She's at work, so can't talk much. 'But I thought you said he was fantastic and it's all just like years ago…?'

Nothing escapes my sister. 'Well, it was. I mean, he was. And he is.'

'So what's wrong?'

I stumble for words and then ask her if we can dissect this later.

Then, I ring Kim on the offchance that she will agree to meet me in her lunch break. She does. I take the train into Newcastle, popping first into the Station Hotel to inspect rooms and book the best one for Patrick.

It's a warm May day, and Kim is wearing a floral dress with a lime green cardigan over it and lime green fifties-style slingback shoes. With her luminous blue eyes and the pink lipstick she's put on, and her blonde hair, she looks strikingly girlie and unintimidating. She orders a Pinot Grigio spritzer and sinks it quickly. But she glances around a lot, as though she has skipped bail, or I'm the ex-con and she doesn't want to be seen with me.

'I just don't think I can do it,' she says, whipping a glance around both shoulders again. I've never seen her this on edge. 'I've spent the best years of my life trying to meet someone and for reasons that are beyond me it just never seems to work out. And I'm just so tired of getting my hopes up, only to repeat the same disappointments.'

The waitress comes to take our order. Kim petulantly says she wants 'nothing' and then calls her back and changes that to a chicken salad. The salad arrives; she comments that it looks oily. She doesn't touch it, but knocks off a second spritzer. I tuck into my lamb burger anyway because I'm starving. 'Kim, there are things we can't control and things we can. You should try to remember that, of all the matches I've sent you, not one of them didn't like you. It was you who didn't like them.'

Her cheeks turn the same shade as the fiery undertip of her nose. 'What was there to like?' she says, with a small sarcastic laugh. 'If I'm paying highly for a professional service, I should be able to meet better men than I would find walking down the street.'

Ah! That's just what they all think! When Kim signed on with me, she came up with a Wish List of what she wanted. Right down to her completely shameless declaration that he should have 'a tanned complexion but not be a foreigner.' He had to be six foot or more, with all his hair, possess the type of physique that said he worked out at least three times a week, and have no hard skin on his feet. On top of that he had to have an income of more than eighty thousand pounds a year. I had four people who matched her ideals — although, admittedly, I took a gamble on their feet. I introduced her to all of them and she found fault upon fault with each one of them.

I catch with a finger the little river of grease that is on its way down my chin. 'I think I know what the problem is,' I tell her.

She tries to drain her glass even though it's empty, and says a sceptical, 'Oh?'

'You remember how you only used to go for blue-collar types? Then when they saw your fancy BMW they seemed to lose interest? You thought they were rejecting you, yet still you went after them. You kept thinking they weren't impressed with you. But the problem was they were too impressed with you — you were out of their league. Now, I've fixed you up with five good matches — in addition to the four that were almost tailor-made to your specifications — and you've rejected all of them, almost all for trivial reasons.' Her eyes have not once blinked. Not a muscle in her body has moved. But she looks like she's ready to explode. 'So I'm thinking either you're now getting your own back — revenge on the male sex at large. Or, deep down, you really don't want to meet someone.'

She doesn't instantly jump to contradict me, but she looks less ready to burst a vessel. I press on. 'You know, all through my teens I had acne. I bought every kind of cream, always trying to hide it. When it finally cleared up of its own accord, you'd think I'd have been overjoyed. But I actually missed it. I missed not having something to be constantly trying to get rid of.'

She scowls. 'How has this got anything to do with what we're talking about?'

'Well, you've got into such a habit of trying to meet someone and it not working, that you'd actually be a bit lost if you met someone and it worked. You've made unsuccessful dating a habit, and in your own way, you're happy with it.'

She does a small, shocked laugh. 'Why would I be paying you then?'

'To feed the habit.'

I watch her and she won't meet my eyes.

'There are such things as the perfect pair of shoes. Or the perfect haircut. There is no such thing as the perfect human being.'

She picks up her fork. 'I really do want to meet someone. You're wrong there.' She spears a piece of chicken, looking downcast all of a sudden. 'I just… I suppose I do have some problems, and sometimes I think it's not worth it — I might as well give up.' She looks up at me now. 'But maybe I shouldn't. Yet. Unless of course, you want to give up on me.'

I wag my fork at her. 'Never.'

She puts the piece of chicken in her mouth.

'Baby steps up the mountain,' I tell her. 'But eventually we'll find you someone.'

Next, in my powerhouse day, I phone Mike to give him the good news. 'I have someone I think you might like to meet.'

I wonder if my decision to set him up with lovely Jennifer Platt is motivated by my own guilt about my reunion with Patrick.

'She's thirty-seven. Divorced. Her name is Jennifer and she's presently employed in trying to set up her own catering business. She'd like to meet someone but is certainly not desperate. In fact, I actually approached her about joining The Love Market, not the other way round.'

I'm finished my brief intro, but he continues to listen. 'I think you're going to like her,' I add.

'Right,' he says, after a second or two of pause. 'Okay. Well, when am I going to get to meet her?'

'I'm going to see if she's free this Friday.' My usual practice is to give the woman the man's number and let them make the first contact. I used to do it the other way round because even though I'm a modern woman I've never been keen on women asking men out. I have noticed that the most successful relationships are the ones that still maintain a degree of respecting traditional roles for the sexes. The most common complaints I have heard married women make are not that the husband has a wandering eye, but that she is expected to wash out the rubbish bin and mow the lawn. But the main reason why I prefer the woman contacting the man to set up a date is because I had one situation where the man wouldn't accept rejection and became a nuisance. Like most aspects of this business, I've learned through trial and error.

'Mike...' I try to tactfully broach this. 'I was hoping that on

Saturday you might take Aimee again. I know you just had her at the weekend, but…'

'You have plans.'

'I might do, yes.'

'Of course,' he says, quietly. 'If I go out with this Jennifer on Friday, I can pick Aimee up Saturday morning if you like.'

I ring off and sit there feeling wormy. Then I ring Jennifer.

'I have a very lovely man for you to meet,' I tell her.

I neglect to add that he's my ex-husband.

Imagining your ex in bed with someone else is the strangest thing. Which, of course, now that I've made those two phone calls, is all I'm imagining. Even though it's rather hypocritical, given that I've just spent the weekend in bed with the man who may have helped wreck my marriage without him ever knowing it. Mike and I weren't great in bed right away. It took time, and love, and practice. Mike was too fixated on whether or not he was pleasing me. And I remember thinking that I probably should have taken more time to get over Patrick. The more we were together, the more we found what worked for us and Mike ended up being an exceedingly good lover. And I realised that loving someone, without necessarily lusting after them, was still love, wasn't it? I didn't have to desire Mike in the heart-slamming sense of the word to care about him, to see myself with him, and to feel empty at the thought of him not being in my life. I'd arrived at love through a whole other way; the journey was different but not 'less.'

Can I picture Mike with another woman, after so many years of being with me? Jennifer gaining the benefits of Mike's years of experience, both in and out of bed?

No.

But picturing him without someone hurts more.

# Twenty-Four

Then Wednesday is upon us.

I check my email before booting out of the door to meet his train. One from Trish. I read it quickly, excited to hear what she thought of my wounded footballer, Liam Docherty.

> Dear Celine,
> Nice-looking bloke. Shy for a footie? Problem though — I was first in line to order, and he told me that he'd buy the coffee because he'd managed to find a parking spot for free!! He's an ex-footballer!! Why would it even be on his radar that the spot came free???!!!

Of course now I am remembering our fake date, how, when the bill came he scrutinized it and then remarked on how he didn't remember either of us having had an orange juice.

I type: *Could he have been joking? Can't see him seriously being afraid of paying two quid to park his car!*

She responds by return: *He DEF wasn't joking!! Extremely serious! SO sad! But still don't think he's for me. Slightly intellectually challenged?*

And I thought he was quite bright. For a footie.

Patrick stands there in my oak-beamed little living room absorbing every last crack and crag on the pale lemon walls. His

164

eyes travel over the tall stone fireplace, clutters of magazines on the pine linen chest in front of the window, the pale green velour cushions against the dark brown leather sofa, the lemon and cream drapes, Aimee's shoes in the middle of the floor, an empty wineglass on an end table that I missed in my tidying up. I had expected we'd go straight to the hotel but he seemed to really want to see my home. 'Are you thinking of putting in an offer?' I ask him.

'It's beautiful.'

'It's old. It needs a lot of work.' I put the kettle on and he seems to get lost in the view of the giant wilderness of moss green and heather that goes on endlessly beyond our back garden.

'It's like Wuthering Heights,' he says.

'But I don't want to live in a novel written in the 1800s, Patrick. I like cities, and traffic and noise and life. Sometimes all this is too confining. Everywhere you go you are known. People know everything you do.'

'But you have a lot, Celine,' he looks around again. 'A lot more than most have. More than I've ever had, certainly.'

'You should try being here in the heart of winter. Endless rain and fog and snow.'

'Do you remember the mist in Vietnam?'

I smile at him. 'Yes. But that was beautiful.' Our gazes fuse together. 'Did you ever go back?'

His eyes comb over my kitchen, somewhere we did renovate when we moved in. Mike bought DIY books and learned how to put down dark-honey wood flooring, install white marble countertops, and change the wall and base units to oak. I painted the walls a brighter yellow than the living room, and sewed white roman blinds for the three windows. He shakes his head. 'I thought about it. Maybe to make a documentary. But Sa Pa has changed a lot since we were there. The Love Market no longer exists. Or at least not in the way that we saw it.' He shrugs, sadly, and then says. 'Who's this?' as the cat staggers in.

'Molly. Mike's cat. She's really old and Mike didn't want to upset her world by taking her with him when he moved out.'

He bends to pet her, and then looks up, his eyes going straight to the picture of Mike and me that I still haven't taken down. Instead, beside it, I put one of Aimee.

'Who does Aimee look like?' he asks.

'My mother, actually. I have a portrait that my dad did of her when they first met and were very much in love. Aimee is the image of her.'

He goes on studying the picture, asking some questions about my daughter. But I wonder if it's really Aimee he's looking at, or if it's Mike he's now studying. 'Does your mother live nearby?'

'She died not long before we got divorced. Breast cancer. She was only in her early fifties. It was terribly, terribly sad. When I think of her life, I think it was such a waste in many ways. She could never forgive my dad, and yet you knew she still loved him. She wrecked herself.'

'Were you close?'

I shake my head. 'I used to think she had no time for me. I got in the way of her and my dad. But now I think in her own way she might have been trying to protect me from the harsh realities of what a bad marriage really was, by somehow trying to push me to the sidelines all the time.' I shrug. 'All I ever really wanted was for her to open up to me. To let me in a bit.

'I held out hope that she might have rallied and been a good grandmother to Aimee. But she was living in York with her third husband when Aimee was little. It's not far away, but she rarely came to see us. And when we tried to go there, we always got a lukewarm reception. She never seemed genuinely thrilled.' I don't tell him that I bumped into my mother and Donald when Aimee was about three. It was in Marks & Spencer's café in Newcastle. They'd come up for a visit, but hadn't let us know.

He ponders me. 'Your dad?'

I smile. 'Good now. He and Aimee go out painting sometimes, now that the weather is good. They go to the beach and he shows her how to capture the angle of the waves, and the change in colour and the movement of the sea. She was pleased as punch the other day. He had bought new colours for her. She kept walking around repeating their names: Prussian blue, cerulean blue, and titanium white.' I smile. I pour boiling water on teabags. 'Didn't you ever want kids?'

He ponders this, and I wonder if he's not going to answer. But then he says, 'It wouldn't have been fair with my life. But I never especially wanted to have a family, no. But then things happen to you that make you wonder how sure you are about yourself, and about what you do and don't want...' He pulls a chair far out from under the kitchen table and sits down, long legs spread. 'A few years ago we filmed a piece on an orphanage in Sarajevo — what had happened to the so-called rape babies — kids born of women who were sexually assaulted by Serbian soldiers. These kids were largely unacknowledged by the state. We brought them candy and toys so they wouldn't be too intimidated by a bunch of guys coming in with all this equipment, which they were at first. But by the time we were ready to go, they were clinging to us and telling us they loved us. They wanted us to take them home. One of them, a little girl of about four, was calling a nine-year-old her mother.' He shakes his head. 'And here was I, doing my work and walking away. All I was really doing was broadcasting their story to sell news, to keep the network's ratings where they wanted them. I could try convincing myself that awareness is key to change, but it's not. Actions are key to change. I used to believe in what I did wholeheartedly. I used to believe my news stories could change the world…' He shakes his head again. 'But there was no good that I could have possibly done for that child. Even if I'd wanted to, you can't adopt them. Bosnians have very strong feelings against removing Bosnian children from their homeland.'

'You were thinking of adopting one of them?'

'The little one who was calling her sister her mother — and the older child too, of course. I couldn't get either of them out of my head for a very long time.'

He looks at me sadly. 'How's that tea coming?'

After I pour us our tea, I log-on to my laptop on the table, and find the video blog of him in Afghanistan. He is sitting in a white vest and jeans, on his blue sleeping bag, in a tent, drinking from a paper cup, looking extremely gorgeous.

He comes and stands behind me, watches the screen for moments. 'That was in Helmand Province. It was somebody's idea of a good segment for the public to see what we look like when the camera isn't trained on us. People seem to think being a foreign correspondent is glamorous, yet look at us — a bunch of smelly guys shacked up together in a tent in the middle of nowhere. I'd just filed a piece on the Taliban for the ten o'clock news. I'd gotten a good interview. It was a great day. Brent in the picture there was editing it.' He points to a big-bellied, hard-lived man in a white vest on the screen. 'I was drinking cold coffee and I'd been awake all night because these guys snored so damned much…' He huffs a laugh.

'So that was a great day?'

'Yes. Actually it was. When you're there it all becomes about the story. It's like being in a room full of heroin addicts. All they can think of is the drug. If they're not shooting up, they're stalking around, working on where to get their next fix.'

'That's your bed you're sitting on,' I say, fascinated. 'Where you slept.'

'I told you it's not luxurious, even in civilized posts. The networks cut back; they don't have the big budgets anymore. So much of the news is reported by stringers who carry their own cameras and do it all themselves. We're the old brigade. A dying breed.' He rubs a hand over his mouth, stares at himself on the screen while I look up at him.

'You really miss it.' Now his reservations about the newsreading job make sense.

He drags his gaze away from the screen, and looks at me with nostalgia in his eyes. He seems more at home talking about his job than doing anything else. 'There were good times, for sure. But now so much is at stake reporting a story. As a journalist you're supposed to be a witness, an impartial observer of the conflict. But in the Middle East you don't observe it, you become part of it. Sometimes you don't know what side you're on.' His eyes have drifted to a place that only he can see. 'So what else have you got on me?' he says.

We look at one another. Then he says, quite out of the blue, 'I regretted not writing to your mother's address, at least to tell you I'd gotten divorced. I regretted not taking that risk.'

I feel tears prick my eyes. 'It would have been horrible timing. Me getting a letter from you saying you were divorced, and knowing that I had really just got married.'

He puts his hand on the back of my neck. 'Yes. Our timing has been off all along.'

Hadn't I recently had the same thought?

His voice from my computer filters into the room, incongruously.

'Can we get rid of that?' he asks.

In bed — the spare room, not my room, that would be too strange — Patrick makes love to me tenderly. Aimee won't be home until after six because my dad is picking her up after school, and taking her to the beach to sketch again. She's building quite a portfolio.

'Were you ever in love with Anya? You must have been, once.' I ask him, after, as we lie there.

'Why must have? Were you ever in love with Mike?'

I think about this. 'Not in the way that I suppose we all associate with being in love.'

He strokes my bare arm. 'I felt I should have been in love with Anya. I think it was my competitive instinct. All my life I'd done well at everything — sport, exams, scholarships. She was just an extension of that for me, I think. If that makes any sense.' He kisses the top of my head. 'Anya was perfect on paper. You'd have matched us, in your line of work. But I just kept feeling I'd got something too easily that I hadn't wanted badly enough in the first place. That my marriage had been a bit of a pot shot. And that's kind of how I'd always felt about a lot of things when I was growing up. I got things easily whether or not I wanted them — and usually I didn't.' He snorts. 'It sounds crazy now, saying that about myself. Maybe I just rode life too highly then. Something in me was unstoppable, and yet there were times when, clearly, I should have stopped myself.'

'I think when you're in love with someone, it repositions how you've felt about everybody else you've met,' he says.

I lie there blinking, wondering exactly what he means by this comment.

# Twenty-Five

On Thursday and Friday, I spend virtually the whole day at the hotel, in bed with Patrick, between school runs and meal-making for Aimee. On Friday, Patrick and I go out for lunch down at Newcastle's fancy Quayside. We sit on a patio drinking beer, and dipping foccacia bread into a pool of olives and oil, then sharing smoked salmon and cream of leek pasta and green salad. It's a warm day. Patrick scrutinizes everything around us and then smiles at me when he sees me watching him.

On Saturday morning, Mike comes to pick up Aimee. 'How was London?' he asks, practically giving me a facial peel with his gaze.

'It was fine.'

'Conference good?'

I forgot I'd told him I was going to a conference. I nod. 'For conferences.'

His gaze travels down the fitted bodice of my Primark denim dress. 'What's new in the dating business then?' When I cast him a look, he says, 'Sorry. Just trying to be sociable.'

'How was your date last night?' I ask him.

He studies me too closely for comfort, his gaze sweeping

around my face like the second hand of a clock. 'I like her. She's a very nice person, isn't she? A pretty woman too.'

Aimee comes downstairs in her new platform wedges, and gives her dad a kiss. 'Have fun,' I tell them both, and watch them walking down the garden path, getting a flashback to Saturdays of old. Our days out. Us clothes shopping while Mike stood soldierly, outside of stores. Aimee prancing around at home in her new purchases, her girlish attempts to act vampish, singing along to Mariah Carey about dream lovers coming back to her. Summer days at the beach — Aimee drawing, me running, and Mike resting on an elbow on the sand, watching us.

When I close the door, I don't feel as peppy as I did before he knocked.

I am barely back indoors when I hear the ping of my email. I click on and see it's from Jennifer. Immaculate timing.

'*I really like Mike!*' she writes.

Patrick and I drive to Swallowship Woods. We lean over the bridge to watch the Tyne River jump and froth over the rockbed. Patrick marvels at the tall redwood trees and the occasional kingfisher and speckled thrush that hops across our path. After that we drive to the coast, and I take him to a place where they serve the best Holy Island mussels I've ever tasted. Before it starts to rain, we manage an hour's walk along the virtually unchartered expanse of buttermilk sand that makes up a portion of the region's thirty-nine miles of coastline designated an Area of Outstanding Natural Beauty. I tell him some of the local history about Grace Darling, the girl with the windswept hair who lived in lighthouses and braved her life to rescue shipwrecked men.

'Do we have time?' he asks me when we get back to the house, nodding upstairs.

We make time.

After a leisurely lovemaking session, and while he sleeps, I go back downstairs and see it's nearly three o'clock. I check on the chicken I am cooking in my slow pot for dinner, and pull out some vegetables to prepare from the drawer in the fridge. I am just putting the kettle on when I hear the front door. By the time I walk down our passageway, my dad is just walking in. I hadn't thought to lock it. His eyes go straight to my dressing gown.

'Aren't you well?'

'Dad? What are you doing here?'

'Visiting. I thought I'd come and see my daughter and grand-daughter.'

'Aimee is with Mike. I thought Saturday afternoon was your life drawing class?'

'Not anymore,' he runs a hand through his plentiful snow-white hair. 'If you must know, I was asked to leave.' He pulls out a chair and sits down. His face, with his new upper teeth, looks fuller, younger somehow.

'Leave?' I watch him pull out a cloth handkerchief from the breast pocket of his jacket, blow his nose, fold the hankie, and put it back. 'Why were you asked to leave, Anthony?'

'For making the models feel uncomfortable.'

I gawp at him. 'You got kicked out of the life drawing class?'

He sighs. 'The trouble with England is that everybody's too uptight. Women are afraid to show their sensuality, and men are afraid to be throbbing male beings. This sort of thing would never happen in France or Italy. A harmless comment about a woman's body.' He takes from his pocket the same hankie that he blew his nose in, and wipes it across his brow. 'Teesh!'

'But we're not in France or Italy!'

He throws up his hands. 'Well, what can I say? More fool us.'

I scrutinise him. 'So what did you say? To the models? To warrant being thrown out?'

'Mo-del. And it was nothing. I commented on a particular part of her anatomy, that's all.'

This is getting worse by the minute. I hide my face in my hands and peek at him through fingers. 'Which part?'

He pulls out a piece of paper. It's a drawing of a small-breasted woman's narrow-hipped body. Between the V at the top of her legs is a wild and wiry crotch.

'It was positively forestlike. I've never seen one like it before. It almost looked like it might be inhabited. I worried that if I got too close I'd be attacked by a band of pygmies.' He smiles to himself. 'But then the idea became quite appealing.'

'Anthony!' I shove his drawing at him. 'You're leaving. Right now.'

As I'm helping him to the door he sniffs the air: 'Something smells good. Are you sure I can't stay for dinner?'

But it's too late. Just as I'm bundling him outside, I look up the stairs. There, at the top, looking mildly awkward, and as though he's just woken up, is Patrick.

'Hi,' he says, and beams a smile.

# Twenty-Six

Patrick spends the night. I get my father to promise not to say a word to anyone about him being here.

I am now asleep on Patrick's chest and hear someone ringing the doorbell like a maniac.

I stumble, fat-eyed with sleep, toward the noise. Opening the door, I find Jacqui in a red dress, bobbing up and down like a person in dire need of the toilet.

'Let me in!' She barrels past me into the house.

I follow her into my kitchen where she turns around and looks at me, white as a ghost.

'What's happened?'

She buries her face in her hands, and starts mumbling. Then she looks at me again. 'So we were all having "going away" drinks, you know, because Cyril is moving to the Frankfurt office… I had about three glasses of champagne, so did he, and the whole time, from me walking into that boardroom, he never once took his eyes off me.'

'Cyril?' We've got a Cyril now to contend with?

She tuts. 'Not Cyril for God's sake! Christian! Who else would I be talking about? Celine, it was so unbelievably charged.

It was total hard-core flirting.' She shakes her head, snivels, sits down opposite me at the kitchen table. 'Anyway, I went out to the toilet at one point and he watched me walk out of the room, and I was sure he was going to follow. My heart was hammering in the loo. I was so sure he was going to walk in and something was going to happen right there… Anyway,' she snivels again, 'he didn't follow me in. So when I came out, I go back into the boardroom where everyone is, and he's disappeared!'

She wipes under her eyes, where her mascara is running. 'I got another glass of champers and I went on a little walkabout. So I go down the corridor that leads to his office, and his door's open, and his little desklight is on… There was no one around, so I walked in.' She hides in her hands again and squeals. 'He was sitting at his desk. Not really doing anything. Just sitting there, like he was thinking. So he looked up. I closed his door, threw myself up against it, fixed him with my most vixenlike look, and said… Come and get me.'

A tiny laugh bursts out of me. 'God,' I say, horrified, 'you said come and get me? What did he do?'

'Well, that's the thing, he just looked at me, and said in a very firm, un-amused voice, "Please open my door."'

Her eyes glass over with tears. She stares, vacantly, as though picturing it all again. 'He was looking at me as though I was some sort of contemptible person.' I feel so sorry for her. She is gorgeous tonight. Her hair in a wavy bob, her bright red lipstick matching her dress that shows off her Nigella Lawson–like curves. My sister doesn't do mad things like this. She never made a fool of herself over a lad when we were growing up. She was always too wise and smart. I hate him.

'Then he just got up, and said, "Please step aside" and he opened his door himself.' She scowls, shakes her head. 'I was mortified, Celine. I wanted to die right there.'

'Please step aside?' I repeat. 'Oh, what a wanker!' I knew I didn't like him for a reason.

'As soon as he'd got his door open, he seemed so relieved. Like I'd been about to attack him or something; it was so weird. Then he just stood there, sort of like the meeting was over and now it was time for me to go. He looked very, very uncomfortable, and so cold all of a sudden — pathologically cold.'

'Oh Jacq! What did you do?'

'I didn't know what to say. So I blabbed something stupid about how all I really meant was "come and get me *another drink*." I just made it worse.'

I pull a taught smile. 'Oh.'

'It was terrible! A part of me was so ashamed, and the other part was furious that he'd embarrass me like that, even though I know, technically, it was me who was embarrassing.' She wipes away tears. 'It was the way he just stood there, as though he was so superior. I am not kidding, he was like a completely different person. Then I blabbed something about how I wasn't getting on with my boyfriend, and I was going through a hard time with my family, and a close friend had just died, and I didn't know what had come over me.'

'Who died?'

'No one died. I was ad-libbing.' She stares at me through glassy eyes. 'I even burst into tears — about the dead person — and then he said, "Well, I'm sorry about your loss." The pompous, self-righteous prick! He sounded like he was some sort of psychologist and I was off my rocker.' Her teary brown eyes flash venom. 'So I said, "Well, er, I'd better go back to the party" and as I walked out, he was already picking up his briefcase to go home. Just like that! So I just walked out of there, walked back to my own office, stood there almost doing something in my pants, and then I got my bag and came right over here.'

'Well, Jacq, there's obviously something wrong with him. No real man would behave like that. He clearly got some pleasure out of leading you on and then embarrassing you.'

She looks right at me, 'But why, Celine?'

'Because he's got problems, obviously. Confidence problems, who knows what? He's probably got a really tiny penis. Jacqui, go home to your boyfriend. Put this past you. Then sit down with the man who wants to marry you, and have a good talk about what the two of you are doing.'

She snivels, looking a tad brighter. 'Thanks.' She shakes her head. 'But I can't go home to Rich. Not tonight. Not like this. After that. After I've come on to some other man. I mean I would have had sex with him right there if he'd wanted.'

'But you didn't.' I pat her shoulder. 'Everybody does something stupid once in their life, Jacqui. No sense in making it more than what it was.'

'Please can I stay here?'

'But…' I am taken aback. 'Where will you sleep? I think you should go home.'

She frowns. 'I've told you I'm not going home. I'll sleep in the spare room! I'll sleep on the sofa!'

I grimace, feeling awful for lying to her. 'It's not entirely convenient.'

She frowns again, looking wounded and confused. Then she looks past my head, and clarity dawns — in the form of Patrick, standing in the doorway to my kitchen.

'Oh,' she says, calming down.

'Hi,' Patrick says. 'You must be the sister.'

'No,' she says, combing him over with wide, watery eyes. 'I'm someone else.'

'Hi, someone else,' he smiles at her.

'Hi,' she says, reaching out to return his handshake. 'And I'm guessing you must be Patrick.' She glares at me.

'Look,' Patrick lays a hand on my shoulder. 'I think I'm gonna take a cab back to the hotel.'

'Are you sure?' I ask him.

He nods, kisses me, and then looks at Jacqui. 'It was nice meeting you briefly. And hey, the guy sounds like a complete jackass. Definitely challenged in the manhood department, as Celine says.'

# Twenty-Seven

Our time together flies. I am starting to feel that where Patrick is concerned, it's the story of our lives.

I tell him I can't come and see him off at the train. I just can't. Memories of him leaving, once, long ago, haunt too much. He understands. His flight back home to Canada tomorrow is something I can't think of when I kiss him for the last time.

Not since that conversation in London have we talked about what is to happen next.

I clock-watch — wondering if there were things I might have said and should have said that would make anything different — until I know his train will have been and gone.

Then I go into Newcastle and land myself at Jacqui's office. I know that she and a few other staff were working the weekend, so I hold it in until we are in the toilet, and then I burst into tears. 'He's gone!'

She watches me unfold for a long time. 'How did you leave it? When are you going to see him again?'

I shake my head. 'Probably never. We didn't talk about it. We were so determined not to have the conversation, that we never had the conversation!' I look up now, from my hankie. 'What do I do, Jacq?'

'Run away with me! I think I'm going to have to get a new job. Maybe in a new city. We could move in together. I would work and you could stay home and be my housewife.'

I smile at her, through my snivels. It takes me a second to realise what she's on about. 'Why? Not because of this stupid Christian episode?'

She parks herself on a toilet lid. 'Oh — him, Rich, everything really. I need a change of track. I have to try and find myself the life I have half an idea that I want, Celine. Newcastle's not exactly the centre of the architectural design universe, either, is it? I mean I always knew when I finished Uni that I'd be limiting myself staying around here.' She cocks her head and looks at me, sadly. 'I really only stayed because of you.'

I am touched. And confused. And panicked. 'But I thought you liked your job? I've never once heard you complain about it. I mean, you complain, but in a happy way.'

'I kept thinking I was all right for now. But maybe now has expired. I do a lot of glorified administrative work really. I mean when I saw myself getting into architecture as a career, it was the creative side I was attracted to. If I'd known I'd be endlessly dealing with sexist contractors, cranky engineers, and basically being some middleman, then I'd have gone and got a masters degree in something else.'

'But everyone has to pay their dues.'

She stabs an index finger into her chest. 'I've overpaid. I'm owed a refund.'

She looks at me now. 'Don't you sometimes wish you'd been born stupid, ugly, smelly so that no one will want you, you'll never get a boyfriend?'

'Born smelly,' I grin. 'Now there's an interesting idea.'

She beams. 'I envy people with simple lives!'

I pat the top of her foot as she sits there looking rather funny on the toilet. 'I don't know anyone with a simple life, Jacq.'

She smiles at me and studies me for a moment or two. 'What you do, my friend — back to your earlier question — is you wait. You wait for him.'

I don't have to wait long. My mobile rings as I am driving out of Newcastle City Centre. 'I miss you already,' he says. 'I don't want to go home.'

# Twenty-Eight

Mike's house is nothing from the outside: a brick-built, Victorian mid-terrace in West Jesmond, just a short walk from the Metro stop. I go to pick up Aimee right from Jacqui's office.

'Have you met your neighbours yet? What are they like?' I ask him, nodding next door.

Mike pulls a tiresome face. 'A bunch of wankers really. Or, he is. Got uptight about my weeds coming through his fence. And they're actually not weeds. It happens to be climbing wisteria. So much for what he knows about gardening.'

I study him, affectionately, remembering only too well the wind chimes. Our old neighbour and Mike had a vendetta going. Pat liked to hang wind chimes off his patio, which was fine until a windy night and you were trying to sleep. Instead of being direct, and telling Pat that they were bothering us, and he couldn't sleep, Mike tried to subtly bring up the topic and the fact that he was a light sleeper. Still the chimes chimed on. So one day, when Pat was at work, Mike took them down. Pat bought new ones. Mike waited until he was out, and took them down too. When Pat brought up the subject of his mysteriously vanishing wind chimes, Mike admitted that he'd taken them down, because Pat had failed to get all his hints about them. This pissed Pat off. Pat bought an even noisier set. Mike took them down. Then Mike had a brainwave: if Pat wanted his wind chimes, it was a sign that noise clearly didn't disturb his sleep. So Mike decided we would start listening to heavy metal music at six o'clock on a Saturday morning. Mike only stopped his nonsense when he noticed Pat's For Sale sign had gone up. I assume his moving out had nothing to do with us, but one never knows.

Mike has on a tight white T-shirt with his black drainpipe jeans. He looks like he's not shaved in a day or two. Unlike most men, Mike was always his most attractive when he'd done absolutely nothing with himself. It was a look that somehow suited him.

'Aimee,' I shout past him up the stairs, wondering when she's coming down. When there's no answer, Mike says, 'Look, will you come in? I want to talk to you.'

I gaze past him down the skinny, dark passageway, into the house that I can already tell has none of the home comforts he's used to. Then I follow him inside.

'Is it about Aimee?' I ask him.

He meets my eyes. 'No, it's about Jennifer.'

I'm startled. He leads me into the living room, which is boxy and devoid of redeeming features, except for a seldom-used fireplace. He's bought an uneventful brown leather sofa — a cheaper-looking version of the one we picked together for our place, and an oversized chair. There is a coffee table, and a brass mirror hung above the fireplace. A wilted plant sits on the sill of the curtainless bay window.

'I don't know if asking her out again tonight is too much,' he says. 'I'd like to, but I don't want to come on too strong. I'm not sure what the etiquette for these things is.'

'Oh,' I say, looking anywhere but into his eyes.

'What do you think I should do?'

He seems to have lost the little paunch he developed in his late thirties and is wire thin now, almost like Mick Jagger.

'When is keen too keen?' he presses.

I am inexplicably exasperated. 'Well, I…perhaps you should wait a few days. It seems a bit…fast.'

He glances over my denim dress that I'm wearing again. 'Thanks,' he says. Then he nods his head to the door. 'Come on, I'll show you the rest of the place. It's not Buckingham Palace but you can have a look.'

In the hall he gestures for me to walk ahead of him up the stairs. I really don't want a guided tour, but now have no choice. As I mount the stairs, I'm aware of his eyes on my bare legs.

'This is my room,' he says, squeezing past me on the small high-ceilinged landing, and pushing open a door. I take one step toward the room and then he edges around me again, so that I am almost in the bedroom, and he's got me hemmed in there. I take a peek. It's just a room with a chest of drawers and a bed in it. Only the bed is unmade. On both sides. Mike always sleeps on the left. And Mike has never been known, in all the years I have been with him, to make a bed. Did Jennifer stay here Friday night? Have they slept together already? Surely not.

'Sorry it's a mess,' he says. I am aware of how close he is behind me.

'Very nice,' I tell him, feeling my face burn up. I turn around, hoping he'll move, but he continues to stand there, blocking me, our faces now only inches apart. A complex energy passes between us. 'Please,' I say, wanting to shut down my mind and the picture I now have of Mike immersing himself happily between Jennifer's legs and, at the same time, wondering why this picture is bothering me. 'Can I get past?'

His gaze is level with my throat. He moves barely half a

foot, enough for me to brush past him, out of the suffocating confines of his bedroom and onto the small landing again. My heart is racing.

'The bathroom,' he says, pushing open another door. Then, 'This is Aimee's room.'

It's clear he's given Aimee the best room. It has a beige-painted drop ceiling on both sides, making a V shape above her bed, a small window, and a double bed, with a dark green eiderdown on it and a collection of fetching patchwork pillows. Aimee sits parked in the middle of the bed, legs crossed, back to us.

'What's the matter?' Mike and I both say together when we realise that Aimee is actually in tears.

'I don't want to go home. I don't want to stay here. I want us to be a family! I don't want two homes. I want one home with all of us in it.'

I sit on the carpet by her legs, letting my head rest beside her knee, in its holey pink leggings, with the denim shorts on top. Mike stands there, watching us, like a man who is first on the scene of an accident, and he doesn't know what to do. I know in years to come that Aimee will remember today, and this feeling of being split between two people. Like I remember. The anger I harboured for years at my parents — toward my dad for having to have other women, and toward my mum for not forgiving him and just getting him to come back. My wishes were born of a simple, naïve heart. I just wanted them back together again. I didn't care how.

Seeing her like this, I suddenly ache for our old life back. Haven't I done to my daughter the one thing I promised myself I never would: failed her as a parent, as I always felt I had been failed, as a child?

'How about if she stays tonight?' Mike says.

'No! I want us all to stay!' Aimee says.

'Aimee, we can't all stay!' I want to hug her but can tell she's angry with me. 'What about Molly, darling?' I get up off the floor. 'We can't leave Molly.'

'I forgot about Molly,' she says, softer now.

I reach and stroke the top of her warm little head. 'Look, I'm happy to go home and see to Molly, if you want to stay here with your dad. Just for tonight.'

Aimee nods, calming right down, and then she says, 'It's okay. I want to come home with you.'

In the car she says nothing. But I am aware of her every breath, her every tiny sniffle. Her hands are locked together in her lap. She sits barely moving a muscle. At a traffic light I look at my own eyes in the rearview and just see oceans of confusion.

# Twenty-Nine

'His name is James.' I phone Trish at work. 'I'm not going to tell you any more, except that you're never going to meet anyone else who is as right for you.'

'Seriously?' she sounds excited. 'Is he going to be able to afford a parking meter?'

'Several parking meters.'

She laughs. 'Speaking of James, have you been in touch with James? As in my James? Do you have a match for him yet?'

'I have, yes. I think he's going to really like her but I don't want to say any more. Client confidentiality.'

'Good then.' She sounds a bit deflated. 'Now back to this other James...'

# Thirty

'To love and other mistakes.' I raise a glass of wine to Jacqui across the pub table. We've not been out for a drink in months.

'Don't keep looking at your phone,' she tells me as I look, almost obsessively, at my phone.

'He hasn't rung me in nearly a week.'

'Look at me,' she instructs me, when she sees my sad face. 'You know he had to go.'

'I know. I just didn't think it would feel so much like…like he's gone.'

'But you know he'll be coming back.'

'Well, that's easy to say. What's to come back for? More walking around London? More endless fantastic sex? More strange encounters with my peculiar family members?'

'I'd take more sex, and less of the peculiar family members!'

'No you wouldn't. You said he was middle-aged and ordinary with an unsociable job.'

'I never said he was ordinary.' She beams at me. 'He's attractive, in a very takes-life-quite-seriously way. And from my brief meeting with him, I think he's nice too. Exceptionally nice.'

'He has a lot to sort out, Jacq. His entire career is hanging in the balance. He says he's done with working abroad, but I'm not so sure it's done with him.'

'But one thing's for sure, he's definitely not done with you.' She beams, as though all her fairytales have suddenly come true. 'He's in love with you.'

I wag my wineglass at her before drinking. 'Ah, but he's never actually said it.'

'Some things don't have to be said.'

'Not all the time. But they should be, once.'

She can't contradict me. 'So what does he really think of us lot, then?' she changes the subject. 'I mean, there's your old man who molests models, then there's me who is about to get engaged, who attempts but fails to molest a co-worker. And we both seem to gravitate to your house to tell you what disasters we are, any time of the day or night, not really caring whether we've been invited. Actually preferring that we haven't because it somehow adds to our drama.'

I beam. 'At least he knows who we really are. What he'd be taking on. Not that he is going to take us on.'

Duffy is singing 'Mercy' and I have to shout over the music. 'Too much stacked against us. We don't even live in the same country. He's got a great career over there, which he wouldn't have over here. Aimee is still in school, so I couldn't uproot her even if I wanted to. And besides, there's no way I could move her thousands of miles away from her father. That would be so unimaginably unfair to Mike, and to her. And imagine her doing it! Imagine her settling! She'd hate me for the rest of my life.' I throw up my hands. 'Plus I have my job here. What would I do over there? I couldn't even legally work in Canada!'

'Those are, admittedly, obstacles.'

'Obstacles are his parents don't like me. His dog likes to sleep between us on the bed.'

'Are you sure you're over Mike?'

The question stops me cold. I'm about to say of course! But what comes out is, 'Can anyone ever be over the person they were married to? Unless that person really hurt them? Mike never hurt me, and I know him more than I know any other human being. Even more than I know my own daughter, I sometimes think.'

She stares at me with so much sympathy that I have to change the subject. 'Have you seen him yet? Mr Somebody's Strange Idea of an Office Heartthrob?'

She looks sadly across the room. 'I saw him this afternoon, by the coffee machine. He did that thing of following me with his eyes — a little bit flirty again, and a little bit smug.' She shudders. 'Ergh, it was horrible. Like a time warp. Like I was Doris Day and he was Cary Grant. Liz said something about him saying the other day that he likes very ladylike girls.'

'Oh, please! He's worried that word has got out. He thinks you've told people, and now everybody's laughing at him.'

'I told you, he thinks he's Cary Grant.'

I have a laugh. 'Cary Grant was bisexual.'

She beams. 'God, I love you. You always make me feel better.' She raises her glass to mine. 'To love and other disasters.'

'Mistakes,' I correct her.


I'm just pulling up in front of the house when my phone rings.

'Hi!' he says, sounding happy.

'Where are you?' I ask him.

'At my desk, in my apartment, staring out of the window, waiting for a phone call.'

He's back in Canada. And life moves on. And everything feels more impossible again, than possible.

'I can't stop thinking about you,' he says. 'In fact, I don't know what I thought about until my mind started going auto-matically to you.'

'That's nice,' I tell him. 'You've just created the perfect fifteen-second sound bite. You should be proud.'

He laughs. 'Look,' he says. 'The reason I called, Celine, is that I wanted to tell you something I should have said a very long time ago. I wanted to tell you that I love you.'

Could he have heard me just talking about him? I laugh a little. 'You love me?'

'I love you,' he says. 'But I have to go now. My other call's coming through. We'll talk more later.'

And then Patrick goes again.

But he's not gone, is he? Not when he leaves me with those words.

# Thirty-One

I meet Mike's Jennifer Platt in Costa's coffee shop opposite the Theatre Royal. She has just been to a meeting with National Express East Coast and excitedly tells me that the head of catering for the train company has agreed to hear out her proposal. She drinks off one latte looking like she hasn't even tasted it and then asks me if I fancy another. I tell her I'll buy.

'I really, really, really like him!' she says, before my bottom reaches the seat, when I return with two more coffees. 'I never thought I would, you know, meet someone this fast.'

I dive into my coffee cup while I remind myself not to show the uber-curiosity about whether or not they've had sex. 'Actually, the most successful matches were lukewarm about each other the first time they met. Generally the average person goes on dates with three different candidates before she meets the one who seems like he might be right. And by that I mean, one she actually ends up having a few dates with and going to bed with.'

Her gaze slides from me, out of the window, and back. She's glowing like a hundred-watt light bulb. 'Mike's interesting, he's mature and sensible, he's very down to earth. He's not crude, like some who make you feel more like a buddy than a lady. He's actually funny too! How we laugh! Just little things he comes out with. And he listens to you. He seemed fascinated with my business idea, although I might have talked his ears off about it,' she tinkles a laugh. 'We really hit it off.' Her eyes are iridescent with new love.

'After that first date, I barely got home and he rang me, and we talked for another two hours!'

Now feels as good a time as any to tell her. 'Did Mike mention how I know him?'

She nods. 'I know that you were married. And in a way, this is why I feel I can say so much about him to you, because, well, you know all this about him, don't you? You'll understand.'

'You're probably wondering why, if he's so fantastic, we're divorced,' I try a laugh.

She tries the same. 'No! I don't believe in judging people. I mean, the only two people who really know what their marriage is like are the two that are in it, aren't they? Sometimes you can think your marriage is all right, and be kidding yourself.'

Why is she so fabulous? And how did she manage to get such massive natural breasts on such a petite frame?

'Is that what he told you?' That last comment sounds like just what he'd say.

'No. Honestly he never got into any specific details about his marriage. When you meet someone, you don't want to bring out all your old baggage, do you? Not right away.'

I nod, trying to swallow the idea of my being old baggage.

'Same as me, I rarely talk about my divorce. Because while I think I'm doing fine now and I'm all right, I don't want someone to sit there looking for chinks in my armour, or then I'll probably start acting like I'm not all right, if you know what I mean.'

'I never asked you why it didn't work.' Because something

about her just made me take her at face value. But now I am
brimming with curiosity about her.

'It's all right. I don't mind saying.' She looks at me with a
certain reconciled expression. 'It was an affair. Not especially
original. I remember thinking that there was so much I should
be feeling — anger, jealousy, sadness — yet all I felt was an
overwhelming disgust. Disgust at myself for not suspecting, and
disgust that he could be with her and then come home and be
with me, sometimes in the same night, as I'm pretty sure happened. It seemed monstrous.' She wrinkles up her nose, and I
notice she's got a rather big freckle on the edge of her top lip,
that looks like a crumb she needs to dust off. I can see Mike
becoming enamoured with that freckle the way he used to fixate
on the small mole on the inside of my elbow. 'But once I made
him leave I was determined not to let his actions ruin my own
self-image. His decision to screw around was a reflection on
him, not on me. I had to keep reminding myself of that. So
that's one of the reasons I don't want to talk about it with Mike
before we really know each other that well. I don't want anybody thinking I've been shaped at all by what he did.'

I drink some of my now unwanted coffee and stare out at
the dashing, neoclassical façade of the Theatre Royal opposite,
one of Jacqui's favourite buildings in the city, thinking she's a
bit goody-goody, isn't she? Just a weeny bit. Then I think, God
that was a catty thought, Celine! She's lovely. She's better for
him than I ever was.

Suddenly she reaches a hand and briefly lays it on the back
of mine. 'You're obviously a very good person wanting to set
him up with someone else and see him happy.'

Tears inexplicably burn in the back of my eyes. I look across
the road, turning my head slightly so she won't see. When I can
speak, I say, 'It was his idea I take him on as a client, not mine.

I didn't want to tell you I was married to him when I set you up because I thought you might think I was weird or something. You know, as though I had no one else to offer so I touted my ex around.'

She laughs. 'Touted your ex around! That's a funny picture!' She cuts her half of the muffin down the middle. 'I'd have thought nothing of the sort. I hope, Celine, that it's not awkward in any way for you, you know, if Mike and I...' She pushes the muffin around the plate, while I hang in anticipation. 'I can certainly promise you that if Mike and I do work out in the long run, I will never try to be any sort of mother to Aimee. Only, I hope, a friend.'

I swallow hard, shake my head a little too enthusiastically. I wonder if Mike knows she's already seeing herself as Aimee's second mum.

'It's not awkward for me in the slightest. You're a client and I took you on to help you find someone. And you were quite right, I want nothing more than for Mike to be happy because he deserves to have everything he should have got from me.'

We smile together, holding eyes, and in one synchronized move our hands go out for our respective coffee cups, and they touch. It's almost as though we are shaking hands.

It's only when we have parted ways at Grey's Monument, she about to go into Waterstone's, and I about to trot down the steps of the Metro to go home, that I remember something. I hesitate there, one foot poised to keep on going, but then I shout back at her.

For a second I think she hasn't heard me and I'm prepared to let it go, but then she turns. 'Did you call me?'

I am already walking over, digging in my handbag. 'I forgot, I brought this with me...' I hold out a folded-up piece of foolscap paper. 'I intended to give it to you, but, well, anyway...

It's yours.' She takes it, looking curious. 'It's just some questions and answers I put down when I was considering taking Mike on as a client. A little exercise I put myself through to somehow reposition him in my mind — you know, as Mike the client not Mike the ex-husband.' I give her a smile. 'I thought that perhaps you might like to have it.'

As it exchanges hands, a shift seems to occur in me. It's too late to take it back. It's gone now. Like Mike, or so it seems, it's hers now, not mine.

# Thirty-Two

Aimee sings along with Duffy, to 'Warwick Avenue' while she has the task of setting the table. It's Father's Day and I have invited my dad. Aimee was supposed to take Mike out with the money she's saved up but changed her mind and wanted to invite him over here. My dad said he wanted to bring Anthea, who he has apparently been seeing a lot of when he's not molesting models, or trying to pick up my clients. Then I casually asked Mike if he wanted to bring Jennifer, and he did. Jacqui is coming alone.

Aimee's little warble on the high notes makes me smile as I bash a piece of garlic and ginger in my mortar to make a dressing to toss over the watercress salad that I'm laying out with the grilled salmon. I'm just adding the oil, when the phone rings.

'Hi.' I hear Patrick's voice, and light up.

I wipe a sticky hand down the front of my apron. 'Hi to you indeed!' Aimee looks at me, witheringly, out of the corner of her eye, and I motion for her to turn down the music.

'God, I miss you,' he says.

'I bet you say that to all the girls.'

'But to you I actually mean it.'

'Ha ha.'

'What are you doing, wearing, thinking… I want the whole picture.'

'Oh!' I laugh. 'Well, I'm making dinner. It's Father's Day and I'm having my dad over.' Aimee casts me another sidelong glance at the conspicuous absence of Mike's name. 'I'm wearing an apron, and I'm thinking, erm, what am I thinking?' I whisper, 'That I'm very glad you called.'

'Oh,' he says. 'That sounds good.'

'Which bit?'

'All of it. I wish I was there.' The dampened note of his voice.

'So what have you been up to?' I ask him, brightly.

'Oh, organizing my office and a few other things. I'm working on an outline for a book on my time in the Middle East. Did I mention that to you?'

'Ah! So you made a start? That's excellent.'

'Finally. Yes. Although I don't have much to show for my efforts. You could say I've been distracted.'

'Have you?' I smile and Aimee goes upstairs, casting me another disapproving look.

'Every time I sit down to think about the Taliban I end up thinking about you.'

'I wonder what that says about me?'

He laughs. 'Anyway, I wanted to tell you something — the reason why I rang. I've decided to take the job.'

I stare at the oblongs of salmon lying on foil on the grilling tray. 'It's a good opportunity for me to establish myself somewhere. I'm thinking I can work on my book at the same time, and maybe it won't be such a bad life…'

I clear my throat. 'Congratulations.' What else was I hoping he was going to say? 'I'm sure it'll be a great life. I'm happy for you.'

Tense silence. Upstairs I can hear Aimee singing along to Leona Lewis's 'Bleeding Love.' 'I gave it a lot of thought. I didn't really see what the other options were.' He sounds like he's explaining himself.

'Of course.' I force a smile into my voice. What was I even thinking his other options were? That he was going to give up his life and move to northern England?

It never would have worked. Because it was never meant to. Stupid!

'You know my dad and Mike should be here soon.'

'Mike?'

'Well, it is Father's Day.'

'Oh,' he says. 'Of course. But I was going to ask you something, before you go…' He hesitates and then says, 'I wanted to know if you'd like to come here in the summer holidays with Aimee? Maybe middle of August?'

'Come there?'

'Yeah. For two weeks, if you think you could persuade her. I'll pick up the cost of the tickets.'

He's going to pay for us to go and see him? I already visualize this conversation with my daughter.

'I could show you Toronto. Then we could go to Muskoka, to the lakes. I have a small cabin up there. I inherited it when my dad died. It doesn't get used very often. It could probably stand a cleanup, but it's right on the water. We could go fishing, boating, have barbeques. Aimee can see wolves and moose and white-tailed deer and black bears. The real Canada.'

'Patrick.' I fill with an inner longing and regret hovering moments ago on that line of doubting him. 'It's a lovely thought. It really is. And I'd like nothing more, I really would.

But I just don't see it happening.' I go back to slapping salmon around, my phone tucked under my chin.

'Hey, don't be so quick to say it can't happen. I've got faith in you persuading her. Just think, Aimee could take some awesome photographs, bring her painting supplies…'

'Well, I'll have to think. But…' I grimace, 'what happens after the lovely holiday is over?'

He sighs, and I wish I could take the question back. You fool! 'Celine, I wasn't thinking that far ahead. I just want to find a way of seeing you again. I want you to see this place, see Canada, see my life.'

When I don't respond he says, 'Well, I should let you get back to your cooking, shouldn't I?'

'Probably.'

'I love you,' he says.

But before I can reply he has rang off.

Mike and Jennifer arrive first. Opening my door and seeing them both standing there is so bizarre that they must see the shock that comes over me before I have a chance to smile. 'Hi,' I say, brightly, but it's too late. Mike's eyes have so many mixed messages in them that it's unbearable for me to look.

'Come in,' I say, noting that Jennifer looks very mod today, in faded, low-rise, rolled-up jeans, wedge sandals — the kind that Aimee would covet — and a sleeveless cotton floral top. She has her longish brown hair pulled back into a messy ponytail.

'For you,' she says, presenting me with an armful of flowers. 'Just a little thank you, for, well, amongst other things, inviting me to your lovely home. It was a really unexpected, but lovely, invitation.'

'Glass of wine?' I ask, quickly turning and trotting down the passageway.

My dad and Anthea arrive about two minutes after. Which is a relief, because Aimee has just greeted Jennifer with a glower and then she gave her dad a possessive and rather protracted cuddle. When I open the door, I'm completely unprepared to see my dad alongside a very old-fashioned, middle-aged woman. She has uniformly dyed dark brown hair that's growing out at the roots, and a cheerless smile. And between the unusually large gap between her top lip and her nose, is a moustache Charlie Chaplin would have been proud of.

'This is Anthea,' my dad says, stressing her name. Anthea and I go to shake hands, and I ignore the fact that my dad is measuring me for my reaction to the sight of his girlfriend. Anthea's and my eyes meet briefly, and then we both make a policy of quickly looking away.

Mike puts new batteries in the smoke alarm for me that has recently started tweeting all day as though we are living under the same roof as a family of bad-tempered sparrows. I keep an eye on the salmon grilling, and Anthea — who seems really nice — and Jennifer chatter away, while Aimee shows my dad her progress on the seascape she's been working on since she and her granddad last went out.

Jacqui arrives in an emerald green strapless sundress, smelling fresh, and bearing red and white wine. When she sets eyes on Anthea, Jacqui's smile takes on a cunning quality, and she keeps trying to catch my eye, so I have to avoid looking at her.

'You're looking very lovely as usual,' my dad sidles up to Jacqui. My father has always had a thing for Jacqui. And Jacqui has always managed to appreciate the charmer he is, and the suave lady-killer he obviously once was. Jacqui's eyes linger on my father's new teeth. 'She smells of sunscreen,' he says to Anthea, about my sister. And I know that my father is the type of man, who, no matter how much he might claim to only have eyes for you, will never be able to resist leering after a passing bit of skirt. His hand lingers on Jacqui's waist, his face reaching to Jacqui's to smell her behind the ears. 'Is it sunscreen?' he asks her, his eyes eating her up. Jacqui grins from ear to ear, at me.

'Isn't she a knockout,' my dad comes over and says quietly to me. 'And single again, too.'

I frown. 'How is she single?'

He leans into my ear. 'If I can't see him, he doesn't exist.'

'It's done, I think!' I prise two flakes of fish apart with a knife and fork. Mike is suddenly standing unnervingly close to me now. My dad has gone back to pestering Jacqui.

'It is,' Mike says. 'You definitely want it out now, or it'll be dry.'

'Thanks. For telling me what I already know.' I smile at Mike. Mike always used to mock my cooking. And while I honestly don't think it's terrible — and it definitely has improved since Mike moved out — I have to admit that Mike was the main chef in the family, and I probably could have learned a few things from him. I pop the tray on top of the oven, and then give my salad dressing a final vigorous shake before tipping it into the bowl.

'I'd better take my jacket off,' he says. 'That looks oily.'

'Excuse me,' I slide past him to turn off the oven. 'Olive oil is replete with heart-healthy vitamins and antioxidants.' I've no idea if it is, but it shuts him up anyway. For a moment he continues to stand there, his gaze the only thing moving as it follows me around.

Molly comes mewing into the kitchen to greet the company. Mike picks her up and cuddles her. 'My old girl,' he says. 'How have you been, eh? Do you miss your old man?'

I turn and quickly catch Mike's eyes looking at me.

The meal goes down well. I have pulled out the leaf in the table, and we sit with the back door open, hearing the birds in the garden. 'We should have eaten outside,' I say, wishing I'd thought to set up the picnic table.

'It might be cold to eat outside,' Anthea says. 'It's warm while you're walking around, but not so great to sit in.' She holds my eyes and I try very hard not to let mine drop to what I've noticed are three or four extremely long moustache hairs amongst the downier ones.

My dad keeps us all entertained. Anthea sits next to him like a fixture, with the unexcitable air of someone much older and more jaded than she probably is. She's not the most feminine of souls, and I don't think this to be cruel, it's just a shock to see the disparity: between what my father used to get, and what he attracts now. He told me that she has been divorced for twenty years. Now, given that my father is in his mid-seventies and she can't be more than sixty, I should be having a very hard time imagining what she sees in my father. Yet it's more the other way round. And I can tell, by the glances she's shooting me, that Jacqui is thinking the same thought. I put their relationship down to an ill-conceived companionship. Curiosity satisfied on that score, I move on to Mike and Jennifer. My gaze shifts surreptitiously between them, and her large breasts, especially when she moves an inch closer to say something to him that must be a touch too intimate for the table to hear. They almost can't be real. Yet I can't see her being the type to go for implants.

'I remember she wore a pea green chiffon dress...' My dad is in the throes of one of his stories. 'It cinched at the waist, and then cascaded to her ankles. Her eyes were the same unusual pea green, and her lips painted cherry red. And when she stood in the sunlight facing me, the skirt of her dress was transparent like a veil, and that was how I painted her legs, through her skirt.' He smiles distantly, appreciating a memory in his mind. 'I remember how she would not take her dress off. Not like the other ones.' My father is off wandering down the dissolute alleyways of his past, searching for a brief imbuement of the man he was, who drank absinthe on Paris's Left Bank, locking heads with the literary intelligentsia, arguing Henri Matisse over Pablo Picasso and transposing into iconic creations young models who all invariably became girlfriends. But none more so than this one, the one with the pea green eyes who let her chiffon dress float off her to the paint-splattered wooden floorboards — or, at least that was the version I heard. They've been known to change. How many times have I heard my dad's nostalgic embroidery? His stories are like supermarket brand wine: they go down pleasantly enough in the absence of anything better to fit the occasion. And you get so used to them that your life would be a much worse place without them.

'Where was Olivia in all this?' Jacqui asks him, in that tone that says, *You old tomcat*. Jacqui always has a way of appealing to my dad's inner Casanova. And for that I know my father adores her.

My dad's eyes darken, as I've often seen them do at the mention of my mother's name. 'Olivia *was*,' he says, after a long pause.

Everybody looks puzzled, but me. I understand now, what I never understood growing up. My mother was his love affair in London. By the time they got to Paris, and I had come along, he was seeing her in a different role. My father had moved on. That's why she never comes up in his stories of that time. My dad was addicted to falling in love; as fast as he fell out of it, he had to fall back in. It was the only way he could live.

A curious thought strikes me. Was Patrick just my love affair in the Love Market? Am I also addicted to the idea of being in love? My dad looks at me, as though reading thoughts that are rattling through my head.

Truth is, I probably made peace with my father a long time

ago, even though I may have fought it. I am probably like him more than I care to admit.

When I put out dessert, Mike says, 'Oh God, it's tiramisu.' He winks at Jacqui. 'She's made this before.' He nudges me, 'Remember.'

'It nearly killed us!' Aimee recoils. 'We were on the toilet for days! What did you have to make that for?' Then she says, 'Like when we went to Spain and she came back thinking she could make paella. She put…' she looks at me. 'What was it? Saffron?'

I shake my head. 'Saffron, it turns out, costs a fortune, so I used the cheaper alternative — turmeric — instead, to turn the rice yellow. Only when I went in the cupboard looking for the turmeric I accidently picked up the cayenne pepper instead.'

Everybody laughs. Mike just sits and stares at me, hollowly.

I tut. 'Anyway, the tiramisu's a different recipe this time.' I peel my eyes away from my ex-husband's.

'How different?' Mike asks, suddenly snapping out of his trance. 'Dare we ask, what have you done to it this time?'

I dunk a big spoon through the cocoa topping, and then plop a serving onto a plate and pass it to him. 'You go first, then I'm sure we'll all find out.'

He takes the plate from me. And as he does, he catches a blob of mascarpone off the side of my hand, with his finger. Then he licks the finger, before picking up his spoon.

'It looks very good,' says Jennifer, winsomely.

Mike's intimate gesture has stalled me for a moment or two. And by the look on Jennifer's slightly discombobulated face when our eyes meet: her too.

After we eat, and I manage not to poison anyone or send them to the toilet, we move to the other room, where we slide further and further down the chairs, pleasantly narcotised by my dad's stories. My father: ever the one to hold court. In a matter of minutes we've traded our cultural injection of early seventies Paris, for Aimee and Mike playing Wii boxing. The four of us women occupy the sofa, drinking brandies, with my father in the armchair, looking bored now that he's no longer the centre of attention. Then Aimee sits one out and Jacqui gets up to play with Mike, my sister's gorgeousness having a way of command-ing the room. My father — for one — suddenly acquires a new interest in the game.

'Your turn now,' Mike says, sometime later, catching me lost in thought. Family gatherings of the past. When we were a fam-ily. He's holding out the Wiimote across the coffee table. It takes a moment to realise that he's giving it to me.

'No!' I flap him away with a hand. 'I'm rubbish at it.'

'Come on, you just have to hit me. Surely it'll not be that hard.'

'You'd be surprised. The intention might flourish but the hand falters.' I grin. I notice Jacqui is beaming a smile but her eyes are measuring Jennifer's reaction. 'All right!' I finally take the thing off him. 'One game.'

He slaughters me in seconds. 'Come on,' he laughs. 'I'm actually letting you beat me!' I aim the thing at the screen and go mad on the Wiimote, not having a clue what I'm doing.

'You're knocking yourself out!' he says. 'Remember, you're the red.'

'Oh yeah!' I laugh. 'I thought I was the green! God, there's no hope for me!' I look at Jacqui who howls, and then at my dad, whose eyes are scampering up and down her legs.

'It's knackering, this!' I moan. But now I am determined to lay him out. I discover a knack for the Right High Jab and land him a good one!

The women say, 'Woooh!'

'Nice one!' says Mike. 'Try doing a big uppercut now. One of these!' Mike socks the little red me right on the chin.

'Ouch!' Aimee chuckles from the floor where she's sitting cross-legged. 'Victory!'

'That wasn't fair! You were distracting me by talking!'

'Oh, that's what it was!' Mike says. 'We just thought you were totally crap.'

Jennifer and Anthea protest, playfully: that kind of comment isn't called for.

'Look, if you turn the Wiimote inward like this to cover your face…' Mike comes to show me, but I suddenly think, oh! I know what he means now about a big uppercut! So I uppercut like there's no tomorrow, and make contact high up on his cheek.

'Ow!' he says, as the others fold up laughing. And then, 'Bugger!' and then, 'All right. I think you've won. You play dirty.'

I instinctively go to touch him and stifle a laugh, thinking, heavens, maybe I have hurt him! 'Oooh, are you all right?' Anthea becomes animated. I feel bad for thinking unkind things about her, but I notice she has a manly way of sitting, with her knees flared, and I can't help smiling. And because I've had three glasses of wine, it tickles my sense of humour more than it would normally do, so I have to stand there and hide my face with my hand.

When I look up again, Mike thinks it's him I'm finding so amusing. But judging by the daggers I can feel in my back, my father is on to me. We hold eyes for a second. Mike makes a big play of touching his cheek. 'I'll survive. If you can fetch me a bucket for the blood, and a needle and thread.'

'I'm sorry,' I tell him, feeling terrible for laughing at Anthea. I glance at my father again. He is still peering at me from narrowed eyes. Mike just goes on looking at me fondly, and when I catch his expression, I can't let go of it.

And I'm no longer laughing. I'm just standing looking at him like this.

As he is I.

And for a while neither of us can stop.

My dad and Anthea are the first to leave. As Anthea goes to the toilet and my dad waits for her at the door, he pulls out an envelope from the inner pocket of his blazer, and shoves it at me. 'Now you've finished wetting yourself over my girlfriend, give this to Sandra for me please.'

It takes me a moment to think. Sandra? Sandra who?

Sandra my *client*!

'Dad!' I growl. 'When is enough, enough?'

'It's never enough,' he says, desperately. 'Please,' he implores. 'I really need you to just give it to her.' My dad's eyes are combing my face in urgent, desperate strides, as though his life depends on my taking it. Then we are both aware that Anthea appears at the top of the staircase. I take the envelope from him and put it in my jeans pocket.

Anthea thanks me and says she's had a lovely day. She gives me a hug, a rib-cracking grasp around my upper back that would register injury on an X-ray.

At the door, Jennifer unknots a creased pink cardigan that she's had tied around the straps of her handbag, and slips it across her shoulders. As she reaches to pull it around herself, the fabric between the buttons of her shirt gapes and I get a private view of a canyon of cleavage.

Mike must see too, because his cheeks flush when we make eye contact.

'Good heavens,' I suddenly say. 'Mike, I think you've got a

bruise!' I go to touch his cheek but stop myself. He touches his face. Jennifer zooms right in on him like she's short-sighted. 'Oh she's right, you do!' she cups her mouth, hiding a smile. 'You walloped him one pretty good!'

'Sorry,' I tell him again. 'How will you explain that at work?'

'I'll just tell people you punched me. What else?'

'While we were playing Wii!'

'I might selectively leave that bit out.'

'Goodnight,' I say, as they walk out. Mike and Jennifer thank me again. Jennifer gives me a snuggle, her big, pillowy chest buffering up against me.

*Q: What made me love him?*

A: Because Mike is the kind of man who loves you limitlessly. He's not slick, isn't a game-player, has no agenda, isn't in competition with you, isn't ever possessive. And yet you have a feeling he never quite lets you out of his sight. When he commits he goes all the way. Mike is in your corner, and he lets you know it all those times you need him to. Mike is guileless; he's not vain, nor is he ashamed of himself.

*Q: What do I admire about him?*

A: All of the above. Plus, he won't be broken. Mike has an inner resilience that comes out in subtle ways. And because you can't break him, that strength rubs off on you. Mike doesn't need to impress anyone. He's had better job offers, chances to make more money, but sticks where he is happiest. Mike is not a patsy, nor is he afraid to stand up for a principle. He will throw a teenager off a train if the lad swears at him. He'll report a bus driver for not waiting for the senior who was hurrying to the stop with her hand out. Mike is what you'd want your little boy to be, if you had a son.

Q: *What does he do to make me feel good?*
A: Makes me laugh. Forgives me. Doesn't take me too seriously, especially when I'm taking myself too seriously. Will tickle me to sleep. Will push me to get out of the house on a day when I don't feel like going anywhere. Will never let me feel sorry for myself unless it's for a good reason. And then, only for five minutes. Encourages me always. Tells me I am beautiful. Often.

Q: *What do I miss most?*

It was the last question. But the one I couldn't pass on to Jennifer. I didn't even commit the answer to paper, it just floats around somewhere in my mind:

How we had a fit. It may not have been perfect. I didn't set out looking for perfect from him in the first place, so I don't know why I was so disappointed. It certainly wasn't the extreme of square peg in round hole. It was what it was.

# Thirty-Three

A writer for *Hers* magazine wants to interview me. She contacts me through my website, saying she's doing a piece on 'Modern Love' and plans to explore international online franchises like Match.com and DatingDirect, and then the smaller boutiques like myself. She says she was attracted to me initially because of the name The Love Market and wonders if she might phone me for a chat.

I Google the mag, and it's got a circulation of 350,000. It would amount to the sort of advertising value that I could never start to quantify. If I ever sit here pouting over my significantly dwindled income since the divorce, and telling myself I have to find ways to grow my business, I might just have found it. Or, rather, it has found me.

No sooner do I type back, *'Yes! I'd love to chat'* than she rings me.

'We talked nearly an hour!' I tell Jacqui, down at my local pub, settling into an aged-velvet corner seat, surrounded by low, oak-beamed walls lined with brass horseshoes and plaques that say things like Good Food. Good Fun. Good Friends. 'Right off she wanted to know how I came up with the name The Love

Market, so of course I told her all about the Love Market in Sa Pa, how I went there, how I met Patrick… She was fascinated. By the time we rang off, she knew the whole story of how you ended up playing matchmaker and bringing him back into my life. So she wants to interview us.'

'Do you think Patrick will be up for it?'

I clutch my half-pint of Guinness.'No! She doesn't want to interview Patrick, she wants to interview you!'

'Me?' Jacqui glares at me.

'She said that since we chatted, the focus of her article was going to change. She was so intrigued that she wants to feature me and the story of how Patrick and I met, and reconnected. She loves the whole angle of how a successful matchmaker is unsuccessful in her own love life, until her sister does a bit of matchmaking and reunites her with her lost love.'

Jacqui looks stunned. 'Well, that sounds like a jolly story, but don't you think it's a bit personal? The whole of the country getting to read about how you had sex with a married man, then thought about him all the time you were married to Mike, and then two minutes after you're divorced, he's back in your life again?'

I stare into the froth on my drink. 'I didn't see it that way.' But of course now I do. 'I don't have to tell her all the intimate details…' I look at her and see disappointment in her eyes. 'Jacq, I'm doing it because I need to earn more money. I have to think of Aimee's future.'

'Sorry, I know. You're right. It just seems odd, them writing all about you. As though you're a big celebrity or something.'

'This isn't about me thinking I'm Cheryl Cole. It's a business decision. Getting The Love Market out there, even if it's via them writing about me, isn't an opportunity I can afford to turn down.'

I peer at her for some sign of understanding, but she won't look me in the eyes.

'I just think when Mike reads it, it's gong to be like rubbing his nose in the whole Patrick thing. How's he going to feel?'

I open my mouth and stagger for an answer. 'Well, he's dating Jennifer now, isn't he?'

'That's completely different. And…well, just because they're going out together doesn't mean anything. I don't believe he's crazy about her. Not for one minute.'

This stills me for a few seconds. 'Look, Jacq, I realise I'm going to have to tell him, at some point. But it's not as though I'm about to get married again! Patrick lives in another country. He's just accepted a job that's going to keep him there forever more!'

'But you are going to have to tell Mike about him if you end up going to Canada next month.'

'I know.' I turn and stare across the bar, my eyes falling on a group of attractive girls being hit on by decent-looking lads holding pints. Does she think I haven't thought about this a hundred times?

She cocks her head. 'Surely, that's not why you don't seem excited about going?'

'Who says I'm not excited?'

She studies me while I try not to look at her. 'I don't know. You don't seem to be. Not massively.'

I open my mouth to speak, but nothing comes out. I take a drink instead.

'It's just because I've not convinced Aimee yet. What's the point of getting all built up about it if it's not going to happen?'

'You know she'll want to go. Canada? It's a huge adventure! She probably won't be thinking much more than that.'

I remember when I went to Greece with my father and his

new girlfriend — the one he had left my mother for. Marie. I was Aimee's age. At first, the idea of going seemed morally repugnant. But a part of me thought: hmmm, I've never been to Greece before…

'Maybe.' When I look at her, she's searching my eyes, as though wondering what distant place my mind has just been off to. 'I will tell Mike,' I eventually say. 'About Patrick, about the article, about everything.'

'Well, just promise me you'll tell him soon.'

# Thirty-Four

Saturday morning, Trish rings me. 'You matched me with my James! Not just any James, but MY James! You even told me you were matching me with James and I didn't even realise! How stupid am I?'

'If his name had been Jasper, I'd have said you should never have been a lawyer.'

She chuckles. 'But how did you know?'

'I just knew. Maybe because on the fake date he kept going on about how fantastic you were, and it was as though he compared everyone else to you and found them lacking. And then there was the way you worked overtime to convince me that you weren't attracted to him.'

'Me?' she chortles dirtily. 'I did that?'

'You did. And then there was something else. You seemed to really really care about him. Something about you lightened when you talked about him.'

She falls quiet. Then says, 'Argh!'

'So how did it go?' I ask her. 'Your date?'

'Oh my God,' she sounds emotional, 'do you want to know how shocked I was? I mean, there I was, I arrive at the restaurant

and I see James sitting at a table in the corner. And I'm like…
hang on, what's he doing here? And he looks up and we both
look at each other and then I think James? JAMES? And I say
what are you doing here? And he says I'm meeting a girl called
Patricia!' She chortles. 'The last time anyone has called me
Patricia was when I was baptised. I'd almost forgotten that's my
real name.'

'I had a feeling that if I told him he was meeting a girl called
Trish, it would have given the game away.'

She chortles again. 'Oh, Celine, it was lovely! We actually
had a date! A real date! We… I don't know, we didn't even
have to try, that's what was so interesting. It just evolved quite
naturally.'

I hear some background shuffling, and then, 'Celine!'
James's voice. Presumably James has spent the night. 'Has anybody ever told you you're quite crafty at your job? But the thing
is, there are a few problems with her. One is, she's a lawyer and,
as you know, I never date lawyers, never have and never will;
they're absolutely despicable, argumentative, uncompromising
people. Two, she's got issues about sleeping with one of her best
friends, as well as some other foibles that I can see being quite
problematic in the long term… Ouch! She's just bashed me
with a feather pillow. See what I mean? And three, I'm really
quite in love with her.'

When I hang up, I sit down on the end of my bed, and all I
can do is smile.


In the week, I phone Kim and break some good news. 'I have
another match for you. He's in the music business. Lives up here
but flies down to London. He's got a flat down there.'

Andrew Flemming is the type of man Kim should be drawn
to. He's an Ideas man, who has an atypical career, is at the top

of his game, is incredibly interesting, entertaining, and he's not at all bad looking.

'He's thirty-nine,' I tell her. 'And he's not opposed to meeting a woman in her mid-forties. I'm going to aim for next Thursday night if that works with you. But I have to tell you, if you don't like him, I have an awful lot of women who will. I'm giving you a chance first.'

'Hmm,' she says. 'I'm going to try really hard not to blow it.'

I then phone Andrew and tell him I am setting him up with a very pretty public relations executive. Being in the music industry, Andrew is used to dealing with 'characters.' And I have to remember that none of the men I have sent her out with have disliked her.

Yet.

On Saturday night, Aimee and I rent a DVD, and when it's over we have the talk. I tell her that Patrick has invited us to Canada.

By the time I get to the bit about me having gotten in touch with him and we've been corresponding, she is already rolling her eyes. 'Mum, I already know that you went to see him in London.'

I gawp at her. 'How do you know that? Did Aunt Jacqui say something?'

'Not really. Just that you'd gone to see an old friend.'

'I went for a conference!'

She gives me that look again.

I study her waiflike upper body with its vest under the T-shirt, and tiny mounds of breasts, her indigo toe- and fingernails. Since she kissed Rachel's boyfriend, she hasn't really talked about boys anymore. Except to tell me that Rachel is in love with Edward in *Twilight*, but Aimee thinks he's lame.

'Well, really, in many ways that's all he is. And I told him
you wouldn't want to go. That you'd have no interest in seeing
a big, exciting Canadian city. You don't want to go to the
Canadian lakes and see black bears and wolves, and go boating,
and have picnics and barbeques. You'd far rather just hang out
at boring old home for the summer, with me and your dad and
all your fantastic best friends who are now back in your life.'

'Why'd you tell him that?' She stares at me like I'm from
outer space.

My overriding memory of Greece is of sitting in a fish tavern
across the table from my father and his Marie. She, with her
hair in a messy upknot, black sunglasses on her head, and a
black caftan-style shirt over her bikini. She dragged on a cig-
arette in a way that said she knew secrets about life that I
would never know. She was twenty-seven to my dad's fifty-
three. The most gorgeous thing I'd ever seen, and I couldn't
fathom what she saw in my dad. Until this holiday, I'd
esteemed my father to be greater than great. Even his dumping
us was something that people like him, who were too good for
the rest of us, did. Yet here he was in his acrylic jumper, with
his furrowed forehead, and his tall stories I'd heard a million
times before. And there was I with my bleached 'eighties' hair,
peering from behind my long fringe that felt like a wad of toilet
paper stuck on there, absorbed in my own personal peep show.
My dad could not stop kissing her. Slow, reverent snogs that
looked difficult somehow, like two people trying to become
unstuck from quick-dry cement. From the other side of a plate
of fried calamari, I watched his hand sneak a fondle of her
breast. I remember her laughing, and my father's tongue shockingly sliding in and out of her mouth, and my eyes widening,
horrified of what might be coming next, and how I thanked
God when she brushed him off to smoke another fag.

I was never going to fall in love. I was never going to be kissed. If you took those two small details out of life, everything else felt like it was going to be simple.

Somehow I will have to manage this trip carefully, if Aimee ever agrees to it. I refuse to ever leave my daughter with that view of life.

# Thirty-Five

I'm tidying my room and folding my jeans when I find my dad's letter to Sandra in the pocket. I had forgotten that I was supposed to give it to her. I sit down on the end of the bed. He has sealed it with a shiny silver sticker, round like a bright ten-pence piece. Worried what's in it, I open it and read:

*Beautiful Sandra…*

*There is absolutely no truth to the rumour that, following her intensive search to find love, Sandra will now fly away with Anthony to spend a fabulous two weeks in the Maldives…*

*In truth, I write this to thank you for your company at dinner. If you ever wish to go out again, to continue our conversation, you have only to let me know. But failing this ever materialising, I hope I can captivate you on an entirely different level. The offer to paint you is one I did not make lightly. So rarely am I moved by my subjects these days, that I cannot help but think you and I can somehow benefit each other.*

*If you would agree to sit for me, I shall repeat to you here, my phone number. 542-1265.*

*Yours,*

*Ancient Anthony*

Ancient Anthony.

I go downstairs, find another envelope to put the letter in, and pop out to the post office.

When I come back I have an email from Lindsay Walsh, the journalist at *Hers*.

> *Dear Celine,*
>
> *Have you had a chance to speak with your sister? When is a good time for me to phone? Prefer some time this week.☺*
> *LW*

'There isn't a good time,' Jacqui says, when I ring her. 'I'm extremely busy at work. I don't think I can do it, Celine.'

I park on the edge of my settee cushion, and stare at the space between my feet. 'You know, stop me and tell me I'm wrong anytime, but I'm getting the impression you don't want to help me out with this.'

Silence. Then, 'Well, you're right in a way. I don't want to be involved in the article, Celine, if you must know.'

I pluck at the threads on my cut-off jean shorts — the ones Aimee made me buy because she said I needed to make myself more trendy. 'But you are the article — I mean, part of it. The whole angle for the story was how there are two matchmakers in the family. Remember? Without you, Patrick wouldn't be back in my life and the journalist wouldn't be wanting to write about me.'

She sighs heavily. I am so confused by her reaction that I have a headache. 'I just don't get it. I don't know why you're being like this.'

'Because it's not me they should be interviewing!' she suddenly says, sounding exasperated. 'I didn't want to tell you this, Celine. But now I've obviously got no choice, have I?' She sighs again. 'It wasn't me who got you back in touch with Patrick. It was Mike.'

# Thirty-Six

'Mike?'

I laugh, a short burst. Then I'm struck dumb. 'Did you say it was Mike?' I say, after a few moments.

'Yes. Mike emailed Patrick. I'm sorry. I wasn't supposed to tell you. That's why I let you just go on believing it was me.'

'Hang on...' I laugh again now, nervously. 'Are you being serious? My God, you are! Mike emailed Patrick? But the email was sent from my computer. Mike never...'

'Had access? Yes he did. When you went to Manchester and he came over. Remember?'

The confusion lifts, and I do remember. Didn't he tell me that he took them out to dinner?

'He came to pick us up. I invited him in because he was a bit early and Aimee had been having a clothing crisis, and she wasn't quite ready. He was downstairs. I was upstairs with Aimee, helping her choose something. I suppose he must have gone on your laptop...'

I always travel with my laptop. This was the one time I hadn't taken it with me. It would have been right there, at the kitchen table. 'Why on earth would he do that, Jacq? He's got no right...!' I stand up and walk around the room, in disbelief.

'So — hang on — he knows that Patrick and I met? That he's been up here? That he's been in our house?'

'Not from me he doesn't,' she says quickly. 'When he told me that he'd emailed, he said he didn't want to know anything about what might happen. He'd just done it and that was it.'

'But why would he even tell you?'

'I don't know. Maybe like all of us, we need someone to tell. Or maybe it was his way of telling me why he believed your marriage broke up — because there was someone else in the background. Who knows? Anyway, he said it quite matter-of-factly. Didn't make a big thing of it. It was the first time I'd ever heard Patrick's name come out of Mike's mouth, but the way he told me, it was obvious he knew that I knew all about him. I'm sure he knew we've talked about him many times. I'm sure Mike knew a lot more than you ever gave him credit for.'

I am stunned.

'But if I were a betting woman,' she continues, 'I'd say that he probably suspects that's why you went to London, yes.'

I look at Mike's photo on the shelf above the table. His eyes again, watching me. Was this Mike's grand plan? To leave me and then reunite me with the one he thought I loved more?

'Why would he do it, Jacq?' I say again. 'I just don't get it.'

'I don't know.' She sounds equally dismayed. 'I suppose you'll have to ask him.'

I arrange to meet Mike in the pub, at the far end of Tyne Green Park. To get him to come, I told him I need to talk to him about Aimee. It's a dark day but dry when I set out. But by the time I am halfway along the riverside trail it starts throwing it down. In my haste to leave the house, I didn't bring an umbrella. Hurrying, my flip-flops make small noises like trapped birds.

Within moments my toes are caked in muck, and my white dirndl skirt soaked. My mobile rings.

'Where are you?' he says. 'I'm at the pub and you're not.'

'I'm nearly there,' I tell him. 'I decided to walk instead of drive. But I didn't bring a brolly.' I push back hair that's dripping styling product into my eyes. I usually run this park, so have no perception of the time it takes to actually just walk it. For some odd reason I remember Aimee getting lost in here when I brought her, when she was about five. One minute she was there, then I bumped into a neighbour and got chatting, and when I looked, she was gone. I can still remember my feet pounding the grass, my heart hammering like I was going to die, my head dizzy from dodging trees and trying to watch my step. How I was calling for her, and thinking, *What if I can't find her? If she just disappears? If someone takes her?* Then, completely unexpectedly, Mike came round the corner with her in his arms.

'I'll come and meet you,' he says now.

'No, stay there. I'm not far. There's no sense in us both getting wet,' I say, but he has already hung up.

I start running. My clothes are stuck to my body now, and I am cold. Nothing like you would expect to feel in midsummer — only in this part of the country where the dampness cuts through when the sun isn't there to lift it. I stop to wipe my smarting eyes, wondering how I'm ever going to go into the pub looking such a mess.

When I stop rubbing my eyes and open them again, Mike is standing right there, about fifty feet away, on the gravel path. A lone figure, against a background of tall trees, cold river, and iron rain.

He has on his light blue skinny jeans, with his white running shoes, and his old beige blazer thrown on top of a white open-necked dress shirt, that he hasn't bothered tucking in, as though he threw it on quickly. He is holding his big black Blaze FM umbrella.

'Hiya,' he says. 'God, you're drenched. Look at you!'

As I walk up to him, my breath coming hard from running, his eyes drop down the front of me, then he holds out his umbrella for me to come under.

I take a step or two closer, so I am sheltered. The rain does an irregular tiptoe on the nylon above our heads. He looks pale, and traumatized somehow. His eyes comb over my dripping wet hair, over my face. He smells of fresh air. There are beads of rain in the quiff of his hair.

'Mike,' I say, hugging my arms about my body.

'What's wrong?' he asks.

I can't go on for a few moments, have to look away from him. A family of starlings fly back and forth between two trees. There is gravel in my flip-flops, small stones sticking to the soles of my feet. 'Why did you email Patrick?' I look at him now.

His expression doesn't change much. But in the darkness of his face, I suddenly see him, as maybe I never have: as someone easily hurt. 'Oh,' he says, 'so she told you. Well, I suppose I shouldn't be surprised.'

'She did. But not for the reasons you might think.' I don't feel like getting into the magazine article thing now. I am shivering and crave to be dry and warm. 'But why, Mike? What on earth made you do it?'

The rain is pelting now on top of the umbrella. It seems to slide down in sheets, riddling the calm grey surface of the river like a hail of bullets. He doesn't speak for what feels like a very long time, almost looking through the rain as it comes down around us. 'You and I didn't work, but that doesn't mean I don't want you to be happy.'

He meets my eyes now, and the bareness of his honesty makes my eyes brim tears.

'What is it they say? If you do what you've always done, you get what you always got? I knew you'd go on wondering about him, and doing nothing about it. So I decided to do it for you.'

The tears roll hotly down my face, now. They're bolstered by a sob. I don't mean to cry — don't even know why I am crying. Mike watches me without huge pity. Then he balances his umbrella handle in the crook of his harm and wiggles his jacket off, gives it to me. 'Here. Take it.'

I pull it around me. It's warm from his body. 'Don't feel bad,' he says. 'It's not your fault any more than it's mine. You tried to make it work, I know that.' He studies me wistfully. 'You couldn't help being in love with somebody else any more than I could help being in love with you. We're both people who tend to reach for things that are somehow a bit far out of our grasp.'

It takes me a while to be able to speak because I'm ashamed that I must have allowed my state of mind to be so obvious all those years. 'Did you really always think I wanted to be with him all the time that I was with you? Because that's not true, Mike.'

'No — maybe not all the time. But enough of the time. I think you wished I'd been him. You had this ongoing thing for him. Most people would have snapped out of it, but you never did.' He pulls a resigned smile. 'I actually happen to think our marriage was a lot better than what you made it out to be in your own mind. But I suppose I always knew something was wrong, deep down. That you weren't really happy.' His face has flushed now. His hair is flattened with the dampness. 'Most people don't have these outbursts, do they? Where they tell their husbands that they're not happy. Maybe once, or twice. But I heard this for years, Celine. Years. The same rant.' His expression seems to blanch with sadness. 'For a long time I thought that if I was good to you in all the right ways I could change that. But then, well, I had to take the blinders off eventually, didn't I?'

I look at this man standing here in the rain, this human being who I happened to meet quite by random when I least expected meeting anyone I could ever care about again. This man who knows more about me, in more specific and intimate ways than any other living soul: more than my mother ever did, more than my father, my daughter, or my sister — certainly more than Patrick. What was the point of it all? What's he going to do with all this knowledge and understanding he has acquired of me now? Wasn't it just a wasted education in another human being? If our marriage had been a mistake, then it should have ended earlier, before there was that expectation that the longer it went on, the longer it would go on. It's like putting yourself through training and entering a race you have no hope of winning.

'I'm so sorry, Mike,' I look at his lean shoulders under the shirt. The goosebumps on his neck. His chest hair poking out; I remember how I would lie and nestle into it, in bed. 'It's not enough. But I am.' My voice breaks.

I bow my head and sense his eyes burning into it. When he speaks, his voice bears this heaviness of heart, with the faintest hint of reproach, which I can tell he is suppressing. 'You know, it would hurt me so much to think that you never found what you were looking for. And who knows, maybe you and this bloke were right for each other. Just because you hardly knew him... I feel like I've known you all my life and that didn't exactly help us, did it?'

I grasp myself around the waist, as though I am caving in on myself. I look at him, and then can't look at him. Because his composure is almost unbearable.

And still we stand here, and the rain pounds the ground around us. Neither one of us suggests continuing this conversation inside the pub. 'I didn't plan to email him, you know,' he says. 'Then I was over at yours, while you were away, and for some reason — I don't know why, your computer was there and I decided to check something on the Internet while I was waiting for them to get ready. Whatever I typed in, there was a list came up of pages last visited. And I saw his name right there — his email address at some college.' He shrugs. 'I have no idea what made me do it. I just thought, put it out there, see what happens. If he bites, he bites.' He laughs a little, humourlessly, when he sees what must be a stunned look on my face. 'I didn't exactly want to say anything to him, so I just fired off a blank email, and that was it…'

'You know he came to London,' I eventually say, as we start walking in the direction of his car.

I glance at him and see his cheeks flush: that look I know so well — the Mike-slightly-pissed-off look. 'I guessed. But I'm really not interested. In fact, it's the last thing I want to hear about.' He looks right into my eyes and we stop walking again. 'I hope it works out for you. But do I have any desire to know anything about him?' He shrugs. 'Nothing.'

I look away, staring across the river until my eyes burn. 'Don't cry,' he says quietly. 'You should be happy. You can have what you always wanted. How many people are in that position? Eh?' He says it without a note of bitterness.

'But what if—' we meet eyes, and I am willing the tears not to fall, '—there's been a mistake?' I find myself whispering.

His eyes scope my face again, and I can see the disarray of him: like a person wrestling with the desire to believe in something that he just can't. 'There's no such thing as mistakes, Celine. Only choices.'

He tightens his grasp on the umbrella handle, while he watches more tears spring in my eyes. 'You have to think of us as a season,' he says. 'We came to an end, but life moves on.'

And then something odd occurs. While he is studying me, there is a moment where his expression changes, and I see in his face a look that used to be there years ago, when he still believed in me. He smiles now — a sad smile. Then our faces move in at the same time; two people thinking the same thought. Before we touch, we pause, as though confirming permission. His hand goes to my waist, the umbrella faltering overhead, his fingers sinking into my wet cardigan. Then we are kissing. At first, a tentative granting of lips meeting lips. Mike's kiss feels new again, after Patrick's. And it's almost like all those years ago, in the car. A small flame fans somewhere inside me, drawing me irresistibly to its heat, but just bobbing slightly out of reach the closer I get and the more his mouth intensifies on mine.

The umbrella drops out of his hand and bobs onto the ground. The rain now is like needles on our heads. Mike's intense grip on my waist, fingers moving firmly to a rhythm. And still our mouths move together, his hands relocating to the buttons of my cardigan now. I freeze, almost. Intrigued by what he's going to do, and, inside, a part of me just going with it. Then the momentum of our kiss picks up again, as he undoes three buttons from the bottom, until he is able to get in there and find bare flesh. Mike's touch has a breathtaking effect. Or maybe the charge in me is partly shock: these same hands that have been on my body so many times that I'd allowed myself not to feel them. Now I feel them as though they are different hands.

We are getting soaked, but he doesn't seem to mind. His hair is plastered now to his head. All he does is hang onto my chilled, bare waist while he finishes kissing me. He is the first to pull away. He smiles, thinly, more with his eyes than anything. Then his gaze doesn't once move from mine as he tugs the sides of my cardigan back into place, and does up my buttons. Like you might wrap up a present that you're going to re-gift.

'Hmm,' he says. Just Hmm.

# Thirty-Seven

'You seem distant today,' Jacqui looks at me quizzically as we sit devouring jacket potatoes and salad in a café in Eldon Square. I have to be in town to meet a potential new client this afternoon, and took this chance to have a bite with my sis.

She studies my silence. 'If you don't have things to tell me, I have things to tell you,' she says.

I smile now. 'Tell me.'

'Well,' she draws a big breath. 'I'm not going to marry Rich.'

I set down my knife and fork, fold my arms, and study her for a moment or two. 'You're not? Hang on, I'm too stunned to speak.'

She laughs. 'All right! So you knew. That's why you're in the business. Because you know things about people that they don't know about themselves.'

'In your case it hardly required supernormal powers.'

'Maybe not… I suppose I've always known I couldn't go through with it. The Christian thing — awful as it was — was a crush that had to happen, to make me see sense.'

'Have you told Rich yet?'

She nods, surprising me. 'He took it quite well. I think he knew. He said half the time he felt we were roommates anyway.

He said he always thought it odd how I was happy to go out without him all the time, how I never really factored him into many of my plans…' She rakes the flesh out of her potato, and then unwraps a small patty of butter and scrapes it on there with a knife. I watch her draw it around the potato until it melts. 'So we're cancelling the holiday, and we're going to sell the flat. But in the meantime,' she looks at me now, 'I have to move out and rent somewhere. But I wondered if I could move in with you, just for a month or so, because I'd like to take my time to look around.'

'Of course. Aimee will be thrilled. You can stay as long as you like.'

She blows me a kiss across the table, and then eyes her potato again, as though she might not want to eat it anymore. 'There's another reason, though, why I don't want to go buying somewhere just yet.' She looks up at me, with her chin tucked, sheepish. 'I've actually applied for a job. To work for Sir Norman Foster, in London.'

Now I really am floored. 'In London?' I gasp. Sir Norman Foster is the famous architect who designed Newcastle's Sage Centre for Music. I know how much she admires his work.

'There's no guarantee I'll get it. In fact, it's highly unlikely, so I'm trying hard not to get too excited.'

I scrutinize her. 'Jacq, you graduated Uni with a first. Your current firm practically took your arm off to get you. I can't imagine there'd be too many people more qualified.'

'Oh, you'd be surprised. They'll be fishing from a very big pool. There are lots more talented people out there than me.'

'You know, I always sensed your restlessness was about more than just you fancying someone else,' I tell her, dousing my own potato in butter now.

She puts her napkin down. 'It was partly the job. But it was mostly Rich. I'm a happy person, Celine, but he pulls me down. That's why I don't enjoy coming home to him. Does saying that make me really selfish and horrible? That I don't want to marry him because of his depression?'

I shake my head. 'No, but truthfully? I don't think that's the real reason. I think you're just not ready to be married to anyone yet. Maybe you need to have a life you love first.' She seems to listen intently. 'It's scary letting someone who loves you go, Jacq — you once said that to me a long time ago, about Rich. But what I should have said is that something always comes along to replace what's gone. It's a bit like digging a hole. You shovel all the soil out, but the earth around it falls in and fills some of it back up again.'

She smiles. 'I like that idea.'

I nod, feeling wistful for a moment. 'Me too.'

# Thirty-Eight

Aimee and I are going to Canada.

Aimee stays at Mike's the night before we fly. I haven't talked to Mike since I told him two weeks ago about Patrick's invitation. It's only when he drops Aimee off at our house that we come face to face for the first time since we kissed. 'Hi,' he says, flatly, avoiding my eyes, seeming to look everywhere but into them.

'Thanks for driving her,' I tell him. Given our flight leaves shortly after two, it would have been a bit of a rush if I'd had to go pick her up and then drive to the airport.

He nods. Now his eyes do meet mine and he looks at me in an almost disturbing hard focus. 'Will you phone Jacqui to tell her you got there safely?' he asks.

'Of course, but I was planning to buy a calling card, so Aimee can ring you as much as she wants. I'm sure she'll have lots to tell you.'

'Whatever you want,' he says. 'So long as I know you got there all right.'

'Do you like my new Skechers?' Aimee, who darted into the house, darts to the door again. She lifts a foot to show me her new pink and brown leather running shoes that she's just put on. 'I'm travelling in them.'

Amazingly, Aimee seems unperturbed by seeing Patrick again, as though it just goes with the territory if she is to have her holiday in Canada. 'Black bears live until they're twenty-three,' she told me the other day. 'I was looking on the Internet. I would have thought they'd live longer. Like elephants.'

'I told you, you shouldn't wear new shoes to fly in,' Mike says. 'Your feet swell in the air. They'll kill you and it's a long time to sit in pain.'

Aimee's bubble is burst. She looks from her dad to me. 'I'm sure it'll be fine,' I tell her, looking at Mike. 'I think it's only older people who suffer from swelling feet. Not someone Aimee's age.'

'Well, take some Elastoplasts,' Mike warns her. Then he says, 'I should go. Have a safe flight.' And then, as a bit of a throw-away line, read by an actor who is not quite talented enough to be entirely convincing, 'Enjoy yourself.'

We arrive at local time 4 p.m. As we proceed through the exit doors into the arrivals hall, I spot him right away, and whatever doubts I've harboured about coming here just disappear. He waves, his face breaking into a big smile.

He hugs me endlessly. I'm conscious of Aimee standing stiffly beside us, so I reach an arm to include her. He kisses me now, a long kiss planted firmly on my cheek. 'Hi,' he says to Aimee, and places a friendly hand on her shoulder. Aimee colours bright red and looks down at her new shoes. 'You must be Aimee.' She smiles at the ground.

A muggy heat hits us outside, as well as the bluest sky with gleaming sunshine. Patrick directs us around wheelie suitcases, past orange taxis, and crawling black stretch limos, through the

horns and shouts, and the shrill whistle of the uniformed parking commissionaire. My first thought is that everything is
bigger: cars, buildings, paths: an immediate outpouring of free-
dom and space. He leads us to his car, talking animatedly, one
hand still on my back, and the other carrying Aimee's suitcase.
In a short-sleeved pale blue sports shirt, and faded jeans, he
looks fit and lean and tanned. And I wonder how many times,
for Aimee's sake, I'm going to have to catch myself before I
reach to attack him with kisses.

And then we are bulleting along the 'freeway' as he calls it,
Patrick still chatting away from the front seat — about our
flight, the weather, about what he's got lined up for us to do —
and Aimee intently observing the vast size of Canada from out
of the back window.

His home is a condominium in an area of the city that he
calls Yorkville. It has two concierges at the gate, one of whom
valet-parks his navy blue Volvo SUV. His unit is way up on
the thirtieth floor. 'I don't think I've ever been in a building
as tall as this.' Aimee stares at all the floor numbers that light
up as we ride the elevator. 'Not very good if you're scared of
heights.'

'I actually don't care for heights,' he tells her. 'I just try not
to look out of the window.'

She blushes and looks at him curiously.

As he swipes his door with a key-card, I am struck by how
unreal it feels to be standing here anticipating walking into the
place where Patrick lives.

'Welcome,' he says, pushing open the door for us.

I walk in, surprised how magazine-interior it is. 'It's all
white!' I laugh.

'Hey, not my doing. The person I'm renting from is an
interior designer.'

Renting? I think. I'd have imagined he'd have owned his own place.

I am drawn to the massive windows behind the white leather couch that overlook a busy intersection of streets. 'Cool!' Aimee, says, coming to look too — high-end stores like Tiffany right below, glass buildings that reflect the sky, broad avenues disappearing in all directions. 'That's Lake Ontario,' he says, standing right behind us, pointing ahead as far as the eye can see. 'And that is Yonge Street,' he points left. 'The longest street in the world.'

'In the *world* or in Canada?' Aimee quizzes him.

'It used to be in the *Guinness Book of World Records*. It's nearly twelve hundred miles long.'

'Twelve *hundred*?' Aimee gawps at him.

He smiles. 'We'll walk it tomorrow.'

'*All* of it?'

He laughs now. 'No. Just the bit that takes us from here down to the lakeshore. Maybe one mile of it.'

'Phew!' she says, looking to me. 'Otherwise I really will need Elastoplasts.'

'Hungry?' He glances at his watch, after we've got our bearings in his place. 'It's just after five. We could go for an early dinner.'

We are hungry, or at least, ready for a proper-sized, satisfying meal. 'Come on,' he says. 'It'll be good to get some fresh air anyway. You can unpack when we come back. Let's go hit a patio in Yorkville and soak up some last rays of sun.'

We go back down in the elevator and walk for about ten minutes until we come to a lively area of bars, boutiques, and outdoor restaurants that feels instantly European, set one block in from the main street. Patrick leads us down a narrow walkway, to one of the less busy patio restaurants in a tiled courtyard that is decked with plant pots spilling colours.

We sit down at a chrome table in the sun. Patrick orders a bottle of Prosecco, and a cranberry and soda for Aimee, which he suggests after the waitress says they don't serve ginger beer. I order chicken with linguine Alfredo, Aimee orders fish and chips, and Patrick, an Ahi tuna salad with a side of yam fries. The Prosecco is sparkly and refreshing. Aimee holds my flute up to the sun and peers at the pale golden bubbles. Patrick sits back in the seat, in his sunglasses that block me from seeing his eyes. His mouth twitching into a pleased smile every time I look at him. We are as much a novelty to him as all this is to us.

When our food arrives, Aimee is so stunned by the portion size that she gets her camera out and takes a picture of each of our plates, which amuses Patrick. 'Mum! That's not a portion of pasta, it's a whole box! What till Dad sees! Can I upload them to Facebook?'

I look at Patrick. 'Sure,' he says. 'You can borrow my computer tomorrow.'

It's true about the size of the food. My enormous oval plate is loaded up with a heap of buttery noodles, and what appears to be two grilled chicken breasts on the top. 'God, I'll never eat all this,' I tell Patrick, laughing. 'My protein allowance for the week!'

'Welcome to North America,' he says.

When we finish all we can manage, it's after seven, which, with the five-hour time difference, is into the next day for us. We walk back slowly, taking a slightly longer route along another narrow street that's full of expensive boutiques, which leads onto a main, tree-lined thoroughfare. Aimee totters on ahead of us in her new running shoes, white footless tights, and a brightly coloured sundress over the top. And from time to time when she's not looking, Patrick takes hold of my hand and squeezes it, before releasing me again.

I spot his building on the corner. When we get upstairs I watch Aimee brush her teeth and then she falls semi-clothed into bed. 'Cool,' she says, enthusiastically, when he shows her the view from her bedroom window. But she's too tired to show much interest for long.

With the blinds open and the city lights streaming in, Patrick and I stand there in his bedroom, illuminated in stripes of white light, kissing, joining foreheads and taking stock of the fact that, somehow, we're together again.

The next few days are a whirlwind through Patrick's itinerary. A whisk up to the top of the CN Tower, one of the tallest buildings in the world, where we eat a very expensive lunch; the ferry across to Toronto Island, for sunbathing. Aimee's shaky attempt to swim. Steaks on the park's communal barbeque. An afternoon in Chinatown, where Aimee is repulsed by the sight of whole fish lying on the 'sidewalk' in the sunshine. We gravitate over the course of the days, from off-and-on hand-holding, to an arm placed protectively around my back, until Patrick's touches and our quiet passion for one another don't need to be hidden so much anymore. Aimee seems not to register it.

And of course I can't help but compare this to holidays with Mike. How, when we'd go to France or Italy, we would inevitably see lovey-dovey couples. And Mike would say 'Why aren't we like that?' And there was really no answer. None I could voice. Because the truth would hurt too much: I am not in love. And I can't make myself be. As though by not feeling it, you were somehow forbidden from trying to fake it, in the hope that in-loveness might somehow grow.

Aimee is enthralled by the shops. We spend a pleasant morning in the Eaton Centre, relieved to escape the humidity and temperatures hitting over ninety. It is an oasis of new and different clothes shops from the ones we've got back home, and far less of a crowd than in the MetroCentre. When Patrick discovers Aimee's interest in shoes, we end up ditching Black Creek Pioneer Village for the Bata Shoe Museum. When he tells her it houses more than twelve thousand exhibits, Aimee nearly dies. Four hours in there is clearly not Patrick's idea of a great way to spend the morning, but Aimee's fascination with the History of Western Fashion, and her rabid delight over a pair of leather platform Oxfords, circa 1973, is almost worth Patrick's pain.

'You can draw. You love shoes. Seems to me you should become a shoe designer,' he tells her, looking through his rearview mirror, when we're on our way home. Bringing his attention back to the road, he just misses the spark that arrives in her eyes.

'Shoe designer?' Aimee repeats, and then catches my eye.

All that, plus Greek food on the Danforth, and a rather romantic dinner for three in Toronto's Historic Distillery District; we are almost worn out by the time Patrick hauls us to Niagara Falls. But Aimee's excitement reaches new levels when we don ridiculous yellow plastic rainwear and take the Maid of the Mist boat ride to the foot of the falls to watch six million cubic feet of water fall over its crest, the equivalent of thirteen storeys above our heads. Patrick tells her the story of the woman and her cat who were the first to go over the falls in a barrel in 1901 and of other subsequent stunts that haven't proven as successful, and Aimee looks at him, part disbelieving, part like she just might want to run out and try it herself.

The photos I snap of Aimee this day show a girl who is as happy as I've seen her in a very long time. And I know that Aimee has had a rough time of things, but we have come through a little way. In the car going back, while I flick back through my digital camera, Aimee thrusts a sketch of 'John Lennon's "Beatle Boot" crossed with an English leather pump circa 1925' over Patrick's shoulder, and then she beams at him, pushing back her hair that's still wet from the boat ride.

On Tuesday Aimee phones Mike on my calling card, while we pull over for a snack on the drive to Patrick's cabin up at Muskoka. She chats animatedly on the payphone, while Patrick and I sit and watch her from a nearby picnic bench. When she gets off the phone, I recognized that slightly subdued look. It's the homesick face, the very one I'm sure I must have had that time my dad took me to Greece with his girlfriend.

The cabin is far more impressive than Patrick has led us to believe. Right on the edge of Lake Muskoka, and a small sand beach, it sits in its own private jewel-sized hideaway among tall trees. We crunch gravel past a small storage shed and then a snowmobile shed, to a 'change house' as he calls it that's as close to the lake as you can get without stepping in. 'My dad built this for my sister and me to towel off in, and to dry the dog,' he laughs. 'My dad must have seen us as little animals in our own right, but for us, our time in this place was all we really wanted from summer. We'd look forward all year to coming here.'

He unlocks the change house to reveal not at all what I am expecting. A small room with a small bed in it, with a cream eiderdown, a pine side table, and a sink in the corner with a small, frameless cracked mirror above it. 'The guest cabin,' he says, looking at Aimee. 'Your own private suite while you're here, if you'd like it. Or you can stay in the main house; it's up to you.'

Aimee turns from Patrick to me. 'Can I stay here?' she asks. 'But what about the bears though?'

'No bears,' Patrick says. 'Except when you go to the toilet.'

Aimee scowls and looks around her. 'Where's the toilet?'

Patrick indicates a wooden shed right next door. 'Don't worry, I'll teach you to use a gun before nightfall.' He smiles at me, as Aimee's jaw drops.

'Here,' he says, opening a tiny connecting door that I only just notice as he walks to it. 'It seems my father thought of everything.'

Aimee looks relieved to see a toilet.

The three nights I'm with Patrick in his cabin with the pine walls, with Aimee sleeping just a glimpse away in the adjacent property, could easily be the happiest of my life. We don't do much except go out on the lake by day; I swim while Aimee sits and draws more shoes, and only once do we go for a long drive looking for a bear or a wolf but disappointingly we don't see any. Just plenty of white-tailed deer, that Aimee takes some good pictures of, and a couple of moose. With each day I wake up looking forward to those two or three hours we have just to ourselves once Aimee has gone to her cabin to sleep.

Patrick tells me a lot more about the book he's planning on writing — a foreign correspondent's inside view of Iraq — and talks surprisingly little of his job. All I know is that he's due to start it by Christmas. One night when we do actually put the telly on, he shows us the man he will be replacing.

'Cool!' Aimee says, well into the idea of Patrick being famous now. 'Won't you get to go abroad though and do those news reports from wars and things anymore?' she asks him.

'Sometimes,' he says. 'I'll do live news reports on location when the need arises.' He looks at me. 'Really, it was the right decision to take it.'

I tell him that I've decided to throw a party for my clients. Perhaps a Christmas party, one that I can get Aimee to help me plan. I'm going to get every client to invite two other single people. 'A masked ball, actually!' The idea suddenly comes to me.

'That's not bad,' he says. 'They can't take their masks off. If they hit it off with someone, they can only see them when they go out on a date.'

In the main cabin, about fifty feet away from Aimee's, I don't feel so bad about the noises I make when he makes love to me, because she won't be able to hear us. As Patrick kisses my shoulder and writes letters on my bare back, he writes the same words he wrote with the tip of a dried-up leaf in the sand, while Aimee suntanned and read a book beside us. 'I love you,' he wrote, and then once I'd read it, he smoothed it away with his hand, as though perhaps he'd never written it.

'*I love you,*' he writes now, only this time he doesn't rub it out.

It's our last night before we return to the city. So I am naturally gloomy. In two days' time we will be flying home.

'What are we going to do?' I whisper. The words are said, but in a way, I hope he hasn't heard them.

'I don't know,' he says. For a second he stops touching me. Then he turns me onto my back, making me look at his face in the moonlight. 'There is part of me, Celine, that says you should come live here. Aimee could go to school here, it's not like you'd be moving to a country where they didn't speak English. You could get a job, or try out your business here, or maybe be happy to not have to work for a while. I'd be earning enough.' His three fingers do a rapid pitter-pat on my shoulder: still this nervous energy in him. 'Aimee could go back to England as much as she wanted — you both could, anytime.'

His fingers stop moving and hover a couple of inches above my skin. 'But it wouldn't be reasonable to drag Aimee away from her natural father, would it? And well, even for my own reasons, I'm not sure I can have you come live here.' He rolls onto his back and stares at the ceiling. His eyes look deeply set, and shadowed. 'I did that with Anya, moved her away from her life. Dragged her off into the unknown. Made her put me and my career ahead of everything else.' He turns to me now, with unfettered honesty written all over his face. 'It wouldn't be that much different, would it? You'd be in the same position as she was in, and I have a feeling it would be doomed. And I just can't have the responsibility of that on me. I just can't, Celine.'

I'm gutted by him saying "doomed". Followed by the *responsibility* word. I've never felt like someone's responsibility before and it just feels like another way of calling me a burden. 'But surely the difference is that you love me and you know we are meant for each other — we have to be, don't we? After all this. Whereas you didn't feel that with her.'

It kills me that he doesn't instantly agree. He seems to give it too much thought, and then says, 'I'm not sure that is the difference. I think it's more about putting too much pressure on the situation. Too much pressure on me to make it work out.'

*Too much pressure on him?*

He watches me as I clamber over him. 'What are you doing?'

I pull on my knickers and a sweater. 'I need air.'

'I'm just trying to be honest with you...'

I am already outside, pretending not to hear. And of course he's right. I couldn't drag Aimee away from Mike. Never. So why am I reacting this way?

He doesn't instantly follow. I sit on the sundeck and stare at the moon, which appears to be suspended by invisible cords on the top of the water, wishing I could undo his words. A thought goes through my head. I want the impossible. That's my trouble. I always did.

Then he's standing behind me. He watches me for ages but

I won't look at him. There is nothing to say. 'I didn't mean it like that. I would love to promise you that we can do this, and it will all work out.' He sits down beside me, gazes at my profile. I won't look at him. 'I have no doubt in my mind that if we'd both lived in the same country — in the same place — it would work out. None. But...' He gives up explaining.

We stay like this for a while, sitting beside one another, not saying anything, just processing all that has been said. Then he stands up, looks down at me for a few moments, and says, 'Will you come back to bed?'

We go back inside. Back to bed. Patrick holds me, but it no longer feels the same.

Something is gone from the holiday. Even Aimee senses it. She draws and colours-in quietly. Quite a collection of shoes she's got now. I wonder if she'll tire of shoes the second we're on the plane and then she'll want to start painting waves again, with her granddad. By the time we're back in Toronto, and I am packing our bags in Patrick's apartment, a part of me can't wait to get on that plane.

I remember my father saying something to me once, recently. That for him it was always the thrill of the chase. 'You can chase dreams as well as people,' he said. 'The dreams are usually better.'

Driving to the airport, it feels like a long time since we were here nine days ago, maybe because we've done so much. Aimee stares out of the back window but with less of a curiosity about Canada than she had when we arrived, her travel bug now satisfied. Patrick and I say very little in the car. In fact, so little that he ends up switching the radio on to fill the silence.

When the girl at the check-in desk asks me my destination, I find myself saying, 'Newcastle,' a little too affirmatively.

'Look, do you want to grab a coffee before you go through security?' he asks, something urgent in him — an urgency, almost, to change the way things seem to be now.

'No,' I say. 'Best not.'

'Hey,' he kisses my downturned lips, as Aimee trots off to the toilet. He lifts up my chin with his index finger, so I have no choice but to look in his eyes. His face is drawn, and as handsome as ever. 'I'm not giving up on us, Celine. You might, but I'm not.'

'I'm not either,' I lie, brightly.

When Aimee comes back from the toilet, Patrick reaches a hand to the top of her head. 'Thanks...' she says, and smiles. 'I've had a really nice time. It's been really great.'

'You've been lovely to us,' I tell him. 'You couldn't have handled us better,' I smile. 'We won't ever forget Canada.' My eyes are telling him so much more, but if I say any more I'm going to cry.

His intense dark eyes look so damned sad. He kisses me again, as I fight back tears. Handing over our passports before we go through the security gate takes me back to years ago, to leaving Vietnam. Only he wasn't there to look at. He'd already gone. A part of me felt I'd dreamt him, and I could be still dreaming him.

Before we disappear, I turn and look at him and he holds up his hand in a wave. And I take a mental picture of him, knowing I probably won't ever see him again.

# Thirty-Nine

I never imagined that I'd find myself celebrating my sister leaving me. But here I am, on this early September day, along with twenty-two other close family and friends, at Blackfriar's restaurant in Newcastle. It also happens to be her 33rd birthday. My eyes move on a continuous loop from Aimee beside me, to my sister at the head of the long medieval table, to my suckling pig, and the monks and buxom wenches serving us, to Mike and Jennifer, to my father and Anthea, who has brownish lipstick on today.

Mike keeps catching my eye across the table. And then we both sharply look away.

Jennifer has tiny hands, like a child's. Her emerald green jumper stretches snuggly over her big boobs. Mike has an arm draped over the back of her chair. Whenever Jennifer talks to me, I feel Mike's eyes on me again. Just as I'm about to ask her how she made out with her pitch to the director of sales for National Express East Coast, Jacqui chinks the edge of her wineglass.

Jacqui has noticeably lost weight since leaving Rich. In a clingy dark brown wool dress to mark the sudden significant turn into autumn, her chest looks bigger, her waist smaller, her hair somehow shinier, and her eyes even more luminous. But sitting here appraising her, I wish so much that she wasn't going that I just want to go and hide behind coats in the cupboard and cry.

'I'm standing here and I'm still rocking on both feet; it's been such a whirlwind from my applying for the job, to the interview, to my hearing I'd got it. Then the trips down to London to find a flat.' She swipes a hand across her brow, 'Phew! But I'm excited!' she sings. 'This is what I haven't felt in a long time. About anything. But it certainly does feel good.'

Her gaze swings itself past me, taking everybody in, including a couple of her friends whom she hesitated before inviting: friends who weren't so supportive about her leaving Rich. 'In getting here I've had to recently make a lot of very tough decisions in my personal life. Ones that some people maybe still don't understand,' she pointedly looks at the naysayers. 'But believe me I have lost sleep over it all, as I take my actions very seriously. Much as I'm excited to move to London, and much as I tell myself I'll be back up here every weekend, and nothing's really going to change, I also know that a lot will.' Her gaze slides to me. 'The one thing I would love to be able to do, and know I can't do, is put Celine in a bag and bring her with me.' She smiles, and her eyes fill. 'Because I'm going to have to find somebody else to drop in on at all hours of the night, somebody else to pop out for a pint with on the spur of the moment, somebody else's personal crises to balance out my own, and absolutely no one is going to measure up! When I've needed a friend, there's no one I could imagine unloading on in quite the same way as I have done to Celine. To me, the fact that we don't actually come from the same parents was just an accident of birth.' She wipes a tear. Then she picks up her wineglass and raises it, surveying the table again. 'I just want you to know that you're all welcome in my new flat in Hammersmith. Only not all at the same time, as it's only a little bigger than the size of my car.'

She flops back down in her chair and some of her friends whoop up applause, and my eyes go over to Mike's only to find him watching me again. We hold eyes for a few moments. Then I try a smile and he matches it for effort.

Aimee and I start planning The Love Market's party, which we have now changed from Christmas to New Year's Eve. As soon as I told her it was a masked ball, Aimee thought it grandly exciting, and wanted in on all the preparations. I thought I'd put her artistic leanings to good use and I've got her designing the invitation.

'Doesn't one of your rich clients own a big castle or something?' she says, when I bemoan the fact that so many of the good venues around town are already booked up. If only I'd thought of the party idea sooner.

The penny drops. 'Gosh! Yes! David Hall, the man who doesn't wear underwear owns the spectacularly fabulous Strickley House!' I had the pleasure to visit it once, and felt like I'd died and been born as royalty. After Kim dumped him — apparently she never saw his house, and I often wonder that if she had, things might have been different — I set him up with Paula Nicholson, a forty-three-year-old wedding photographer who was the granddaughter of the chauffeur to the Duke of Northumberland. I don't know why, but I thought the connection was neat. Plus, when she's not shooting a wedding, she has a thing for artfully capturing stately homes and castles. She had an exhibition of her photography a few months go, in Newcastle. I went to see it, and contemplated inviting my father. But only briefly.

So far her relationship with David Hall seems to be going well. 'Well, it's a long shot but I could try to find a way to tactfully tell him that I am desperately seeking a venue for the party — to which he is, of course, invited.'

Aimee scowls. 'Why doesn't he wear underwear?'

Patrick wants us to go there for Christmas.

Even though we're only in September, he says he wanted to plant the seed early. But my head feels like it's spinning, given that we've really only just got back from Canada. Contemplating another trip is…impractical.

Me, who has craved more adventure in my life, doesn't know what to do with it when I get it. I pace in front of our window, staring out at the rain over the misty moors, holding the phone. Then I tell him all the reasons why I don't think we can come. Aimee will want to see her dad over Christmas. Obviously. I have the party, and the invitations are about to go out. So there will be a tonne of things to do. No one likes travelling in the winter.

'I miss you,' he says, cutting me off. 'At least in the summer I had your visit to look forward to. Now I don't know when I'm going to get to see you.'

'Maybe Easter,' I tell him, feeling defeated by the logistics of a long-distance relationship. Yes they can work. If they are a means to an end. Not if they are an end in themselves. 'How's your book?' I try to change the subject.

'I can't focus.'

'Are you looking forward to starting your job?'

'No.'

It's not fair that he loves me, I think. The Beatles were wrong. Love isn't all you need.

'Hey,' he says, brighter. 'I was looking up long-distance relationships on the Internet. We should go on a date.'

'Date?'

'What we do is, we pick a time. We both make the same meal. We buy the same bottle of wine. Then we rent the same movie and watch it at the same time.'

I find myself smiling. 'What? And then let me guess, when the movie is over, we have phone sex?'

'No I think we're supposed to do that while we're making the spaghetti. With no clothes on.'

I chuckle. I love the way he makes a light come on again, when everything seemed dark. 'Somehow I can't picture us doing that at all.'

'Me neither,' he says. 'I think that would just make me lonelier than I already am.'

# *Forty*

I spend all day Wednesday putting together some preliminary plans: phoning caterers, contacting a client who is an event planner, for a DJ recommendation, researching costumes. I find a site on the Internet that sells exclusive, handmade ostrich feather masks that Aimee's going to love. Then I suddenly think, well, hang on, we can put feather boas in vases instead of flowers. It'll be fun and far cheaper.

David Hall agreed to loan me his house. Well, part of it. He said it was the least he could do — given that I'd introduced him to someone he was falling for — plus, he said, the house has needed a party for a long time.

I went over there and saw the room that he thinks we should have it in. Now I have the whole place envisioned: a couple of chrome martini bars decked in silver tulle and strung with silver and gold minilights, nests of silver Christmas balls on high-top tables, silver candelabra, silver and gold tableware — I must find out where to rent it. And it might be fun to kick things off with a dance lesson! I'll invite an instructor to teach everyone the Viennese waltz. Or should I do the merengue? Perhaps the waltz will be more original. Plus, it encourages intimate contact.

I am so busy scribbling notes as ideas come to me that I almost forget I promised to take my dad out for afternoon tea.

He is already seated, in Lovejoy's Tea Room, in the village, when I get there. I watch him for a moment or two, as he sits there unaware of me. His square military shoulders in his best navy blazer. His spectacular, snow-white hair. I try to imagine if I had no parents left, and I can't.

'Sandra is going to sit for me,' he says.

I groan. I lay down the small menu card as I already know I'm having the clotted cream scones, like I had last time I brought him here. Then I smile at him.

> She walks in Beauty, like the night
> Of cloudless climes and starry skies
> And all that's best of dark and bright
> Meet in her aspect and her eyes.

I quote this to him. I don't know why.

'Lord Byron,' he says.

'I remember you reciting it to me when I was little. I must have only been about four or five.' I also remember asking him to paint me. And he never would. He said he didn't paint anymore. And when I pressed him he got angry. All I wanted was my dad to paint me. If he'd loved me, I'd have thought he'd really have wanted to.

He nods. 'You were. Just a little girl.'

I notice he's wearing one of his cufflink shirts — his best shirt, for the high-tea-ness of the occasion. 'I've always remembered those lines for some reason,' I tell him.

'She phoned me after I wrote to her,' he says, back on Sandra. 'She wants me to draw her nude.'

'Will there be a nurse present?'

He scratches the edge of his David Niven moustache. 'Who for? For me or for her?'

We titter. 'How do you manage it, Dad?' I ask him.

'Manage?' He looks around for the waitress, impatient to get his scones, having acquired a sweet tooth with age. Then he just smiles.

> So, we'll go no more a roving
> So late into the night,
> Though the heart be still as loving,
> And the moon be still as bright.
>
> For the sword outwears its sheath,
> And the soul wears out the breast,
> And the heart must pause to breathe,
> And love itself have rest.
>
> Though the night was made for loving,
> And the days return too soon,
> Yet we'll go no more a roving
> By the light of the moon.

The middle-aged waitress has arrived and stands there, in her white frilly apron, entranced, until my dad finishes. He orders for us, makes a slow assessment of her legs as she walks away. 'It's about age conquering the restlessness of youth,' he says, of the poem. 'Byron of course made me look like a saint. You know his half-sister bore a child by him... The day I stop being in love, and believing in love, is the day I know it's time to die.'

I'm not sure if that last bit is my dad talking, or Byron, but it makes me melancholy.

He looks around the small room with its ten or so tables taken up with those of us who still appreciate loose-leaf tea, pectin-free jam, and the smell of baked goods cooling on a rack. 'I'm just saying that age and time, and living and life are supposed to dull those senses and desires but sometimes, for some, they don't. And they never did for me.'

'Are you talking about Anthea?'

He looks at me disapprovingly. 'Anthea needs companionship. I light up her life.'

I beam a smile at his egotism. 'Anthea isn't your true love then?'

'*Jacqui* is my true love.' My sister's name lingers there. 'I miss her,' he says. 'Every time I look at that woman a part of me blazes like a forest on fire.'

'I miss her too,' I tell him. My dad's declarations about Jacqui get more grandiose every time.

'Do you miss Patrick?' He looks at me quizzically.

Before I can answer, he says, 'There are two kinds of people, Celine: romantics, and everyone else. Romantics will never truly be happy, and yet they know a fuller happiness than others. It's a blessing and a curse.'

'I'm not sure if Patrick is a romantic.'

'Well, romantics always think they want to be with someone just like them. But in reality it doesn't work.'

'What was my mother?'

'She was you.'

I widen my eyes at him.

'Much as you don't see it or want to believe it. You think you're not like her because she was bitter and you aren't. But she had reason to be, and you don't.'

'But I'm not a negative person like she was.'

'She couldn't let go, and it made her negative. When you're a romantic, and you're in love with someone to such an exalted degree, and then that love starts to fade, the natural instinct is to devalue everything that comes after it. Then, as though in some cruel turn of fate, what you are left with is far worse than what you would have had if you hadn't met them. You are exactly like her. You hold on to your vision of how you want things to be, instead of accepting how they are. That's how your marriage failed.'

He looks across the room wistfully. 'You know, your mother was the only woman whose portrait I ever painted and kept. I wouldn't — I couldn't — sell it.'

Yes, the postcard-sized oil he did of her, when they first met, he gave to me shortly after her funeral. That I haven't been able to look at since for some odd reason. One day — someday — I will. When I am ready to go there.

He looks at me quizzically now. 'Why did I never paint you?' he says. Then he shakes his head. 'Madness. I will one day. If you'll let me.' 'I'll let you,' I tell him, and smile. We hold eyes.

'What I'm trying to say to you is, if you're feeling that Patrick isn't matching you ideal for ideal, that's a good thing not a bad thing. He's being prudent when you can't be.'

The waitress sets down a doily-lined, silver tray with four fat, golden scones on them. My father ploughs right in.

And I think, is Patrick just being prudent?

Or does he just not want me enough?

# Forty-One

Mike comes to pick up Aimee for their Saturday thing. Only he's early, and she's still over at a friend's, so I invite him in and offer him a cup of tea. It's a rotten, rainy night, and in the kitchen we try to talk overtop of the knock-knock of the loose downspout.

'I'll fix it,' he says. I open my mouth to protest, but he's already outside, removing the small key to the garage that I keep behind the back door — to let himself in to get the stepladders.

He's up there awhile. I keep looking out to make sure he's all right. Drops of rain cling to the fading rose bushes like hundreds of the world's tiniest fairy lights. It suddenly strikes me that Northumberland is beautiful. The mists. The rain. The vastness beyond my window. I do want to live here. And Patrick was right: I do have a lot to be thankful for.

Mike is quite soaked when he comes back in, and he takes off his jacket and puts it over the back of the kitchen chair. Then he goes to the sink first and washes his dirty hands, while I re-boil the kettle.

Thanks,' he says, taking the mug of tea from me. Mike always used to be busy fixing things around the house. So in a way this feels normal. I have one of those surreal moments where I still feel married to him; I can't believe he ever left.

'Patrick asked me to go to Canada for Christmas,' I find myself telling him, punctuating our silences. 'But I'm not going. I said it wouldn't be fair to you and Aimee.'

He was about to take a drink. Stops. 'Well, how about if you could persuade Aimee to have Christmas with me and Jennifer, and you go to Canada by yourself?'

I put down the mug that was on its way to my lips, but don't answer him right away. 'I would have thought you'd have jumped at the chance,' he says.

I watch him, and try to read him but it's difficult. It's as though there is a blanket laid over his emotions, which has the duel effect of buffering us both from them. 'Well, the thing is, I don't think it's going to work with me and Patrick.'

He looks at the space on the floor between his feet. 'Oh. I'm sorry.'

I go on watching him, but he doesn't look up. 'Are you in love with Jennifer?'

He goes on studying the floor between his feet as though he's looking at it for an answer. 'No,' he says. 'But I do enjoy her company.'

He holds my eyes now. We sit here, listening to the rain, in this study of one another. Then Mike says, 'See the thing is, I suppose there's something I've always known about myself, Celine. I only ever wanted one woman. And I married her. And unfortunately for me I'm still in love with her.'

# Forty-Two

His mobile rings. He hesitates, and then reaches to the chair, to his jacket pocket. He looks at who's calling, and puts it back in the pocket. 'It's Jennifer,' he says, and huffs, ironically. Then he says, 'I should go.'

He plucks his jacket from the back of the chair, but he doesn't immediately move to leave.

'Don't go,' I tell him, quietly.

He looks at me now, tiredly.

'We should talk,' I say. But I'm not even sure what I plan on talking about. I want him to leave. I want him to stay.

He frowns, half shrugs. 'Celine, you're with somebody else. Fine, there are glitches, but I'm sure you'll work it out. And I'm with Jennifer now.'

'I thought you said you didn't love her?' I clear my throat.

'That doesn't mean that I'm not really fond of her, or that I never will be in love with her. We can hope, right?'

His eyes cut into me and mine drop away from his face. Then he walks around me, kisses me once on the cheek, and walks down our passageway to the front door. I hurry after him and just as he's opening it, say, 'Why did you kiss me? I mean — before.'

He sighs and shrugs again. 'That's a good question. I don't know. I shouldn't have. I couldn't help myself.'

He reaches for the door handle. 'Mike, I really need you to tell me if you don't think it's over between us.'

I stop him with my words. He lowers his head for a moment or two, and I can't tell if he's welcoming this or if he's irritated. When he looks up again he talks to the door rather than look at me. 'You know, there was a time, Celine, when I hoped it might not be.' He turns to face me now. 'When I emailed him, there was a small part of me thinking that if you got back together with him and it didn't work out, then I might get you back.' He shakes his head, almost laughs. 'Mad, eh?'

Then he glances upstairs, in the direction of the bedroom that we once shared. He seems to be thinking or taking stock. 'I don't feel like that now,' he says.

His words take me aback. Yet there is not a part of me that doubts him. I see it clearly in his face — something that Mike might not yet have even realised about himself. Mike has stopped loving me. He may claim differently, but he's still harbouring a fantasy; it can be a hard habit to get over.

'I think it was just something I had to go through. I had to hold out some hope I'd get you back, just to lessen the pain of losing you. But now I know I'd never want to go back. Thinking you're happy isn't the same as being happy. I know that now.'

He continues shaking his head long after he stops speaking. 'I don't know what you're really asking me, or really saying, but I hope you're not even thinking that you want to get back together, Celine. We had our chance. Now you have to take a chance on somebody else, and so do I.'

'Are you going to marry her?' I remember what he said long ago, about how we learn things: that just because you're in love doesn't mean you're going to be happy, and just because you're not in love doesn't mean you'll be any worse off.

'I don't see me marrying anyone again, actually,' he says. 'I think being married to you was probably as good as anyone could really expect marriage to be. But if that's as good as it could ever be, well then it's not worth it.'

He watches me passively, while the blood rushes to my head and my heart hammers. 'But the good thing is, if I do marry again, and it doesn't work out, I know it'll never feel as bad as this, so there's some comfort in that. Because this has been pretty bad, I have to admit.'

He nods me up and down, as though he might follow this with 'Goodnight,' or 'I'm going now,' or something. But nothing.

When he's out the door and halfway down the path he turns and looks back at me. 'Don't kid yourself, Celine, you don't want me back either. Not really. And you know you don't. Not deep in your heart. Go with your heart,' he says. 'You're the kind of person who should, maybe more than others. It's the only thing that works for you.'

# Forty-Three

The party preparations, and Christmas, consume me. A month to go, and I have seventy confirmed guests, most of whom intend to bring a friend or two. Paula — David Hall's photographer girlfriend — is going to take some snazzy photos, hoping to land us in the local newspaper. My event planner client referred me to the world's finest hors d'oeuvres caterer who knows how to do things with an asparagus spear that boggle the mind. And Trish, who claims she's an expert in alcohol, has been having tonnes of fun designing weird and wonderful martini concoctions that I'm going to serve. All I need to find is my dance instructor and I'm all set. Aimee claims she doesn't want anything for Christmas, only the right to spend up to a hundred pounds on buying things for her costume.

The article on The Love Market came out in the November issue of *Hers* magazine, angled slightly differently. They ended up sending a photographer here to shoot me, and a lovely picture of me led the piece. Because of the publicity, I've had eight phone calls from women keen to join, and, interestingly, one from a man: a thirty-nine-year-old consultant heart specialist. He filled out my personality questionnaire and sounds interesting. By his picture he looks quite nice, and while I don't have time to fake date him, I suggested he come to the party.

Aimee has a copy of the invitation she designed pinned up on her wall. 'It's good,' I tell her.

'I'm crap at art. Granddad says my wave looked more like an unclipped toenail.'

I tut. 'Your granddad thinks being hard on you will motivate you.' I remember how he used to encourage me to draw. But because I knew he was trying to mould me into an image of himself, I deliberately made myself fail. 'He liked the sand dunes you did.'

'He said they looked like breasts.'

I groan.

She wipes the back of her wrist over her cheek. 'I'm useless. I can't even get a good mark when I copy somebody's exam.'

'You copied somebody's exam?'

'Once.' She flushes. 'But I copied the wrong person. He was even dumber than me.'

'Aimee! Don't ever call yourself dumb! I never got good marks in school and I've done fine! There's more to life than being measured against everybody else. Sometimes you have to just be proud of what you achieve for yourself, and stop comparing yourself to other people, or you'll never be happy. There's always somebody better, cleverer, prettier.'

'You really don't think I'm useless then?'

I smile. 'On a scale of one to ten — ten being the least useless you could ever be — you're a seven.'

She looks horrified. 'You could still try much harder to beat your dad at Wii tennis. You could try putting a load of dark laundry in without washing my white blouse with it. You could get a Saturday job as a farmer.'

I see her smile.

'But other than that, I can't really think of anything else that's useless about you.'

On Thursday night, before we officially roll into December, I do what I know has to be done. The decision toys with me and tests me. I believe in it with every ounce of me one minute, and then I doubt it. I doubt it so strongly that, for once, I'm sure about everything, suddenly, in my life: and I'm so relieved. Until I'm besieged again with the reality that I want to fight, but can't.

I phone Patrick, and when he answers I tell him that I can't do this anymore.

'Having you come back into my life made me believe in something. And you know what? It's a lovely dream. But I don't honestly see how it can be anything else anymore.'

I'm done, but he goes on listening. After a long silence, he says a very quiet, 'I'm sorry you see it that way.' And those few words, and the way he says them — disappointed, but not crushed — make me wonder if I was right: that Patrick has loved me, but perhaps he hasn't loved me quite enough.

'You were the one who said we were dreaming,' I tell him.

'I know, but I didn't mean it. I knew that as soon as the words came out of my mouth.'

'Patrick, I just know that I can't get on with my life, talking to you nearly every day on the phone and not being able to really have you in my life, and having this be so open-ended.'

'When did you decide this?' he asks, sounding a bit more human again.

'Maybe when I heard you were taking the job.'

'Celine...' Exasperation.

'I'm just saying that's when I knew it was impossible. I'm not blaming you. You have to work. I understand that. Who would not understand that?'

'But if I hadn't taken it, I'd have probably gone back abroad again — to what I know, to what I've done for twenty years — so how is this different?'

I laugh now, a little. 'It's not. That's the point. It doesn't make it any better; it just makes it the same. And for me, I just know I'm not the kind of person who can keep coming over there to see you, having such a fabulous time, falling more and more in love with you, and then having to come home, and live my life looking forward to the next time, however many months away that will be.'

'Celine…' he sighs. 'Aimee's nearly a teenager. In a few years she'll be grown up and moved out, and you can go and live and be who you want to be, and do what you please.'

I laugh again. 'A few *years*? Patrick, no!'

'Why not? We waited fifteen to meet again; what's a few more?'

'Just…no.' I shake my head. 'And the funny thing is, I think I already am who I want to be. In some ways I'm already doing what I please now. Maybe this is all too much too fast. Maybe I have to get used to me being on my own, it just being me and Aimee. I might have to start with that.' If I were my own client, would I not be asking myself if this is just another slightly more storybook version of the classic rebound situation?

'I don't know what to say,' he says. 'I really don't. Except that I disagree. Strongly.'

'Let's just agree to leave it,' I tell him. 'To recognise what we had for the lovely thing that it was. And leave it.' Then I say the hardest words I've ever said. 'Goodbye, Patrick.'

Jacqui comes back up for Christmas and we celebrate it with my dad and Anthea, and Mike. Jennifer was invited to a cousin's in Dundee, and Mike said he didn't feel like going. We eat turkey with our paper hats on that Aimee made, and listen to Bing's 'White Christmas.'

After, we watch two films, my father squeezed on the couch in the middle of Anthea and Jacqui, and we drink copious amounts of red wine, and pass around various boxes of chocolates, some better than others — the handmade ones that Jacqui bought in London, definitely the star. Around six o'clock my company starts to go home.

We won't have many Christmases together like this, I think. But I'm pleased we had this one. I know that by this time next year, we will all have moved on, becoming more sure of the new steps we have taken. There will not be this need to gravitate to what's familiar. Because it won't be so familiar anymore. That's just the way life is.

When I see Mike off at the door, he kisses me once on the cheek. Mike won't be coming to my party. He's going up to Scotland to spend New Year's with Jennifer. As I watch him walk down the garden path, in his skinny jeans with his thigh-length sheepskin jacket, I realise something that not so very long ago would have made me come apart at the seams: I will always love Mike. I will love him equally as much as I have always loved him.

But Mike was right. Mike knew something I didn't know at the time: that I don't want him back. Divorce is like hacking down a mature tree; it leaves an unsightly gap and you want something to quickly grow in its place. You find yourself staring at it and remembering not why you cut it down in the first place, but only how nice it used to look. But eventually you can look at it and a part of you forgets it was ever there.

# Forty-Four

David Hall's stately pile opens its doors to, among the more notable: a masked red devil, masked playboy madam, masked phantom of the opera, masked Cinderella, a masked black cat, masked Batgirl, masked Batman, and four masked court jesters. Jacqui wears a stunning silver-sequined floor-length gown and is, she tells me when I can't guess, 'a masked Hollywood actress at the Oscars.' She tuts. 'Isn't it bloody obvious?'

'Which one?' I ask her over the top of Barry White singing 'Let the Music Play.'

'Angelina Jolie and Kate Winslet all rolled into one,' she grins under disco lights, showing white teeth lined in ample red lipstick.

'When are you coming home?' I ask her.

'Never.'

'Please?'

'Sorry. I'm never coming back up to this dump.'

'Don't call Newcastle a dump! Just because you're a Londoner now!'

She laughs. 'I'm just happy down there now! Except for

missing you. It's almost perfect. And maybe almost is as good as any of us gets in this life.'

'Oh. My. God!' Someone taps me on the shoulder as Jacqui and I are trying to move a giant candelabra that got placed dangerously too close to the edge of the martini bar. When I turn around it's Trish and James. 'Your dress!' she says. James whistles as I do a twirl for them.

'I'm one of the professional dancers on *Dancing with the Stars*,' I tell them, holding out my arms to show off the dramatic slit bell sleeves of my frock that I ordered from a second-hand ballroom gown shop off the Net.

'It's the most stunning thing I've ever seen!' Trish says.

I look down at myself, still amazed that, other than a minor little let-out around the hips, the dress fits me so well. It's aquamarine, with an asymmetrical neckline and a low waist that leaves my entire back bare. The bodice is what the description called 'cracked ice' lace, and the skirt is a full soft charmeuse satin. As it came with a wrap that I knew I'd never wear, I had a seamstress cut it up and sew a mask out of it. Aimee helped me choose my high silver stilettos — insisting on only one thing: that she could buy the same pair.

'What are you?' I ask Trish, happy to see her and giving her a hug, and then introducing her and James to my sister. She's wearing a white towelling bathrobe, a white towelling hairband pushing her hair back off her face, and a bright orange silicone eye mask with two holes in it for her to see out of.

'Can't you guess? I'm a spa diva!'

'Oh!' I chuckle along with Jacqui.

'Truth is, we went to the costume rental shop and they didn't have much left. So we had to use our imaginations, which was quite hard, given we don't have one between us.'

'And I'm…well, guess what I am?' says the extremely hand-some but un-costumed James who has his arm around her like a man who never wants his arm to be anywhere else. I can feel Jacqui doting on them with her eyes.

I look him up and down. 'Well, unless I'm missing some-thing, you're a man in a T-shirt and a pair of jeans, with a navy blue mask around your neck — which breaks the rules by the way! You know I said it's supposed to be faces covered all night. No masks off until midnight! Then you finally get to see the person you've met.'

'But I've met her already!' he says, squeezing her into him. 'Thanks to you. But then I'd met her before you. So, truthfully, I'm all confused.'

'But this girl has so many *issues*!' I joke, remembering his comments about the last ten women he dated.

'I know,' he says, 'and I love every last one of them.' He kisses the side of her head. Then she turns her face to his, catch-ing his lips while they're still there. 'But you still haven't guessed what I am.' He lifts up a foot to show me a pair of navy blue fuzzy socks.

'You're a person with no shoes,' Jacqui says.

'Close,' he says.

Trish is grinning at me, besotted with him. Sometimes you see two people together who just look so right for one another. And they are it.

'I'm a passenger on a British Airways flight,' he tells us. 'You know, socks, mask…' He pulls a tiny toothbrush out of his pocket and waves it at me.

'If you misbehave we'll make you clean the toilets out with that,' I tell him.

He laughs. 'If I get drunk enough I'll do it without being told.'

'So are you going anywhere nice, Mr BA Passenger?' Jacqui asks him.

'Actually, on Monday we're off to Barbados for two weeks,' Trish answers for him.

'To get engaged,' James adds, and Trish nudges him, spilling his martini.

'We're NOT going to get engaged!' she says, as though the idea is unthinkable. James winks at me, secretively.

I laugh at her. 'Still trying to convince me you don't want him?'

'I've given up on that,' Trish says. 'Given I'm clearly so crap at hiding how I feel.'

James pulls Trish away toward the bar.

'He's quite tasty,' Jacqui says. I think she's talking about James, but then I see that she is indicating across the room. To a tall, masked, blond man in hospital scrubs.

'That's Dr Michael Hill, a thirty-nine-year-old consultant heart specialist at the Freeman Hospital. He filled out my personality questionnaire. Contacted me after he saw the article in *Hers*. Remember that article that the journalist had to completely restructure because of you?' I tease her.

'He's a doctor and he came dressed as one?' she laughs. 'Oh dear! But he looks very sexy. There's something about him.'

'So you want to meet him, then?'

She grins. 'I don't want to meet someone who reads women's magazines.'

'He doesn't. His secretary showed him the article. Apparently they've all been trying to set him up since he got divorced. And he doesn't want to date nurses.'

'Interesting,' she says. 'How about architects?'

'Oh come on,' I drag her over there.

'But you can't let me like him!' she says. 'And you can't let him be as good as he looks! Please! Not now that I live in London, and I'm just getting my life sorted! I can't fall in love with a man back up in Newcastle!'

'Of course not,' I tell her. 'I'll try to guarantee it.'

The music changes to Earth, Wind and Fire's 'Let's Groove,' even though I specifically warned the DJ not to get into cheesy seventies music until everyone was seriously pissed. But somehow it has the effect of drawing everyone to the dance floor. After I introduce Jacqui to the doctor, I go and work the room, and I'm happy to see Sandra, my spa owner and father's muse, chatting away animatedly to my wounded footballer Liam Docherty, and Liam looking happily ridiculous in a masked red devil costume. I'm just deciding not to bother interrupting them when she waves me over, excitedly. 'Oh, Celine,' she hugs me as Liam asks her what she's drinking and walks over to the bar. 'I've been meaning to phone you since before Christmas but I was so busy at the spa. I wanted to tell you how the sitting went, with your dad.'

'Oh! I didn't know you'd actually done it. I thought you might have just been putting him off.'

'No!' she says. 'I was very keen. I mean, obviously not at first.' She laughs. With her enormous boobs spilling over her gown, she looks like one of the most pornographic Snow White's I've ever seen. 'I did it as a treat to myself for Christmas. Had my staff work a few miracles on me,' she laughs again. 'It was lovely. I never expected I'd feel so comfortable with all my clothes off, but he put me completely at ease.'

'He did?'

'Yes. And his drawing was wonderful. I couldn't believe it was me. So when this all gets over and things settle down a bit, I want you to come over to the spa for a free massage and see it.'

'It's at the spa?'

She beams. 'I had it framed and hung it in the powder room. If anyone asks me who did it, I'm going to give them his card.'

'I don't think my dad has a card.'

'Apparently he's getting them made.'

'Oh!' I hide my grin in my hand.

'I was fat as a teenager. It took me years to lose the weight. Then I end up in the spa business, but somehow never lost the self-esteem hang-ups.' She throws up her hands. 'But your dad made me think that maybe I don't have to be so hard on myself all the time.'

'This music is SO cheesy,' Aimee comes and pokes me in the back, right as Liam returns with Sandra's drink. 'And so is she...' Aimee rolls her eyes at Sandra. 'She didn't realise she was beautiful and now she knows she is! Pu-leeese!'

I laugh. Then I cuddle my little Tinkerbell in her short green minidress, with her white footless tights with holes poked into them, and her silver mask on a stick.

'Mind my wings,' she says.

I look at her feet, in the same high silver stilettos as mine. 'You'll have bunions by the time you're nineteen,' I tell her.

'Don't worry, I'm not going to be dancing to this lame music.'

'What are you drinking?' I ask when she picks up a martini glass from a high table.

'A martini, of course,' she says and takes a sip. 'Without alcohol.' She looks across at the cute young barman who always thinks I'm a prostitute, who I 'hired' for the night, on loan from Karma restaurant where I went on my fake date with my ex-husband. 'Mark made it for me.'

I take it from her, sniff it, and give it back to her. 'I'm going to do random sniff tests, so you'd better be on your guard.'

But she's too interested in watching Mark.

I survey the room. A great turnout, and most did bring a couple of guests. David Hall, dressed as Mr Darcy, said that only Kim had guessed who he was. He's a perfectly good sport about having his house taken over by about nearly two hundred people whom he's never met before. Kim, otherwise known as Elizabeth I, is here with Andrew Flemming, my client in the music business. When I go over and ask her how it's going, her first words are, 'Nice house,' as she looks around.

'It could have been yours,' I say.

'But he'd come with it.' She smiles. 'And no, actually. It's not "going" with Andy. You seem to think I'm here with him, but I'm here by myself. As is he. We just happen to be talking.' She smiles. 'We've been on four very good dates. He's lovely — the first man you've introduced me to who has absolutely nothing wrong with him.'

Nothing hanging out of his nose? No patent lack of shoulders? He didn't pick up his fork before she picked up hers? I'm floored. 'What's wrong then?' I ask.

'There's just no chemistry,' she says.

Finally. A real reason to not see him anymore. And, alas, one I cannot fix.

'This is progress though, isn't it? In a weird way?' I hug her.

She chuckles. 'I think.'

'Who is this hunk?' Jacqui comes up to me and whispers in my ear. When I look to where she's pointing, a part of me dies. Over by the Christmas tree, a diminutive highwayman is talking to a masked devil in a miniskirt, wearing horns.

'How did he get in here?'

Jacqui chuckles.

The diminutive Dick Turpin has got his beige pants tucked into knee-high boots, and is wearing a long purple velvet cape.

For one moment his two masked eyes meet mine before look-ing away. He grins at me, and I would recognise those teeth anywhere.

I notice, as we dance and chatter and drink, and swipe hors d'oeuvres from trays the second they come near us, that Jacqui and Michael the doctor seem quite engrossed in conversation. When we have to take our partners for our lesson in Viennese waltz, Jacqui and Michael take the floor, and Jacqui sends me a look that could contain pornographic content. At one point, when we meet in the middle of the floor, she says to me, 'He's fabulous! We totally hit it off! I think he's really into me! But why does he have to live in Newcastle?'

Diminutive Dick Turpin dances his way over to me with a tall young thing in a red minidress. 'She's a horny devil,' my dad says, touching the pointy things on top of her head. 'See…horns.'

'Yes, Dad, I think I get it.'

He dances his way back across the room.

As we approach midnight my mind briefly goes to wonder what Mike and Jennifer might be doing. A joylessness crosses over me as I stand there dancing in the middle of the crowd, a colourful moonflower pattern of lights spinning around my feet. But only for a second. As Slade brings in the New Year with 'C'm On Feel the Noize,' everyone takes off their masks, and I hug and kiss my daughter, my sister, my father, and I realise something. It is no longer the year I got divorced. We have moved on, technically only by minutes, but it feels like miles.

'Can we phone Dad?' Aimee comes and puts her arms around me, while I'm chatting to Jacqui.

I hug her back. 'You know what, sweetie, I think we should let your dad have a good time and surprise him with a call in the morning.' I adjust her wings.

'But it is morning!'

'I know. But we'll wait until we've been to bed and woken up again. Then we'll ring him. Okay?'

When Aimee flits off, Jacqui raises the tip of my chin so my eyes meet hers. 'Sad thoughts are not allowed. Not tonight.'

'I know.'

But the sad thought I'm thinking is not about Mike.

I pick my moment and then I make my escape.

In one of David Hall's many bathrooms, I take my mobile out of my clutch bag. Sitting on the toilet lid, I punch in the numbers. It'll only be 7:30 p.m. in Canada. He could easily be at work, because he'll have started his job now, no doubt.

It rings and rings, as my heart beats and beats harder. Then I know he's not going to answer, and I sink inside. It clicks over to his voicemail.

'Hello,' I say, a moment or two after his recorded voice stops speaking. I force myself to smile so I sound more cheerful.

'Patrick…it's New Year's, and I just wanted to phone you and say…' I put my head in a hand. 'It's supposed to be a new year and I'm supposed to feel happier than this. But I miss you.' I leave the words there until I can get myself around other ones. 'I actually didn't mean to ring you and say that. But there it is. I really do. I don't know what it means, any of it…'

*Be happy*, I'm about to add, but it sounds so final.

I click my phone closed. Downstairs, Elvis Costello is singing 'Alison.'

I go on sitting there, not wanting to face anyone just yet. I redial his number, just to listen to his voice again, giving myself a chance to add something else, and then I hang up without saying anything. I stand up, straighten out the skirt of my dress, and go back to my party.

When I go back into the room, my sister says, 'Where have

you been?' She looks urgent, and a bit shaken up. 'Go outside,' she says.

I frown, scrutinizing her for more.

'Just go!' She gently pushes me.

My first thought is that it's my father getting it on in the bushes. I prepare to be extremely embarrassed — and to murder him. But something tells me it's not that.

When I step outside into the moonlight darkness, I see right away that there is a taxi at the door, not fifty feet ahead of me. There is a man getting out of the taxi. And I know this man, and my world becomes a surreal sort of still. It's the stature that's unmistakeably him. And even if he had been wearing a costume and a mask I would have still recognised him.

'Patrick?'

My mouth has gone dry. My heart is a strange clash of disbelief and delirium.

'Yes,' he says. He puts his suitcase down on the path, and the taxi pulls off. And then we are standing there, in the gravelled grounds of a twilit stately home. In the year 2010. A year as yet untarnished with screw-ups and resolutions that we'll fail to keep. He holds up a hand, with his mobile phone in it. 'I think I might have just missed your call.' He replays my message on speakerphone. I hear my anxious voice blurting out everything that I blurted out. Then a ring off, and then another call. This time nothing said, only the sound of Elvis Costello's 'Allison' playing in the background.

I breathe out, into my two hands clasped over my face. 'What are you doing here?' I ask him, when I recover myself.

He puts both hands in his pants pockets, tilts his head, and looks at me. 'Actually, I got invited. Aimee sent me an invitation.' He smiles a little when he sees my bemused expression. 'Sorry I'm a bit late.'

'You've come all this way to see me again?' I shake my head in disbelief.

'Yes.' He takes a couple of steps toward me. Then he takes something out of the inside pocket of his jacket. The jacket he was wearing that time I thought I saw him in London. The same one he wore when he came to meet my train. He was right: he actually doesn't own that many clothes.

He hands me a piece of paper with something written on it. 'My new address,' he says.

I take it off him and read in the dim light. Have I drunk too much? 'London?' I frown.

'I've rented a flat. For a year. I'm going to give myself that time to focus on my book. And I'm going to be free to see you as much as you're willing and able to see me.'

I am too stunned to respond, and while I stand here, his eyes do a slow wander over me, from head to toe and back. And then he smiles. He looks young, and handsome, and happier than I've ever seen him. And for the first time, relaxed, in an odd sort of tense way.

'But your job?'

He is already shaking his head. 'I didn't take it. I had doubts about it all along. I didn't want it enough. Or what I should say is I wanted something else more.' He takes hold of my warm hands in his cold ones, and clasps them there, and looks at me with that same vigorous intensity that I always associate with him. From inside the house, Seal is singing 'Kiss from a Rose.'

'I told you before that there would be a way. That I made a mistake once, and I wasn't going to make the same one over again.' He smiles at me. 'I don't say things I don't mean, Celine. I meant every word of it.'

He pulls my hands now and relocates them round his back, wrapping his arms around me, and resting the weight of his head on the top of mine. Our breaths merge around us in the bitter night air. 'We've got a year to see how it goes. It's not perfect, but can you live with that for now?' He kisses the top of my head.

I look up at him, and whisper. 'I can live with it for now.'

*The End*

## Acknowledgements

A huge thank you to Kim McArthur and her team for editorial direction, the wonderful cover, and all the enthusiastic selling-in. Thanks as always to my literary agency, and agent Jane Gregory, and to Stephanie Glencross for her feedback on the manuscript as it developed.

I have to thank all of my unsuspecting single friends whose stories helped inspire *The Love Market*, and those who read it, or chatted constructively about it, as it was coming along — mainly, Dana, Kelley, Luigi, and Stefany, plus all my other friends and family who are supportive in their own ways.

To my mother, who is always the first one to read my drafts, and is the most reluctant to say anything negative, until I have prodded it out of her, then she lets me have it. To my husband, Tony, for his endless support and faith, book in and book out, since "day one" when I decided I wanted to write novels. Thanks to David Terry too, for a bit of legal info about divorce.

My sincere appreciation goes to the book trade who are responsible for getting my novels in the stores, and to those who have written lovely reviews in the media.

And last but not least, thanks to readers who have bought my other two books, and those who write to me and inspire me to write more. I love reading your comments. Please keep them coming to www.carolmasonbooks.com